JUN   2018

TWO-FACED

ALSO AVAILABLE BY A. R. ASHWORTH

Souls of Men

TWO-FACED

An Elaine Hope Mystery

A. R. Ashworth

CROOKED
LANE

NEW YORK

Copyright © 2018 by Russell Ashworth.

Published in the United States by Crooked Lane Books, an imprint of The Quick Brown Fox & Company LLC.

Crooked Lane Books and its logo are trademarks of The Quick Brown Fox & Company LLC.

Library of Congress Catalog-in-Publication data available upon request.

ISBN (hardcover): 978-1-68331-589-6
ISBN (ePub): 978-1-68331-590-2
ISBN (ePDF): 978-1-68331-591-9

Cover design by Lori Palmer.
Book design by Jennifer Canzone.

Printed in the United States.

www.crookedlanebooks.com

Crooked Lane Books
34 West 27th St., 10th Floor
New York, NY 10001

First Edition: July 2018

10 9 8 7 6 5 4 3 2 1

For Anna, who is always there for me through
thick, thin, and writer's block

PROLOGUE

April, Hartland Point, Devon

I'm alone now.

Elaine stood in the front drive of her stone cottage and watched the red taillights of Peter's car disappear behind the hedges at the end of the lane. The afternoon squall had cleared the air, and she turned her gaze out to sea. In the dusk, the steady mariners' beacon at Hartland Point flashed in syncopation with South Point Light on the island of Lundy, both in counterpoint to the crash of surf on the rocks two hundred feet below.

"Excuse me, DCI Hope?" Police Constable Buntyn's clear young voice startled Elaine. "Is there something I can get you, ma'am?"

Alone, except for Buntyn. She reminded herself not to think aloud. The uniformed officer stood at the door of her stone cottage. His shift would end soon, and another young officer would take his place. She turned to walk back to the cottage. "Still here, Buntyn?"

"Yes, ma'am. I was on my rounds until just now. PC Carter checked in. She's passing Titchberry. Five minutes out."

"Then you'll be home soon. Good night. Have a nice evening with the family."

Elaine had objected to having watchers because one

constable, even if armed, wasn't likely to stop a hit man. If her life were at risk from a gangster like Anton Srecko, he would be ruthless. Why endanger a nice young officer with a growing family? But her case officer had insisted, so young PCs from Bude and Bideford appeared every day, like clockwork.

Her cane sank into a deep patch of gravel, and she lurched to one side before catching herself. Buntyn moved to help her, but she held up her hand. "I'm all right. Damn low spot. Have to go slow."

Elaine didn't excel at going slow. Every day she damned her condition with a litany of curses that had grown too familiar.

Damn me for rushing into that brothel without backup.
Damn the Met for not getting backup to me in time.
Damn Anton Srecko for planning my murder.
Damn Nilo Srecko for beating me, shooting me, cutting me.
    Raping me.
I killed him. I took a life. Damn me.

The perverse ritual never brought her a step closer to peace.

Darkness had fallen. When she reached the thick wooden door, she took a last look at the ocean, nodded to Buntyn, and went inside. A cafetière and mugs cluttered the table between the two blue leather chairs in the sitting room. She could carry only one item at a time securely, so clearing up meant multiple trips back and forth to the kitchen. She wouldn't bother. The cleaner would clear it away tomorrow.

Peter's scent pervaded the room. She breathed deeply. His clothes always smelled like rosemary and citrus. He still loved her in spite of her scarred face, her hobbling, hesitant gait. This afternoon she had allowed him to take her in his arms and kiss her. He had held her for what seemed like hours, but when she finally had pushed him away, she saw it had been only a few minutes.

He was the first man she had ever considered making a life with. He was the only man she'd allowed to touch her since the rape. And she'd pushed him away. She felt so different now, about life, about purpose, about the future. She didn't know when she would feel anchored enough, at peace enough, to see him again. When she would be able to give, when she would no longer rage.

Scratch's insistent meow interrupted her thoughts. She poured a bit of kibble into his bowl and took her evening medications while the huge grey tabby crunched and purred. After he was done, she washed and put up the bowl, turned out the light, and together they went into the bedroom. She sat at the foot of her bed and scanned the photos she had taped to the wardrobe mirror.

If Peter had come in here, he'd think I'm mad. The cleaner and therapists all do.

Nilo Srecko's macabre morgue picture—grey face, half-closed eyelids, slack mouth, the two-inch wide incision at the base of his throat where she'd plunged the knife. He'd put a bullet through her leg and sliced the same knife across her face.

In a recent session, Elaine scoffed when her therapist talked about how she shouldn't actively remind herself of pain. Looking at the picture now, she reconsidered the advice and then asked herself why that bastard's photo was still there when he was dead. Surely gone to Hell, if there was such a place. She pulled the picture from the whiteboard and ripped it to pieces. She would damn him forever, but he hadn't devised the plot that had nearly killed her. Nilo was a young psychopath, too volatile to plan anything more than two steps ahead.

Elaine's gut knotted as she stared at the other picture—Anton Srecko, his skin so pale, his eyes so cold, his photo might as well have been a morgue shot. He was the bastard who had set her up to be killed, and he was still alive. She left Anton's picture where it was and lay back on her bed, staring at the ceiling.

She laughed, a deep-toned upwelling that began at her diaphragm and rolled through her throat and filled the room. Three men from her life. She killed one, wanted to kill another, and drove away the third.

Peter. Until today, the last time she had seen him was eight weeks ago at his house in London. They had made love. His heart had pounded against her chest, her heart against his. Separate heartbeats converged to synchrony as their bodies joined.

Would he ever kiss her like that again? Would she ever again shiver at his breath on her neck, his touch on her skin? She shook her head. Fool's questions.

You're not ready, Lainie. You'll never let yourself feel that until you let go of the fear and the rage. And you can't do that until you've delivered justice to Anton. You've got no proof, so find it.

Recover. Go back to duty. Build the case.

ONE

Monday, nine months later, Camberwell

The canary-yellow pom-pom on Joanna Christie's woolen hat made following her ridiculously easy. The portly woman bounced as much as walked along the pavement. Periodically she entered a shop or greengrocer. When she emerged, the ball of yellow yarn atop her head again became a splash of colour bobbing in a stream of dark-coated women going about their daily London lives.

As Elaine watched, Joanna grappled with her fully laden shopping bag—Ms. Innocent Housewife on her errands. *Safe and sane, business as usual.* Elaine gritted her teeth at the thought, felt the rage rising in her at the sheer perversity that the woman in front of her still had her career, her life, her future.

Elaine took a deep breath, relaxed her shoulders, and focused on quieting the demon inside her. Despite her anger, she reminded herself she was a police officer, constrained by the constable's oath she had taken the day she started the job sixteen years before, when she had sworn to accord "equal respect to all people."

All people. Saints and sinners, cops and killers.

And who am I to judge Joanna? The woman was merely getting on with her life—a widow, a receptionist who worked hard to keep food on the table and pay for her daughter's education. The last time she had met Joanna, Elaine had threatened to charge her as an accessory to murder, which might have ruined her daughter's chance to go to university. The tirade had been all bluster and empty threat on Elaine's part, and Joanna had called her bluff.

So it wasn't like the two of them were strangers, which was all the more reason to take care and pay attention to tradecraft. Elaine's black hoodie, loose-fitting jeans, and boots offered reasonable street camouflage, but her six-foot height meant she towered above the mostly female shoppers around her.

Slump, Lainie, shorter steps, let the gap grow. The chill wind of January ruffled her hood and threatened to strip it back from her head. She pulled it closer around her cheeks and kept her eyes on the pom-pom. Her weak right leg slowed her down, but she usually could keep up with her marks.

The yellow pom-pom stopped at a shop window. Elaine veered left towards a pub entrance just as a trio of pierced twenty-something men burst out, jostling her and throwing her off balance. Her right leg buckled, and she instinctively clutched at the nearest man, falling against him, close enough to smell the whisky on his breath. Startled and defensive, the man took the front of her hoodie in both hands and swung her against the wall with a curse.

"No! Don't touch me!" Elaine drove her fists upwards between his hands, gripped one of his wrists, and twisted him around. His friends began advancing towards her, so she shoved the man into them hard enough to force them to catch him.

As she did, the wind ripped her hood back, exposing her face. The men's voices changed from growls of aggression to astonished exclamation. "Christ, what the fuck happened to her?"

Elaine squared her body, weight on the balls of her feet, willing herself to stay steady. "Whatever happened taught me how to deal with shits like you."

A small crowd of spectators, mostly women, had gathered,

forming a semicircle on the pavement. Snatches of their murmured conversation rose, loud enough for Elaine to hear.

"Did you see what she did . . . ? Good on her . . . What happened to her face?"

The aggressive young man had slipped to his knees on the pavement, holding his arm tight to his body. "I think you broke my shoulder, bitch." His blanched face contorted with pain and anger. "Jesus haitch—call the fucking rozzers, Eddie."

Elaine held out her warrant card. "No need. Detective Chief Inspector Elaine Hope, at your bloody service. Or perhaps I should arrest you for assaulting a police officer."

The man struggled to his feet, assisted by his friends. Some colour had returned to his face. "Oh yeah, right! I'm the one with the busted shoulder! How was I to know you was a copper?"

"Nothing snapped." Elaine jerked her head towards a CCTV camera located above the pub entrance. "I think the video will show who attacked whom. Do you make it a habit to attack anyone who happens to jostle you?" She made eye contact with each of the men in turn. "Or were you looking for some rough?"

A police car pulled to the kerb. Two uniformed officers emerged and made their way through the gaggle of spectators. The older of the two uniforms acknowledged Elaine. "DCI Hope. Do you need assistance?" He appraised the man who was still holding his arm. "Or does he?"

Elaine shook her head. "I'm fine, Officer. I think it's sorted. Unless one of these gents has something to say."

The injured man spoke. "No, we sort of bumped each other and slipped down. Bit of a misunderstanding is all. If it's alright, I need to get my arm checked." The three men exchanged glances—sufficiently cowed for Elaine to nod in agreement.

"Right, then. Go get that arm tended," the uniform said as the men walked off. "Do you need a ride to the station, Chief Inspector?"

In her mind, Elaine cursed her misfortune. Joanna Christie

and her ridiculous pom-pom could be blocks away by now. But she had time to find her again.

"No thanks. I'm going the other way." She watched the two uniforms get in their car and drive off.

A woman's voice cried out behind her, shrill with anger. "You! Still a bully and getting away with it."

Elaine spun around. On seeing Elaine's face, Joanna's tirade halted in mid-accusation, her mouth open, aghast. After a few moments she managed to stammer on.

"Jesus, I had no idea." Joanna took a deep, wavering breath. "Was he the one? You know, who . . ." She fumbled with her bulging shopping bags, but she never took her eyes off Elaine. "To do that to you, I mean."

Elaine smiled down at the flustered woman. A head of cabbage teetered on the lip of Joanna's uppermost bag, threatening to dive to the concrete at any moment. *Time to make a friend, Lainie.*

"Here, let me help with that. Can't have your supper smashed on the pavement, can we?" Elaine took hold of the bag, secured the cabbage, and nodded at the entrance to the pub. "You look like you could use some fortification. Tea? No, wine. My shout. Why don't we find a nice private nook in here and have a chat?" She held open the door and stood aside. "After you."

Joanna glanced at the spectators and at the shopping bag on Elaine's arm. Without further words, she trundled through the open door. Elaine smiled to herself. In her career she had found bestowing a small kindness could force action and confirm another person's character. Joanna Christie was not evil. She was, however, easily led.

The Cave of Bacchus was one of the hip, new drinking establishments that had sprung up across London in the last five years or so. Rather than traditional coziness, it featured smoked glass tables with formed plastic stools, designer beige and pastel decor, and sconce lighting in rose and blue hues.

Elaine saw no oak panelling, no overstuffed leather cushions, no dark wooden tables marred by decades of heavy cutlery. The bar sported no pump handles a competent barmaid could pull to deliver an honest pint. No yeasty smell of spilled ale. *Christ, not a cask ale in sight.* Instead, the Cave offered mostly white wines, a few reds, designer vodkas, and fruity liqueur miasmas, many of which were chilled with a spurt of liquid nitrogen.

Peter and I could never feel comfortable here. Nelson's Glory is our pub, and it always will be. No, that's wrong. It was our pub, once. Never mind that.

She shook Peter from her thoughts and focused on Joanna Christie, who said, "This used to be a nice pub. The Gander. Comfortable. My husband and I came here every now and then, before he died." She looked around vaguely as if she were trying to find where they used to sit. "I've passed this place every week for fifteen years since, and I haven't stopped in. Can't tell you when it changed into . . . this. Why don't they want people to just be comfortable anymore?"

"Let's sit there." Elaine pointed to a booth in the back corner. "Doesn't look comfortable, but there's room for your shopping."

They decided on a moderately priced carafe of pinot noir. Elaine poured and they sat, gauging each other. Joanna shed her yellow wool hat and drained her glass. Elaine refilled it and spoke.

"First things first. I won't apologize for what I said about your employer the last time we met. I know Anton's just criminal scum underneath his slick suit." Joanna started to speak, but Elaine held up her hand. "I hope you're keeping well clear of their extracurricular activities. But I do apologize for including your daughter in that rant. I hope she made it to uni and that she's doing well."

"She went up for autumn term. Durham. Trev's."

Elaine raised her eyebrows. "She picked a good one. I was at Durham. Castle. That's University College."

"Mm-huh, right." Joanna sat back and studied Elaine. "Good for you. You listen to me for a change. Mr. Anton's a hard man, but he pays me well. You made an enemy there."

Yep, she stays for the pay cheque. Elaine replied, "I'm a cop. If I go a week without making a new enemy, it's a week lost. They dock my pay." She poured herself a half glass of the wine. "I was serious. You're in jeopardy there. The Crown Prosecutors could make it tough on you, even if they don't charge you. You could be forced to testify."

Joanna sneered. "Bollocks. I'm just the receptionist."

"You don't have to be directly involved. You keep the diaries of who he talks to, where he goes, and when he returns. Who visits him. If the Met suspects something, if they need to piece together a chain of events, they'll look to you for answers. And you'll have to supply what they want, best you can, or get charged with obstruction." Elaine lowered her voice. "Mrs. Christie. Joanna. Didn't you ever wonder what Nilo actually did for Anton? Didn't you ever feel threatened by him?"

Joanna shifted in her seat and swirled her wine glass. "Nilo was a wild boy."

Elaine spoke barely above a whisper. "Wild? Bloody hell, Joanna. He killed a fifteen-year-old girl because she wouldn't have sex with him. Your daughter isn't that much older."

"You never proved that. And leave my daughter out of this."

"It never went to court, but forensics eventually matched his DNA on her blouse. We have his DNA for Geri Harding too. The estate agent who worked for Anton. Nilo fucked her, broke her neck, and dumped her body in a bathtub of bleach."

Joanna darted a look at Elaine's face, then returned to studying her wine glass. The initial anger had drained from her face. She now appeared uncertain, wary.

"Be glad you didn't see what he did to her." Elaine took a sip of wine. "Oh, and there was that solicitor who was murdered, Greene. Granted, there's no solid evidence, but my money is on

Nilo for topping Greene. Do you think he would have done any of that without orders from Anton?"

"I'd rather not talk about this." Joanna picked up her cap and started to gather her shopping bags.

"Please stay—I haven't answered that question you could barely ask. Outside, before we came in here."

Joanna froze, half out of the booth. Her eyes scanned Elaine's face. When she relaxed back to her seat, Elaine continued.

"I wish I had amnesia about it, but I don't." Elaine took a deep breath. She could never talk about the assault without first collecting her emotions. "I confronted Nilo in a brothel he ran. First, he blew a young woman's brains out. Then he used the same pistol to blow a hole in my leg."

Elaine pulled back her hoodie and smiled. "After that he pounded me with his fists. These aren't my own teeth. He broke three ribs kicking me. I don't have a spleen anymore. When I was down, he took a big knife, like the commandos use, razor sharp, and sliced my face to the bone."

Joanna's mouth twisted and she swallowed hard, appeared to gag. Elaine leaned forward, steeling herself for the admission. Every time she had described it—to the Met investigators, to the Professional Standards officers, to her therapist—she felt like she was coughing up her soul. Months had passed, but it hadn't gotten easier.

"He threw me over a table. I struggled. Fought like hell. But blood was flowing into my eyes, and I couldn't see. I couldn't move my right leg. I remember trying to push myself up. Tried to throw him off me, but my hands kept slipping in the blood. I felt him cut away my pants. I couldn't stop him."

For long seconds they stared at each other, Joanna mesmerized by dread, Elaine silent in pain. Two women, sharing horror.

"And then he raped me, Joanna." Elaine's voice trembled. "He bloody raped me. I killed him, though. See, he dropped his knife. I found it and I jammed it into his neck, right here at the bottom." She held her fingers at a spot an inch above her collarbone. "Up to the hilt they told me, and it was true. I saw the post-mortem photos. It cut through his carotid and slashed his vena cava, so the autopsy said. He bled to death before my mates and the ambulance got there."

Joanna's eyes rounded. Her nervous fingers turned the wine glass on the table in front of her. At last she spoke. "He'd gotten in trouble with Mr. Anton over women. There was an accounts clerk in the office, pretty girl, but a bit dim about men. Gossip had it that the company paid her to stay silent." She sniffed. "For months I didn't want to believe what had happened to you. I read the news reports about it, but I never imagined. I didn't want to think about the remarks he made about my daughter, the look he got when he talked about women. There have been other things, people in the office I don't like . . ." She sniffed and sipped her wine.

Elaine sensed she wanted to say more, but when Joanna remained silent, she said, "Later, we found out Anton had brought Nilo to London because he'd raped and beaten a girl. She lived, but she's crippled for life. The number-one son of the Srecko family was a murderer and rapist. And they were grooming him for bigger things."

Elaine held eye contact. A tear crept down Joanna's cheek. "That's the family you work for."

TWO

Monday night, Kensington

The bar in the small hotel off Queen's Gate in Kensington reeked of old leather, smoky single malt whisky, and Penhaligon after-shave. Fiona sat with her back to the wall, sipping red wine and despising the smug male clubbiness. As usual, a black-tied waiter had escorted her to a small table far from the door. Her husband, Jonny, was at a police conference in Manchester. It was unlikely any of his colleagues would be drinking here, but there was no point being indiscreet. A perfectly turned-out fiftyish woman meeting someone like Jacko meant only one thing to most people.

There were no other women in the bar. Two men, well beyond middle age, judging from their paunches and age spots, leered from a table across the floor. Fiona didn't return their glances. After fifteen minutes she rose, taking her clutch purse, leaving her half-finished glass. Alone in the lavatory, she assessed her make-up, applying a dab more powder to mask the crow's feet that had begun to show at the corners of her light blue eyes, tilting her long, fair-skinned face to and fro in the light, inspecting it for flaws. She poked at the few streaks of grey that silvered her honey-blonde hair. Finally, she touched up her lipstick and stood straight. The black dress dipped low enough in front to reveal the pearl-and-Swarovski crystal pendant nestled in her cleavage. Restrained aristocratic sensuality.

She smoothed the fabric over her slender hips and turned slightly to the side. Just the image Jonny would want. Mature, svelte, pliable. Not that he ever wanted anything beyond a look, these days. Two years ago she had damned him for that, but now she was reconciled to the reality of having his friendship, nothing more.

It was close to the proper time, so she returned to her table. After a few discreet seconds, the barman approached her with an envelope. "For madam." She opened it once he had retreated to the bar—310. It wasn't their usual room. Fiona opened her clutch and extracted a ten-pound note. She placed it on the table and walked to the lift. The barman would pocket the money and put the wine on Jacko's bill.

On most of their nights together, Jacko sat in the hotel chair, blathering about his latest courtroom exploits and directing her movements as she slowly undressed until she stood naked before him. Tonight, however, he mumbled, directing her to turn this way or that, bend forward, lie back. No hoots, no gropes. Fiona wondered if he had lost a case.

One thing hadn't changed. Their coupling was all about Jacko—from his obscene taunts to her scripted submission and adulation. She mouthed the requisite words of praise and ran her fingernails up and down his flanks as he pounded away. Whisky-tainted breath enveloped her. His amber eyes stared down. His sleek black hair glistened with sweat. Droplets coursed over his cheekbones and dripped from his chin onto her breasts.

At last he groaned and again took his place in the chair at the foot of the bed, berating her about what a whore she was. She stared at the ceiling as he ranted, her tears tracing quiet paths from the corners of her eyes to the satin of the pillow.

After two minutes of abuse, Jacko seemed to tire. He walked

to the bathroom and came back towelling the sweat from his body. "Get up and get dressed. We have somewhere to go."

"I need to get home. Jonny's . . ."

"Fuck Jonny. He's in bloody Manchester. Do you think he gives a damn? He knows where you are, and he knows what I do to you. Shower, then get dressed. Quick."

"Where are we going?"

"Not far. To see a friend."

"Oh Christ, Jacko. Not that." Her voice rose. She stood to retrieve her clothing. "I'm sick of this! I won't go . . ."

He laughed. "No, not that. He's bought a flat. You're artsy. You could advise him on decorating." He put his arms around her. His fingers caressed her cheek.

"I'm not a decorator; I own a gallery. I won't go and I don't care what you threaten to do to Jonny. I'm sick of you." She tried to push him away, but he held her fast. He curled his fingers in her hair and pulled her face close to his.

"Do you think you have any choice? You're nothing to Jonny but a show wife. An arm-candy aristocrat. That hundred-thousand-a-year inheritance you brought with you doesn't go far past keeping your ridiculous art gallery afloat and paying tuition for those whelps of yours. Am I right? I'm all that keeps Little Jonny Wanker from pulling your kids out of that overpriced boarding school and sending you all packing. He'd be better off without you and that pile of Hampshire bricks you call a family home. Now, clean up and get dressed."

★ ★ ★

Bright halogen lights reflected off the stark white walls of the flat. Fiona stood by a window, sleek in her long cashmere coat. She felt like an actor in an absurd Victorian tableau. Four figures, three of them wondering, *"What next?"*

A man she didn't know, and had never seen, knelt in a

corner. He was dressed in a striped tie, crisp white shirt, and black pants. He turned his face towards her, wordlessly imploring. But what could she do?

She looked at Jacko, who stood a few feet to her right, quaking so hard Fiona thought he would collapse. Rivulets of sweat rolled down his face, much more profusely than when he had been fucking her.

She tore her gaze from Jacko and focused on the slender man standing between them. He was dressed in black, from his rubber-soled trainers to the military-style balaclava that rendered him unrecognizable. His gloved hands held a sawn-off shotgun.

Dark eyes assessed Fiona through the balaclava. "Why did you bring your friend, Jacko? I didn't tell you to bring anyone. You should have left her at the hotel."

Jacko's mouth moved, but no sounds came out.

"Is that all you have to say?" Balaclava said. "Oh, Jacko. You're such a fuck-up. You've got to learn to keep promises, mate. How could you think bringing her would make anything different? Trying to bribe me with her again? Letting me see the goods?"

"Again?" Fiona glared at Jacko, then at Balaclava. "I'm no fucking friend of his."

"He offered you to me just last week. Said you're beautiful." His eyes assessed her. "He said there's nothing like a mature woman who knows what she's there for. Why would you ever get involved with that tosser? I had no intention of taking him up on it. You weren't part of the debt."

He lifted his shotgun, the barrel inches from her face. "But now you're here, and that creates a problem."

Fiona's knees buckled. She braced herself on the windowsill. Drops of her urine splattered against her ankles. "Oh, God please. I have children who still need me. I didn't even want to come here. Just let me go."

The man looked at the puddle on the floor. "How embarrassing for all of us. Don't you think, Jacko? So sorry, lovely lady."

She squeezed her eyes shut. *Please, Jonny. Take care of Andy and Stella.*

The shotgun blast staggered her against the wall. A roaring sound filled her ears. She screamed to prove she wasn't dead, then forced her eyes open. Nausea knotted her gut and pushed at her throat. She scrabbled at the window latch, flung it open, and vomited.

THREE

Elaine twirled a fork in the can of tuna and plopped a second good-sized scoop into Scratch's bowl. The big grey tabby jumped to the tabletop, purring and rubbing his head on her hand.

"Sorry, mate. You may be the man of the house, but you eat on the floor, not the table." She shifted his bowl to a mat next to the fridge. Scratch dived after his dinner and crouched, alternately lapping at the tuna and purring. She watched and considered that her cat was more appreciative in his behaviour and fastidious about his eating habits than most people she knew.

Why would she not let him eat on the table? She loved him, stroked him, and fed him regularly. Every night he shared her bed, purring in a steady drone until he fell asleep, usually draped across her leg. All in all he had a good life and let her know he appreciated it. Yet she wasn't ready to concede sharing her dinner space just yet. *Limits are limits. You gotta keep something for yourself, Lainie.*

Elaine removed the tray of lasagna from the microwave, picked up a fork and a glass of merlot, and sat down at the kitchen table. She pondered the day's events while her laptop started up. Was it a coincidence those two uniforms arrived so quickly? If a bystander or someone in the pub had reported a fight, it would have taken several minutes to respond. But it had been only what—forty-five seconds or maybe a minute before they showed up? And they had known her name. Over thirty thousand officers in London, not counting City of London and Transport Police, and one random uniform knew her immediately? She didn't believe in coincidence.

Her laptop was up, so she put those thoughts out of her mind and typed the account of the tail and the confrontation into her note-card app.

She had learned nothing. No new leads to follow. No actionable evidence. But you never knew when a pattern would emerge. It could happen any day. Still, she hadn't found any new connections since she had returned to London from the Devon cottage where she had recuperated.

By this time half the lasagna was gone, as was her appetite. *Save it? No.* The fridge was packed with containers of half-eaten meals. Some day she would clean it out. Or maybe she should start cooking again.

She laughed. *Right, Lainie. When you can look at a kitchen knife without retching in panic.* She dumped the lasagna into the bin, poured herself another glass of wine, and retired to her bedroom, with the single note card.

She stood in front of the huge pinboard that occupied most of one wall. The board was divided into three columns. The "Leads" column on the left was bare. Only a few note cards dotted the central "Evidence" column, low down on the wall to denote their relative unimportance. The "Background" column on the right was half full. Lots of background, damn little evidence, no leads.

Above the pinboard, she had taped two images. One was a picture of Anton Srecko. His pale complexion, close-cropped hair, and grey eyes matched his lethal, soulless character. His smirk chided her for her lack of progress.

The other image was a simple black silhouette. She hated

Anton, but he was the enemy she knew. There were others she didn't know.

The silhouette's formless ignorance had begun to bother her more than Anton's smug familiarity. Someone, quite likely someone she had worked with, eaten lunch with, and tipped a pint with, had betrayed her. Any of her fellow coppers could be the shadow she sensed behind her.

Up until now she had focused on finding evidence that would incriminate Anton. Granted, she had plenty of free time. Her superiors had decided that she should return to service gradually because of her physical injuries and post-traumatic stress disorder, so she worked only half time at the College of Policing, and she could choose her hours. Even with that, she couldn't follow everyone who worked for that monster, all day every day. The paucity of evidence and complete lack of leads spoke to the futility of that approach. Could she be going about her investigation backwards?

Elaine lay back on her pillow, one arm crooked under her head. She was tired. Tired of the constant dull pain in her leg, the stabbing jolts behind her right eye, and the accompanying flashes of light. Tired of the opiates. Tired of the startled, flustered and then agonizingly polite responses she got from people at the market or in restaurants. Mostly she was tired of her fellow coppers. The way they stepped to the side when she passed in corridors. The way they avoided casual conversation, as if her rotten judgement and piss-poor luck would rub off on them.

She was tired of being the cheese, standing alone.

It had been a long day. She would think through it some other time. She padded to the shower, twisted the lever to hot, and opened it full on. God, but her leg ached. She popped a pill, undressed, and stood naked in front of the full-length mirror on her bathroom door. Surgery scars tracked across her abdomen. Others crisscrossed the splash of the bullet wound and the hollow place on the outside of her right leg. The socket under her right eye still drooped slightly. She needed a few more procedures to erase the slicing scar that jagged from her right temple, across her cheekbone, and down to her jaw, but she didn't think she would have it done. *No. That's mine. My memento mori.*

Elaine laughed aloud and stretched out her arms. She curtsied from side to side as if she were accepting applause. "Here I am. Look at me, rozzers. Here's what you get when you think you're some kind of saviour. Constables and sergeants, look and learn. I'm your fucking memento mori. Body and soul."

The hot shower roared behind her, fogging the mirror from the top down as steam flowed over the glass door. Ready. She swung open the door and stepped into the flow, the needle spray piercing her face, penetrating her scars, flaying her breasts and her back. She doused her body with rosemary and lavender cleanser and began to scrub. Her skin reddened under the scouring of her loofah.

Afterwards, she curled on her bed in the warmth of her thick, emerald-green bathrobe, with Scratch nestled in the crook of her knees. She rejected sleep as long as possible, her thoughts fencing with the opiates whirling in her bloodstream. Sleep began to overwhelm her consciousness. This was the limbo time when doubt and terror rose from her soul.

On most nights, in her sleep she saw Nilo's face, felt the burning knife at her cheek, gagged at the metallic smell of the slick redness all around her. Jerking awake, screaming in panic. How long could she remain driven by rage? How could she truly return to her career? Did she pursue the Sreckos only because little else seemed to matter anymore?

But tonight Peter stood over her. The image of his slightly crooked nose and deep-set blue eyes, framed by shoulder-length dark hair, lifted from somewhere in her heart.

Is that me moaning? I can't close my eyes. The light hurts, so white. Loud sounds, hissing, beeping, people barking. Too much. He's leaning over me, telling me he's here, better now, blocks the glaring light. Oh God, I can't breathe, can't—oh God, my chest—

She screamed awake and bolted from the bed, yanked open the French door and burst onto the veranda, gasping in the cold air, her heart thumping. Being outside, no matter how cold, was preferable to her enclosed bedroom. At last her breathing slowed as she regained control. She went back inside and sat on her sofa, her head in her hands.

I died. The nurse told me I flatlined. She said Peter kept trying. He willed me to live. He loves me. Will I ever know why?

FOUR

Monday night, Kensington

Fiona ran, her coat billowing. She was only ten steps out the front door of the house, but Jacko was already halfway to the car, parked a block away.

"Jesus, Jacko, wait!" She stopped, grasped one of the Victorian wrought-iron railings that separated the pavement from the basement steps of a house, and tore the spike-heeled pump from her left foot. As she lifted her right foot and reached for its shoe, her hand slipped, and she fell into the bars. The shoe in her hand clattered into the darkness. She heard the alarm on Jacko's car bleep twice, and saw the lights flash.

"For God's sake, wait for me!" She looked for the errant shoe but couldn't see it. In the dim light, she saw Jacko opening the car door. There was nothing for it but to run as fast as she could. "Jacko, you coward! Wait!"

Her bare feet slapped against the freezing pavement. The motor of Jacko's Jaguar roared to life. Fiona slipped between two parked cars and bolted across the street without looking. She was thirty feet from her goal when Jacko roared away towards Old Brompton Road.

Fiona slowed her pace and stopped, winded and gasping. What could she do now? A car door slammed behind her, and she turned to see another set of taillights pulling into the street near the house she had run from. The murderer? Her moment of panic subsided as she realized the car was moving in the other direction.

Where to go? Someone had certainly heard the shot or her screaming, so she still had to get away. Walking home barefoot was out of the question. Her feet already felt like they were freezing, and she lived in Mortlake, miles away on the other side of the Thames. Three blocks north she could certainly find a taxi near the cafés and hotels that clustered along Queen's Gate.

The lights of a busy, brightly lit neighbourhood pub glowed across the road. As she stepped into the light streaming from the pub windows, she looked down at the front of her coat. The cashmere was bloody in places, with small gobs of God knows what clinging to the fabric. She slipped into the shadow of an overhanging tree and swallowed hard against the nausea that again rose from her gut. Ahead of her, street lamps stood every thirty yards or so, on alternate sides of the street. No pedestrian, or taxi driver for that matter, would miss seeing all that gore. Nor would they miss a barefoot blonde carrying one shoe.

She took a huge breath. There was nothing to do but brave it out. Fiona walked past the pub, keeping in the shadow of the trees. A man and a woman embraced in the street light next to the pub entrance. "The Onslow Arms," the sign said. "Cask Ales Fine Wines Gourmet Dining." With each step, her bare feet sent needles of pain up her legs.

At the next intersection, she noticed a builder's rubbish skip sitting in the shadow of a large ash tree, a few yards down a small, curving side street. She turned the corner and climbed onto a crate next to the skip. What luck—it was half full of builder's waste. She pulled her small clutch purse from the inner pocket of her coat and slipped it into her bodice. After shifting some boxes, she was able to stuff the coat and her shoe under some plasterboard and plastic sheeting. It would have to do.

Without the coat, Fiona began to shiver, and the icy pavement had by now removed all feeling in her feet. She laughed at herself. A few minutes ago, she'd been a barefoot, middle-aged slag, walking down the street in a warm, but blood-soaked, coat. Now she was a barefoot, middle-aged slag, walking down the street, shivering in a sleek, windblown, black dress. Hell, two hours ago she had been the gorgeous wife of a high-placed public servant, meeting her lover in an exclusive boutique hotel.

How times change.

Fortunately, no one paid any attention to her until she reached Old Brompton Road and Queen's Gate. It was London, after all. Thank God, a taxi was at the corner rank. Horns blared as she scurried across the busy road.

"Are you all right, lady?" The driver's face showed concern as he watched her shiver.

She climbed into the back of the cab. "Yes, thanks. Just lost my coat. Mort—" She stopped. One of the CCTV cameras had probably caught her climbing into the cab, so giving the driver her home address would be like calling the police. She thought quickly. "Mortlake Station, please." She could walk from there.

She saw the driver's eyebrows rise when he heard the address. "Right, then." He passed a package back to her. His voice was kind. "Here's a fleece to help you warm up."

She took it and wrapped it tightly around her shoulders and over her legs. "Thank you so much. It was hellishly cold out there without my coat."

The driver studied her in the mirror, so she averted her face and snuggled into the corner of the seat. Questions stirred in her mind. Why had Jacko taken her with him to that god-awful place? Why hadn't he let her leave the hotel? And why were she and Jacko still alive? Wouldn't the killer have eliminated the only witnesses? She had no answers, but she was married to a Metropolitan Police Commander, and she knew eventually detectives would come to her with other, more damning questions.

At last the taxi trundled west on the A4 towards Chiswick Bridge. Fiona wriggled deeper into the blanket and watched Kensington roll past. Part of the debt, the killer had said. It made sense that Jacko thought of her as payment. Two years ago she'd agreed to just that kind of arrangement. How could she have imagined that was the right decision?

She'd think of that tomorrow. Right now she had to figure out how to get home from Mortlake Station without being seen. The damn CCTV cameras seemed to be everywhere.

FIVE

Tuesday morning, Kensington

Detective Constable Philip Bull stopped his aging Ford Mondeo a few feet short of the blue-taped police cordon. Beside him sat Detective Sergeant Simon Costello. Bull and Costello could not have been more different physically.

Bull was nearly six feet tall and dark-skinned, with a shaved head that perched on a thick neck and powerful shoulders. His off-the-peg suits never seemed to fit properly. Costello was slight and fair, six inches shorter than Bull, with a full head of blazing red hair. He favoured tailored suits.

They peered through the windscreen at the procession of outrageously expensive, nearly identical, marble-white and cream-brick colonnaded homes that marched along each side of the chic South Kensington street. Along the pavement, black wrought-iron railings separated the upstairs and downstairs entrances to each house.

Yellow-vested police moved along the line of cars parked on each side of the street, peering into the windows, jotting down number plates. Others stood at strategic points along the pavement. Several plain-clothes detectives stood singly, muttering into mobile phones. White-clad forensic technicians glided purposefully in and out of the house two doors up the street on their right.

Costello grunted. "The place is crawling with coppers. Why did they call us out?"

Bull lowered his window and flashed his warrant card at a uniformed officer approaching the car. "DC Bull and DS Costello. Okay to leave it here?"

The officer checked his clipboard. "Initials here." He pointed behind the car. "Pull in back there. DI Novak's inside."

Bull closed his window and reversed the car. "Dunno. You're a DS. Didn't they tell you?"

"Right. Now they tell me everything," Costello said. "I meant to ask, how's Liz? Haven't seen her in months."

Bull hesitated before he answered. "Better."

"She's been back on duty how long? About six months?"

A drop of cold rain caught Bull in the eye as he angled his large frame out of the driver's door. He blinked hard and pulled the collar of his coat tighter around his throat. The car chirped as he clicked the lock. "Closer to seven. Let's get inside." At the stoop a small "For Sale" sign sported a telephone number. Bull and Costello pulled on their scene suits and entered the house.

The interior was empty of furniture, rugs, and any evidence of habitation. White travertine floors, white plaster walls, crown mouldings, ceilings, every shadowless angle blurred by halogen lighting from track lights installed in the ceiling.

"This place is bloody clinical," Costello said, as two white-suited technicians hurried by, each wearing blue paper booties and carrying aluminium equipment cases.

"Like some sci-fi movie set," Bull replied. "I wonder if the owners of this place made guests wear a scene suit? Wouldn't want to shed lint or skin cells all about."

Costello led the way down a wide corridor with arched entries into adjoining rooms. In one room a dark, weeping woman dressed in black skinny jeans and a red woolly jumper stood next to a window, talking to a pair of detectives. "Guess she found the body."

As they approached the end of the corridor, the smell of fresh paint mixed with the odour of death and faeces. Bull made a wry face. "Novak must be back here. And the body too, if my nose is right."

They passed a kitchen on the left, paint cloths covering counters, two ladders leaning against cabinets. They turned right into what once might have been a large study or perhaps a conservatory. A double window in the back wall stood wide open, allowing cold wind to whirl around the room. Despite the fresh air, Bull sensed the clinging odour he had learned too well during two tours in Afghanistan.

Costello grimaced. "Good god."

In the far corner of the room, the body of a man slumped, on his knees, facing the wall. His hands were restrained behind him with a cable tie. The middle of his head was missing, as if an explosion had cut a path rear-to-front, leaving only ragged flaps of flesh attaching his ears to his shoulders. Dried blood and matter blackened the back of his shirt and stained the floor behind him. The wall several feet on each side and up to the ceiling was streaked with heavy gore. Two crime scene investigators had stretched a body bag on the floor. From their gestures, Bull assumed the CSIs were discussing how to remove the body with the least disruption to the scene. Or perhaps they were debating how to keep what remained of the poor sod's head from falling off.

A detective squatted on a steel stepping plate near the window, talking to one of the technicians. His sleek hair and trim, tailored suit didn't look very cop-like. He reminded Bull of an upper-class amateur detective from a 1930s mystery novel. The only thing missing was a monocle—and a white scene suit to prevent contamination of the crime scene. Bull couldn't believe it. He elbowed Costello to get his attention, and silently mouthed the words *scene suit*. One after the other, they moved across the floor, careful to stay on the stepping plates the CSIs had laid out.

"DS Costello, DC Bull." The detective spoke in a crisp, clipped style. "I'm DI Novak. Glad you're aboard." He tipped his head towards the corpse. "Most likely dead a couple of days. Male, average height, muscular, long dark hair." He pointed at a trail of blood-matted hair hanging from a fragment of scalp. "Ponytail, maybe. I estimate forties, but hard to tell. Professional appearance. Possibly handmade shoes. Nails manicured, but his hands are thick, calloused like he's done manual work. Execution style. Shotgun from a couple of feet. Splattered most of his head over the walls and into the plaster. Lots of blowback. Whoever did it got quite a bath."

The CSIs had enclosed what was left of the victim's head in a large, clear plastic sack. The detectives watched as they uncoiled the body and laid it out on the black body bag. The front of the shirt was as covered with carnage as the back. Through the sack, Bull could tell there wasn't enough face left for identification. Perhaps some of the teeth had survived. Once the body bag was zipped, Novak returned to his briefing.

"Blood spatter shows the window was shut at the time of the shot, opened after. Why? No sign of forced entry, nothing in the flat to steal. The killer left the door to the room closed. The flat's for sale. A woman from the property company found him. Costello, run the house-to-house along this street and the one behind. The usual. Focus on the last twenty-four to seventy-two hours, Tuesday through today. Bull, stick here with the forensics blokes and then with the medical examiner. Get the post-mortem results to me ASAP. Questions?"

Costello spoke. "It rained hard most of Sunday right up until dusk. Rain might have washed or damaged the splatter on the open window. Any sign of that?"

Novak assessed the slightly built detective, then turned to one of the technicians. "Did it look like spatter had washed off the window? Water on the floor?"

The CSI thought for a moment then shook his head. "No, sir. There were small flecks of brain matter adhering to some of the glass panes. No sign of puddling. Except for this. He pointed to a stain on the floor near the window. I think it's urine."

"Let us know when you're sure." Novak gave Costello a crisp nod. "Good point, Sergeant. Helps narrow the time of death. Focus on Sunday night to now, then." He looked at Bull. "Anything else? No? Ring me as soon as you have anything."

SIX

Tuesday afternoon, Hendon

These chairs are bloody hard. Elaine had forgotten the cushion she usually took to meetings, and her right leg had begun to ache. She glanced at the wall clock, then let her gaze wander. A hundred or so officers, plain clothes and uniform, filled the room, listening to the latest issues and developments in neighbourhood policing. As she watched, several of her colleagues flicked their eyes towards the clock on the wall. The wall clock was at the front, right above the video screen, where bored coppers could see it without craning their necks. Constant glancing made the presentations seem interminable.

She had returned to work before her compassionate leave was finished, so her superiors called her College of Policing assignment "light duty." Last week she had written a research paper illustrating the effect of dog ownership in reducing burglaries. One of the sergeants had just finished presenting it, to polite applause and few questions.

Twelve years in murder investigation, and I'm writing about dogs. Compassionate assignment, my arse. It's bloody hell. "I'm fucking useless," she muttered under her breath.

The Superintendent, seated next to her, leaned over and whispered, "Sorry, what?"

"Nothing, sir. He did a good job." *Dammit, watch yourself, Lainie.* He nodded politely. "Quite right, DCI Hope."

She knew *useless* was too strong a word. Community policing was multi-faceted, and each aspect presented its own challenges. What strained her was inventing reasons to be away from her desk so she could continue to investigate the Srecko operation. But she was here, so she might as well listen.

The next speaker, a female commander in charge of one of the East London boroughs, presented the results of her social media scheme to reach more young people in her area. The goal was open communication, and she had certainly succeeded. Youngsters messaged and tweeted with her local force at an almost overwhelming rate. Success! But the forward-thinking commander didn't reveal to her audience what the young people were actually saying. According to the Met rumour mill, at least half the messages contained advice about where she could store her truncheon—public opinion varied on that topic. During the Q&A, Elaine briefly considered mentioning the Law of Unintended Consequences, but held her tongue. Her comment wouldn't have been well received.

The Chief Superintendent in charge of the programme next introduced a certain Detective Inspector Mehta from financial crimes, who would talk about real estate transactions.

Elaine closed her eyes. It had been a dreadful night. The bloody dream had awakened her at about two o'clock in the morning. As usual, she hadn't fallen back to sleep once the panic subsided. She dozed off and on until her alarm buzzed at six AM.

". . . deeper blue boroughs are those in which property values have risen fastest over the last two years."

Elaine caught herself as her head began to nod. When she looked up, the slide on the screen portrayed a colour-coded map of London neighbourhoods.

". . . and if we overlay the map to show purchases in the last five years by offshore companies, it becomes apparent that . . ."

Her eyelids were drooping again. If she let them close, she'd doze off, and that wouldn't do with all the commanders and assistant commissioners in the room. Elaine wasn't exactly well loved among those exalted ranks—more of an embarrassment, although none would admit it to her face. She knew they all were waiting for an excuse to fling her out the door, especially if her firing could be construed as sympathetic. If only she could convince them she was right about the Sreckos.

Wait. Offshore companies? What was he saying? Dammit, Lainie. Stay focused!

". . . the boroughs with the highest rise in property values also show the fastest rising incidence of offshore ownership. Given that most of these companies are based in banking havens such as the Channel Islands, the Cayman Islands, or in some instances Eastern European nations, actual ownership is difficult to ascertain."

The DI's voice was soft and soporific. Elaine forced her eyes open. Perhaps, if she could hire him to stand at the foot of her bed at night and give this presentation, she wouldn't need a sedative. *Eastern European nations? Christ! What did I miss?*

". . . so these so-called 'friendly' solicitors first set up shell companies in these havens, where banking laws are a bit looser, and financial scrutiny is almost nonexistent."

Is that what Jackson Greene was doing before he was murdered? Setting up shell companies for Anton Srecko? There was that Cambrian Estates company that was based in a little old lady's council flat in Cardiff. It was owned by some other shell company in Macedonia or Montenegro or somewhere. Damn the pain meds. Focus, Lainie!

". . . and this is what we call Lights Out London. Not the song title. Significant portions of our most exclusive neighbourhoods are dark most nights because of absentee owners. Crooks and gangsters, usually from Eastern Europe, are buying property at outrageous prices so they can launder the money they've stolen from their governments or made from smuggling drugs and cigarettes." Mehta paused. "And, increasingly, human trafficking, which is becoming more pervasive and much more profitable than most of the other criminal endeavours."

Elaine's pulse quickened. *That's what the Sreckos were doing.*

". . . some of our oldest and most trusted property companies are being exposed to criminal prosecution because a few of their unscrupulous agents and managers ignore our proceeds of crime laws and accept this tainted money."

Is that why Geri Harding was murdered? Had the estate agent stumbled onto something?

". . . an unrecorded conversation here, an under-the-table payment there, a hefty solicitor's fee, and presto—the estate agent walks away with a fat commission; the criminal has a shiny new flat for his girlfriend; and property taxes rise for the legitimate property owners in the area. The property stays vacant most of the year, so business at local shops suffers. Questions?"

It was starting to make sense. The Imperial and Republic Group company the Sreckos owned might be all about money laundering. Elaine shot her arm into the air and stood before the DI could acknowledge her. "DCI Hope here. Suppose money laundering like you describe was a property company's main business? Maybe their only business? Have you ever encountered that?"

DI Mehta shook his head. "Not to my knowledge. Not since I've been in Operation Sterling. I suppose it's possible. I could check with Revenue and Customs. Perhaps it's happened in another city."

Elaine pressed. "What about business properties? Have you seen much laundering activity in office blocks or industrial estates?"

The superintendent interrupted. "Pardon, DCI Hope. We're out of time here, and we have a very busy schedule for the rest of today. Perhaps you and DI Mehta can take the discussion offline? Thank you."

Elaine made eye contact with Mehta, who nodded. This might get interesting.

SEVEN

Tuesday afternoon, Kensington

The house-to-house was completed far too quickly for Costello's liking. He gathered the team around him on the pavement. "Given your speedy return, I assume the neighbourhood is full of fast talkers. So what have you got? Anything interesting?"

One of the younger uniforms raised his hand. "No one's home, Sarge. A lot of the houses we knocked up, no one's there. Right, Simpson?" The officer next to him nodded. "We were on that back street." He looked at his notebook. "Lecky Street. Like it's a ghost town. The residents we spoke with don't recall anything unusual."

Another officer spoke. "I had two interesting interviews. Both of them were women, Russian or from over there somewhere. One said her father's business owns the house. The other one was older, two kids playing in the room. Said her husband was a government minister. Ukraine, I think." He flipped open his notebook. "Yes. She said he was in Kiev."

"Interesting enough for a second interview?" Costello asked.

"Well, I asked that first one, the young one, what kind of business her father owned, but she was vague, like . . ." The officer looked at his notes and read aloud. " 'He owns a lot of them. I don't pay attention, so I don't know what he does.' She had a heavy accent. Sounded bored." He turned to another page. "This other one said she and the kids are just here for the shopping. She was dripping with jewellery worth about a year of my pay, I reckon."

"That ties with one of the gents I spoke to." One of the female uniforms pulled out her notebook. "Older fellow. Ronald Caddigan, lives at number twenty-three in the mews. We asked about the vacant houses. He about blew his top. Rattled on, all militant, about foreign owners who look like criminals, coming here and buying up houses for outrageous sums. Then they're only in the house for a couple of months a year, maybe the summer. But they'll pay whatever the owner asks. He said his property value has almost tripled in two years, so much that he can't afford the taxes and he's thinking about selling up. Said his family had lived in Kensington over a hundred years. Now he'll have to move to a flat or maybe get out of London entirely. He was upset, wanted to know what we could do about it."

"Not bloody much," Costello said. "Not anything, unless you advised him to grab the lolly and run." He looked up at the darkened sky. The dusk was fading, and more raindrops were falling. "Right, then. Get back to the nick and write up what you have. Then get your sorry backsides home and to bed. Morning briefing at six thirty."

Tuesday night, Brentford

Scratch hopped up on the bed and sat next to Elaine, blessing her with his presence. When she crooked her finger and rubbed under his chin, he stretched his neck, and the locomotive purrs began. The clock indicated ten. She thought she might as well see what was happening in the world, so she clicked on the TV.

". . . found by a decorator in an empty South Kensington flat. The dead man remains unidentified at this time. Detective

Inspector John Novak has asked anyone in the vicinity of Onslow Gardens and Fulham Road, South Kensington, between Wednesday and Friday morning, to come forward if they saw or heard anything suspicious."

Damn wretched irony for the poor dead sod. Anonymous fame. Novak, eh? Last I heard he'd been transferred to the National Crime Agency. Haven't heard much about him in the last year. Or has it been two? As she watched, Costello and Bull walked through the background of the news video. She smiled at the sight of them. She and Costello had been on the same murder investigation team for three years. Bull had come on board just over a year ago. They had been two stalwarts of a great team. Costello's brains and quick-witted experience; Bull's massive presence, dogged persistence, and fierce loyalty.

That was all before, though. Before that one time she didn't read the situation right. Before that Serbian goon beat up Liz. Elaine let her head fall back against the pillow.

Before I went into that godforsaken brothel without backup. A cardinal fucking sin.

If she hadn't, maybe Ximena would still be alive. The young prostitute had wanted out of the game, had wanted to go home to Spain.

If I had waited a few more minutes, maybe Nilo would have surrendered. But Elaine thought somehow the bastard knew she would come in after him. She could have broken him in an interrogation. She knew it. But she had killed him, and Anton still walked the streets.

She shifted her attention to the TV. The dead man's forty-five seconds of fame were over. The newsreader now droned on about hooligan damage that had occurred during New Year's celebrations. She clicked the TV off.

The newsreader had said Onslow Gardens and Fulham Road, which was right in the middle of South Kensington, one of the darkest blue neighbourhoods on Mehta's map at his Lights Out London presentation.

She'd last spoken with Simon Costello two weeks ago, when she went to his promotion party after he'd made sergeant. Maybe it was time to touch base with him. She dialled.

"Costello. Hello, guv." She enjoyed Simon's Irish accent, which contrasted well with her easy Scottish burr.

"Hi, brand-new Detective Sergeant Costello. I saw you and Bull on the news. What's your position on the team now that you're a sergeant?"

"H2H today, then DI Novak put me on the incident room beginning tomorrow."

"Ah. High visibility. I'm sure you'll do splendidly. Look, I know you've had a long day, so I won't keep you. What do you know about the house where your poor sod was murdered? Anything on the ownership? Reason I'm asking is I saw a presentation on that area of London today. I'm doing some research into foreign ownership, empty houses, and I'm curious."

Costello laughed. "We used to take bets about whether you were psychic."

"Good. The more who fear my superpowers, the better. Although, I think over the last few months my therapist has largely taken them away. It sounds like you've something to tell me?"

"Big, empty house. Up for sale in a neighbourhood of other big, empty houses. This one's divided into two large flats. Just under four million each. An interesting item is that there was no forced entry, no sign of lock picking. If it was locked, someone had a key to get in. All the estate agent's keys are accounted for."

"Previous occupants?"

"The locks were changed after they left, so . . ."

"So either the estate agent is lying, or some keys have gone astray."

"Could be. It's owned by a company called Boxe-Berkshire.

DI Novak says it's an old one, upstanding. He put one of the new DCs on it."

"Upstanding." Elaine sighed. "Ever since our last case, I get a hollow feeling when I hear that word applied to a business."

"I hear you, ma'am. I've been a bit less trusting of reputations since we sussed out Anton Srecko and his IRG company."

"Have you ever dug through the online archives at Companies House?"

"No, but that's where Cromarty got the company info when we were on the Srecko case, so if anyone knows how, he does." DC Evan Cromarty had been the researcher on Elaine's last team. His digital abilities were renowned.

"Right. Thought you might say that. I'll give him a call. By the way, how's Novak to work for?"

Costello hesitated before he answered. "I'm reserving judgement right now. I could say he's a bit unorthodox, but it's only been one day."

"Thanks, Simon." Elaine rang off. She felt the old excitement of being on the trail of something real, moving towards finding leads. And the more leads she had, the closer she was to building a case.

Tuesday night, Notting Hill

"Don't get more out of control than you already are. You're on thin ice."

Bluster. Jacko realized he shouldn't have answered when his mobile rang. He looked at his right shoe and wondered when the new scuff across the toe had appeared. Probably when that little bitch threw it at him last week. He'd ducked, and the shoe caromed off a bureau and lodged behind the bedside table. Time to be cool. "*Tranquille*, René. You need to learn patience. I gave you a payment last month."

"That was for three months ago."

"I've been a couple of payments behind for years, and you've not gotten tetchy. You took my winnings last week."

"You don't win often enough, Jacko. I need to think again about the interest rate."

"We had an agreement."

"You think you are dealing with one of your English gentlemen? Or a bank? *Non, mon cher avocat.* When we settle, we will settle out of court." René's soft laugh pierced Jacko's nonchalance. The fucking Frenchman was dangerous when he was quiet.

"I'm strapped. No readies for a couple of weeks. Give me a few days. I'll call you back."

"A few days?" Again, René's soft laugh raised the hair on Jacko's neck. "Not too skint to take another English *salope* to that boutique hotel last night. Blondes, brunettes, at least one redhead. Your taste is going to bankrupt you, Jacko. Maybe you need to consider a motel on the motorway."

This conversation had become as tiresome as that love-struck little shoe slinger's tear-fuelled anger. "Maybe you need to consider who you're talking to. I wasn't born yesterday. Gambling and fucking are time-honoured vices. Imprudent. Certainly immoral. But not illegal."

"You witnessed a murder and didn't report it."

"Perhaps I should report it. You know, I think I know why you wanted me there, but I want to hear you say it."

"You won't report it. And you need to know we mean business."

Jacko laughed. "I'm supposed to believe you're going to kill me before I pay you the twenty-five thousand quid? I don't think so."

"If we can do that, we can do other things."

"Other things would only delay payment."

"Who's the blonde? Why did you bring her? It doesn't say much for your discretion."

"Your man should have killed her when he had the chance. Come to think of it, why didn't he?"

"He only expected you."

Jacko laughed louder and longer than he needed to. "Only expected me? You mean he only brought one shell? What a fucking amateur!"

"He had no instructions about her and didn't want to use his pistol. The blonde is the wild card. I need her name, Jacko."

"You'll get your money. It's late and I have a trial tomorrow." He rang off.

Fiona wasn't a wild card, she was his ace in the hole. He couldn't squander her.

EIGHT

Wednesday morning, Kensington

"Good morning, boys and girls. I'm Sergeant Costello, and I'll be running the incident room."

Bull smiled to himself. Costello had opened the first morning status meeting using Elaine's standard greeting, so he was falling back on comfortable routine. It's what people do, especially when they've learned from the best. DCI Hope had been Bull's first boss in homicide, and Costello had been on the team too.

Bull turned his attention to what Costello was saying. "I'll assign actions and liaise with other units. DI Novak is senior investigating officer. He'll be here in a few minutes. We'll be operating out of Kensington nick. We should have CCTV footage for public cameras within two blocks around the murder scene by later this morning. Some of you will be assigned to that. DC Bull, DI Novak wants you to follow up with Dr. Kumar on the post-mortem, and then check with shops and businesses, especially that pub"—Costello referred to his notes—"the Onslow Arms, to get copies of their CCTV. This evening we'll go back and resume the house-to-house, as residents are more likely to be home. I've posted assignments on the board, so check there and get going once DI Novak adjourns our little soiree. He'll be here in a few minutes. Questions?"

A DC on the other side of the room spoke up. "Sarge, we've all been assigned to this team sort of hodgepodge. From all over."

Costello shrugged. "The guv said the other teams were stretched, so they had to cobble together a new one."

The DC scanned the room. "Seems they pulled us together awfully quick. Novak hasn't been on murder for over a year."

"It's DI Novak or Mister Novak. Or sir." Novak's voice came from the back of the room. He took his place at the front next to Costello. "I apologize for being late. DC Bull, the post-mortem?"

Bull glanced at the wall clock. "I talked to Dr. Kumar ten minutes ago. He starts in about a half hour. I figure I have time to get there."

"Good. Liaise with forensics. Keep me posted. If you can't find me"—he jerked his head sideways—"then DS Costello."

Bull nodded. This was unusual. A sergeant usually liaised with outside resources.

Novak pulled out his mobile and pressed a few buttons. "You now have my number. Call when you have something from Kumar. And get hold of the crime scene report. Leave now. You can catch up on everything later with DS Costello."

Bull's mobile rang as Novak's call came in. He swiped "Decline" as he turned and left the meeting. "Right, sir."

Wednesday morning, Mortlake

"Don't you think you should see a doctor, darling?" Jonny's plummy Oxbridge tones resonated with social position and self-satisfied privilege. In fact, he was the son of a Welsh tailor, had excelled in his local comprehensive schools, and had attended Bangor on a scholarship. Jonny liked playing roles.

Fiona pulled her duvet further up over her face and groaned.

It would be a blessing if she withered and died in bed. "I think it's a flu bug. I'll feel better soon."

Jonny sat on the edge of her bed. His sleeked black hair and crisp white uniform shirt showed he was ready to leave for his office at New Scotland Yard. "You were in bed all day yesterday. You didn't even call the gallery. Siobhan actually called me, she was that worried. She said you hadn't phoned the gallery, and you weren't answering your mobile. I—"

"I know, Jonny, I know. You were worried. You told me that last night." When Jonny recoiled at her tone, she reached out and put her hand on his knee. "Sorry. I need another day in bed is all. Siobhan runs the gallery far better than I do. Besides, she'd rather be there alone with that skinny, fawning toy she keeps—Oliver, or whatever its name is this month."

"That's harsh. I didn't get that impression at all. She was worried. This isn't the flu, and you haven't once peeked out of your bedroom since I got back from Manchester. So I'm concerned too. It's not like you, Fee."

Couldn't he leave her alone? He was so good at talking her into a corner. Just like thirty years ago when that copper had caught her stoned, sleeping in her car with a half-smoked joint in the ashtray. This time the cop was Jonny, perfectly turned out in his uniform, immaculate hair, stubble-free face, and gleaming teeth implants. She needed to buy some time.

"So, what am I like, Jonny? Tell me who you think your little Fee really is. And while you're at it, tell me who the hell you are now. Right now, today. Are you who you were when we met? Commander Jonathan Hughes, all macho in his starched white shirt, black tie and trousers, and mirror-shined boots? Or are you who you were three years ago, when you came out to me? Or maybe you've decided to reinvent yourself again? What is it this time? Now you want a sex change? Commander *Joan* Hughes?"

Jonny's face reddened. He spluttered. "Lie there, then.

Wallow in it, whatever it is." He turned and stormed from the room.

Fiona waited for the slam of the front door, but it didn't come. He was probably fuming in his study. She lay staring at the ceiling, her arm crooked over her forehead. It would only be a matter of time before the knock on the front door. How long would she have? Thank God, she'd left her lambskin gloves on when she'd followed Jacko into the Kensington flat, so no fingerprints.

But DNA was a different story. Before she was married to Jonny, she'd given a blood sample so they could record her DNA, in case she was the target of kidnapping due to her aristocratic pedigree. The National DNA Database was used for criminals, so she doubted her sample was there. But it was on file somewhere.

A web search the previous day had told her that it was difficult to extract DNA from vomit because of the stomach acid and DNA from food she'd eaten. But she'd puddled on the floor. Successful DNA extraction from urine required the presence of skin cells—women's urine typically contained more than men's. And there was always the possibility the CSI technicians would find a stray hair.

What worried her most was CCTV. The closed-circuit cameras that blanketed London made it almost impossible to move undetected down many streets, especially in upmarket areas. She still had the dress she had worn, so she needed to get rid of it. And what would happen if—when—they found her coat and shoes?

Perhaps the police wouldn't show up unannounced. Perhaps they would have a quiet word with Jonny and ask him to bring her to the station for questioning. She knew she couldn't stay in bed forever, but what should she do? It seemed to her that no matter what she did, her life would be ruined. Jacko hadn't returned any of her calls. He'd left her to fend for herself. No surprise there.

Who could she turn to? No matter how deceptive Jonny was in his personal life, he was true to his professional oath. She knew that much. Telling him would force him to choose between her and his career. She was a witness and she had destroyed evidence, so there probably would be charges. And if he were forced to choose between her and his career, he would probably divorce her. If that happened, she would have two more years to find another husband. Minus any jail sentence.

She could visit Aunt Peg at the family pile in the country. Peg was always good for a cup of tea and a sympathetic ear. Fiona could lay herself up and lick her wounds.

She closed her eyes. That's it. Go to Hampshire, show Peg and Uncle Fritz some love, and, if the weather held, walk the meadows and ride horses until the police showed up. She breathed deeply in satisfaction at the thought.

"That was a huge sigh."

Jonny's voice startled her from her reverie. She opened her eyes to see him gazing down at her from the edge of the bed.

"Look, Fee. I don't know what's going on, but why did you turn on me? I know I haven't always been upfront with you, but I'm the same man I was when I left on Sunday. We were fine then. You were busy, looking forward to planning your new exhibition. Now I'm back, and you're acting like a twelve-year-old with a dead pony. Why don't . . ." His face relaxed into resignation. "What did you do, Fee? What happened?"

Fiona rolled over so she wouldn't have to face him. "No. I don't want to talk right now. Why don't you go to the office."

"Did Jacko hurt you? He's a sick bastard, sweetheart. I ought to know."

She sensed him standing still for about ten seconds, then felt his weight on the bed as he leaned over her. She felt his lips brush her hair, scented the citrus in his aftershave. She spoke when she heard his footsteps move towards the door. "Jonny? I may go down to Hampshire this afternoon. I haven't seen Peg in a couple of months, and I need to check on the house. Maybe visit the kids at school. Ride. Get some fresh air."

"That sounds nice. You know whatever you need is alright with me. I'm meeting late tonight, but you know you can call any time. If I can get away early Friday, maybe I'll join you there on the weekend. We can bring the kids up from Winchester. Have a barbecue if the weather stays nice."

Her bedroom door clicked shut. *Meeting late*—two code words, along with *weekend conference*, that years ago had become the encrypted death of her marriage. Two code words that had propelled her—and Jonny too—into the nightmare their marriage had become. Everywhere she turned, she was trapped. When she heard his footsteps recede, she curled in a ball and wept.

Wednesday morning, Fulham

Bull took the small vial of waxy VapoRub out of his pocket and smeared some under his nose. The strong menthol and eucalyptus scent didn't completely mask the odour, but it certainly helped. The exhibits officer and photographer had done the same. Apparently none of them had gotten used to the smell of death. PC Dixon, who had been first on the scene, stood by to ascertain that, yes, this was the same body he had originally discovered at the house on Selwood Terrace.

Dr. Kumar, the medical examiner, had made his initial observations and begun to remove the victim's clothes. It wasn't a straightforward task. The blood had dried, so it was a matter of softening the cloth with water and cutting the still blood-stiffened clothes from the body. Once that was done, they could carefully inspect what was revealed, then wash off yet more blood. The photographer documented the process. The exhibits officer described the items into a recorder as he bagged them.

"Shoes, loafers, black leather, Marks and Spencer label. Soles slightly worn under ball of foot. Heels worn on the outside."

"Trousers, black, wool blend, Marks and Spencer label."

Kumar and his assistant disrobed the body, moving from the feet upwards.

"Well, this is impressive." Kumar's assistant had peeled the shirt from the victim's back. He looked at Bull and jerked his head towards the corpse. Bull stepped closer.

As the water sluiced the caked blood away, an eagle with two heads facing in opposite directions emerged. The eagle's wings extended across the man's back and over his shoulders. Three distinct words were written in Cyrillic script above a red and yellow shield on the eagle's breast. Rinsing more blood revealed a tattoo of a tiger wrapped around the man's upper arm.

Bull pulled out his smartphone and took some pictures. Once he was sure he had good shots of the tattoos, he dialled Novak.

"Sir, something you might want to see. It looks military. I'm sending images to your mobile."

"Yes." It was half a minute before Novak mumbled a few unintelligible words.

"Sir? I didn't receive you."

Novak cleared his throat. "Serbian Volunteer Guard. Tigrovi. An Arkan Tiger. Crime scene report?"

"Preliminary in about an hour. I'll send the link."

"What next?"

"Back to Kensington to check for CCTV cameras."

"Okay. Good work." Novak rang off.

Wednesday morning, Hendon

Elaine gazed out the window of her office at the College of Policing. Despite the boredom and busywork, or perhaps because of it, she'd been given a decent playpen. From her south-facing window she could see over the railroad tracks and Colindeep Lane, to the neat rows of semi-detached homes in West Hendon.

Her early morning conversation with Cromarty had been forty-five minutes well spent. When she'd arrived at the office, she'd had no idea how to begin the web search. Cromarty's tutelage had shown her where to start. He'd also recommended that instead of focusing strictly on Srecko's Imperial and Republic Group, she expand the search to include a second company and look for connections. She reasoned that Boxe-Berkshire, the company Costello had mentioned, was a decent bet for the second company. She had to start somewhere, if only to get the hang of how to conduct a search. Plus, if she turned up anything, she could share the knowledge with Costello and Bull. Doing that might be one way to show the Met that she was ready to return to murder investigation.

First, the government website for Companies House allowed her to download lists of the two firms' directors and their numerous subsidiary shell companies, all of which she loaded into a spreadsheet Cromarty had sent her. She sorted the data and used two of the software tools Cromarty had provided—he called them "macros"—to match the various lists against one another and against property ownership rolls from a different address database.

She worked for several hours, and after two more calls to Cromarty for advice, she used a police application to chart the addresses on a map of London. At last her efforts resulted in some interesting correlations. Neither IRG nor Boxe-Berkshire owned many properties outright—both were investors in numerous shell companies. This wasn't unusual for real estate firms. It was the nature of the business to form investment and development partnerships focused on a single location, then dissolve them once the property was built or sold. However, both firms she was investigating tended to have directors who lived offshore, and a few of those directors overlapped. For the London properties, she'd noted several clusters of locations where subsidiaries of both companies owned adjacent buildings or properties nearby.

Now Elaine held in her lap a sheaf of papers that possibly contained the first actionable information she had found in months. After Tuesday's presentation, she and Mehta had agreed to meet Thursday morning, but he hadn't rung her to set the time and place. Joanna Christie had seemed sympathetic when they had parted Monday. Perhaps she would be inclined to help provide information.

Elaine stuffed the papers into her bag. Joanna first, then Mehta.

NINE

Bull pasted the web link for the crime scene report into his email and sent it directly to Novak, copying Costello for posting with the team's online files. Then he began the drive back to Selwood Terrace.

On the way, Bull dug into his memory. Communist Yugoslavia had broken up after the fall of the Soviet Union. The problem was that during the Communist rule, from 1946 until 1991, all the ethnic groups had moved around, gotten mixed up. And then, in 1991, the borders were redrawn. Several countries had appeared almost overnight.

Not everyone liked the new borders, especially the ethnic Serbs living in Bosnian territory. In 1992, the Serbs drew a long, crooked line and called everything on their side the "Republika Srpska." They declared only ethnic Serbs, who were mostly Orthodox Christians, could live there. A lot of Muslim Bosnians and Catholic Croats happened to be living in neighbourhoods on the wrong side of the line. Those areas needed to be "cleansed." When the Orthodox Christian comrades were finished, tens of thousands of civilian Bosnians and Croats were dead.

Bull's thoughts shifted back to the matter at hand. Should he tell Liz the victim was a Bosnian Serb? She'd been a wreck after the Srecko investigation. It wasn't only what had happened to her that caused her emotional trauma, but also what had happened to Elaine. No, he couldn't keep it from Liz. She was a copper too, and they were as good as married. He wanted to be married, anyway. Sometimes he wasn't sure how she felt about being together.

And what about Elaine? Should he pass it along to her? If he did, what would she do with it? For all her good traits, she could be impulsive. She might start asking Novak about the investigation. Then the question would be who had broken security, and Novak would look at him.

Loyalty could be such a pain in the arse. Maybe Costello would have some ideas about how to manage it.

Fifteen minutes later, Bull slid his aging Ford Mondeo into a space on Selwood Terrace, a few houses along from the murder scene, and assessed the territory. One block behind him was the Fulham Road intersection, with its small shops and boutiques featuring designer furniture and women's clothing. Ahead on the left sat the Onslow Arms pub, and two long blocks beyond it roared the busy intersection at Old Brompton Road, with its coffee shops, cafés, and pubs, all of which served the traffic generated by the posh boutique hotels of Queen's Gate.

Anyone leaving the murder scene likely would pass through one of those two intersections. Bull decided to start at the pub and then interview the businesses on Old Brompton Road. He set a "Police" placard on the dashboard of the Mondeo and walked to the Onslow Arms. Low green walls separated the pavement from the pub's terrace, which contained several small tables sheltered by green fabric awnings. Hanging baskets overflowed with red and yellow blossoms, similar to those in the display at a flower shop he'd seen on Fulham Road.

The large barman, middle-aged and florid, smiled a greeting as Bull pushed through the door. "Not open yet, mate. Give us ten." When Bull held up his warrant card and identified himself, the barman's face took on a serious scowl. "Ben Pleasant, proprietor. The murder up the street, right? Sad business. You'll want my CCTV."

Bull nodded. "I noticed the camera on the corner of the building. Would you have the video from Sunday through Tuesday? I'd like to upload it to our site, if you don't mind, Mr. Pleasant."

"No worries." Pleasant leaned into the door to the kitchen. "Kerry? I'm going up to the office. Watch the front, please."

A stocky, chestnut-haired young woman bounded through the door and took her place next to the proprietor. She studied Bull up and down. "The police about the murder, Dad? Can I listen?" Kerry spoke slowly, as if her mouth were full. Given her almond eyes, Bull considered that she might have Down's syndrome, but he wasn't quite sure.

"Not now, luv. Need you to watch the front. I'll be back in a sec." Bull followed him up a set of narrow stairs.

On one side of the landing at the top was the entrance to what Bull took to be a small sitting room. Apparently, Pleasant and Kerry lived above the pub. The office on the other side of the landing was barely large enough for the two men at the same time. Pleasant sat at a desk crowded with a tray containing mail, pamphlets, and various invoices, and a flat desktop computer and its accoutrements. He clicked the mouse, and the computer began wheezing and whirring. Once it had started up and the CCTV app was loaded, Pleasant stood and smiled awkwardly as he squeezed past to let Bull sit. "Pardon. They didn't build as large in the 1820s."

The video controls were straightforward. Bull clicked the mouse to advance the picture to Sunday evening, started the clip, and fast-forwarded it to noon on Tuesday, which is when the first police arrived at the scene. Once the segment was uploaded to the Met's cloud site, they returned to the front of the pub and sat at a table. Pleasant offered a pint of hand-pulled cask ale, but Bull declined. He had a busy afternoon ahead of him, so he pulled out his notebook and pencil and got to the point. "Were you open Monday evening?"

Pleasant nodded. "Normal hours. Kerry and I were here, along with Jason, who's the cook, and Tamara, the server. Closed at eleven. Went upstairs at about midnight."

Kerry set two glasses of fizzy water on the table and hovered over Pleasant's shoulder, shifting from one foot to the other. Her grey eyes never left Bull.

Pleasant indicated two men standing at the bar. "Kerry, we're open now, so it would be helpful if you could see what those gentlemen want."

"Okay, Dad, but then can I . . . I mean, we might have . . ."

"I won't be a minute, sweetheart. Go take the order, please."

Kerry slouched back behind the bar. Bull could see her talking with the men, then pulling one of the ales. She knew what she was doing.

Pleasant followed Bull's eyes. "We lost her mother two years ago. Kerry has mild Down's syndrome. After she finished school, she stayed to live with me. Said she wants to learn to run a pub. I'm all right with that. She's been amazing. When something's on her mind, she has trouble focusing. Still, she can stand on her own feet if people give her a chance."

"It looked like she wanted to tell me something. If it's all right, I'll interview her when we finish."

"Sure. Mondays are always slow. It hadn't rained, but it was cold and damp. No one was on the terrace, and I was inside the whole evening. I didn't hear or see anything out of the ordinary. Not that made me notice. Tamara isn't here today until four PM. Do you want to talk with Jason?"

Bull shook his head. "We'll send a uniform around later. I'll just speak with Kerry now, before I go." He drained his glass of water in a gulp and immediately realized the mistake. The fizz would want back out shortly.

Bull felt the pressure building at the bottom of his throat as Kerry sat down across the table. He swallowed hard and began. "Your dad says you were at work all Monday evening. Is that right?"

Kerry nodded and studied his face. "I wasn't working the whole time, though."

He swallowed hard again. "You took a break? Did you go outside?" The belch erupted as he finished the sentence. He held a napkin to his lips and turned his head away.

Kerry giggled. "Do you like it? My dad calls it Vesuvius water. It does that to me too."

Bull nodded and smiled self-consciously. "It was sensational. Tell me about your break."

"The weather is nice today." She looked at her father, who was taking an order from a customer. "Let's go outside and sit in the sun. Want some more Vesuvius water?"

Bull laughed and shook his head. "One eruption per day is my limit."

Kerry led him out the side door of the pub. They sat on one of several rustic benches set against the wall.

"It's more private out here." Kerry tilted her head back and closed her eyes, allowing the thin January sunlight to bathe her face. "You asked about my break. I came outside. My friend Wallace was going to meet me after he got off work. He works at the Sainsbury's grocery, down Fulham Road, and he gets off at nine. It's not far, so he walks. He gets here in time for my break. But that day he got off late, like five or ten minutes." She opened her eyes. "Is this too much detail?"

When Bull looked up from his notebook, she was leaning over, reading what he had written. "No, Kerry. It's fine. It does what we call establish context. Helps everything fit together."

"You have neat handwriting. I try to make mine that neat."

Bull smiled. "Thank you. I might forget something, so I have to be able to read what I write. What was special about this break? Other than seeing Wallace, I mean."

Kerry blushed. "That was pretty special. I hadn't seen him in almost a week." She appeared lost in thought for a few moments, then continued. "But something different happened. I heard a lady screaming at someone, and then two cars sped off up the street."

Bull gave her a steady look. "Now, be very careful about being accurate. Could you tell where the lady was?"

Kerry pointed. "That way, towards Fulham Road."

"And could you make out what she said?"

"She screamed at someone named Jack. I think she called him a coward. Right after that, a big black car squealed its tires and sped off up that way." She pointed in the opposite direction, towards Old Brompton Road.

"You said there were two cars."

"I only heard the other one. I didn't see it."

"All right. What else can you tell me?"

"Wallace said the big car we saw was an old Jaguar saloon. I think he said 'XJ'? Does that make sense? He likes cars. He has lots of books about them."

"What time was this?"

"I take my break at nine thirty. So this must have been at about nine forty-five, just a few minutes before I had to get back in."

Kerry appeared deep in thought, so Bull hesitated a few seconds before prompting her. "You look like you're thinking about something. Did you see or hear something else?"

"Well, I don't know for sure if it was her. The lady who screamed, I mean. But a few minutes later, a lady passed on the far side of the street. She was kind of in the shadows, so I couldn't see her very well. Wallace had just kissed me goodnight and was hugging me. I saw her over his shoulder."

"Do your best to describe her. Think back to that moment."

Kerry closed her eyes, then took Bull's arm and stood up, dragging him to his feet. "Face me," she said, "and bend over a bit. There, that's about right for Wallace." She stared over Bull's shoulder. "She was blonde, and she had on a long coat—tan or maybe light green. She was in the shadows, so I couldn't tell."

"Is there anything else you recall?"

"There was one other odd thing I noticed about her." Kerry squinted her eyes in thought.

"What's that?"

"It was pretty cold that night. I could see my breath. And she was walking funny. Careful, like her feet were hurting. Or like she was barefoot, but . . ."

"Thanks, Kerry. One last thing. Did you hear any loud noises after you came outside?"

"No. I don't remember hearing anything like a gun."

Bull pondered. "Do you think Wallace might have heard something?"

"I don't know. He didn't say anything."

"We'll want to talk with him to see if he remembers something. How can we contact him?"

After Kerry pencilled Wallace's name and address in his notebook, Bull took his leave and walked to the street.

The murder house stood fifty yards away, still cordoned with blue and white police tape. A scenario coalesced in Bull's mind. He imagined that some minutes after the murder, at least three people left the house—the woman and perhaps two men. The woman was scared, possibly panicked. Was she screaming "Coward" because she was being left behind? That might fit with the car roaring away. Given Kerry's description, was the woman hurt or barefoot? Was she carrying her shoes—an odd thing to do on a cold night—or had she lost them? If so, where? Not in the house, and the uniforms hadn't seen any during their street search.

Bull pulled out his mobile and dialled Costello. Skipper, I think we may have something to follow up. A witness at the pub says she and her boyfriend heard a woman screaming and saw a black Jag speeding off. Just after that, a woman walked north on Selwood towards Old Brompton Road. The time fits."

Costello was quick. "So the officers reviewing the CCTV need to be looking for a black Jag in a hurry. I'll note it. Where will you be?"

"Going to get the CCTV from local shops along Brompton Road. They might have caught either the woman or the Jag. Then, if you don't have anything else, I'm going to see if I can interview the boyfriend."

"Good work. Stop back at the nick once you're done."

Bull ended the call and decided to trace the possible steps of the unknown woman. If the woman had been left at the scene by the cowardly Jack, then she would have been on her way to somewhere she considered safe—either a nearby residence or a place where she could catch a cab. That meant the hotels on Queen's Gate and the restaurants along Old Brompton Road.

The day was sunny and mild for early January. Bull unbuttoned his overcoat and started walking north up the concrete pavement. The colonnaded houses scrolled past, almost identical in their cream brick and white marble, differing only by their black-, red-, or green-painted doors and the plants in the pots on their front stoops. Every few yards, a plane tree shaded the walk. At night, the overhanging trees would have shadowed someone keeping close to the houses and their black railings.

As he passed, Kerry waved from the terrace of the pub, where she was serving tea to a grey-haired couple dressed in warm tweeds. Bull raised his hand in acknowledgement, and continued.

A half-block further on, he passed two workmen loading a skip in a white fog of plaster dust. Their shovels rasped the pavement. Paper masks shielded their noses and mouths from the fine powder that ghosted their boots and clothing. Bull remembered the months he'd spent working in the building trade before he joined the Royal Marines, and how his two tours in Afghanistan had altered his professional ambitions. After that experience, he'd seen more rewards in policing than plastering.

He stopped. The crime scene had shown evidence of heavy

blowback from the shot striking the victim. The woman's coat would have been stained, probably quite noticeably, with blood and body matter. She had been wearing the coat as she hurried along past the pub. Kerry hadn't noticed any blood, so it wasn't apparent from a distance. But the woman must have worried someone would notice when she reached an exposed, lighted area.

Up to now, no witnesses had come forward with a story about a blood-soaked woman limping along the side of the street, nor had any taxi driver reported a blonde in a bloody overcoat. So she'd either taken it off and folded it to hide the stains, or dumped it somewhere. There was no way to know which she would have done in a panic. The CCTV might confirm whether she had it or not.

Bull gauged the street ahead of him. Old Brompton Road was still a long block and a half away. Houses lined the side where he stood. On the other side, an iron railing and a tall hedge enclosed what looked to be a grassy park. A sign on a gate warned "Private Garden for Use by Residents Only."

He turned back and flashed his warrant card at the workmen loading the skip. "Did either of you find a coat, a nice one maybe, in your skip?"

The older of the two pulled his paper mask to the side. "When would that have been?"

"Yesterday morning. Were you here then?"

"Yep, but didn't see nowt like no coat in there." He looked at his younger mate, who shrugged and shook his head. "Lorry brought this one yesterday morning and carried away t'other." He readjusted his mask and resumed scraping up the debris.

Eight or nine businesses remained that Bull still needed to contact. He pulled out his mobile and texted Costello to assign uniforms to search the private garden.

TEN

Fiona looked at the two Aran knit jumpers lying on the bed and wondered why there was never enough room in one suitcase. No hard luggage, she decided. Just the large carpetbag. She stuffed the jumpers into the bag, along with two pairs of jeans, a sports bra, knickers, thick woolly socks, and some warm flannel pyjamas. Her bedroom at Waleham House was eternally cold.

She had remained in bed until she was sure Jonny had left, unwilling to chance an accidental meeting in the kitchen or hallway. There was no sense coolly pretending nothing had happened.

She stood in her bathrobe, cosmetic bag in hand, and considered the image in the mirror. *This is what damn near fifty looks like.* The array of bottles and potions lined the vanity like a regiment of expensive French commandos, steady and determined, courageously battling the inevitable in a doomed suicide mission. With a sigh she decided she would give them a reprieve this weekend. She would be home, answerable to only Peg and Fritz. She stuffed her cosmetic bag into a drawer just as her mobile sang.

Peg's deep country voice boomed across the miles. "Fee! I got your message. Of course I would love to see you this weekend, and for as long as you like, dear. It's your house, after all."

Fiona held the mobile a few inches from her ear. Peg always bellowed on the phone like she was calling across a pasture, trying to be heard above her pack of baying hounds. She was nearing seventy years old and had spent most of those years outdoors. It was lifelong habit.

"It's so good to hear you, Peg. I've just finished stuffing my bag, and I'll be off in a few minutes. Do you need anything from town?"

"Just you, dear girl. I took Trooper out yesterday. He still enjoys a good gallop now and then, but not for long, and I'm afraid he and I aren't much for fences anymore—just low hurdles. I give him a little bute with his feed. Arthritis, you know—the plague of us all—and it makes him so cranky, but he's always been good for you, so there. I'm glad you'll be here. Fritz and I always look forward to it."

"We need to have a talk. I miss you."

Peg hesitated before replying. "It's been what—two months? Since the beginning of the school term, I suppose. Will Jonny be with you?"

Fiona cringed. "He said he would try to join us Saturday. He has some work thing or other going."

"Mmm. You sound—I don't know—sad. What's wrong, pet? You can't fool your old auntie, and it's wicked to even try."

"I'm leaving in about a half hour." Fiona glanced at her phone. "I'll be there around five-ish if the M3 isn't rammed. We can talk then."

"The kettle will be on, and I'll lay out your jodhpurs and boots. Fritz gave them a good polish after you left last. They were in such a state after you long-reined Trooper in that muddy paddock. I'll ask him to look at Andy and Stella's kit. They may want to ride this weekend."

"They're in Italy, luv. A school trip to study Renaissance art. Tell Fritz ta, and I love you, Peg."

A brief call to the gallery reassured her that Siobhan and

Oliver had everything under control. She shook her head. She should sell that bloody albatross. She had lost interest in it months ago.

Her mobile weighed in her hand like a pistol. Call Jacko again? He'd probably let it roll over to voicemail as he had the last four times she had called. No point right now. What more could she add?

Her large detached house was in a tight enclave of similar Italianate homes that overlooked the Thames south bank. She exited through the electronic gate at the end of the narrow access lane and turned west down Mortlake High Street, past the brewery, towards the A316. As usual, construction clogged the highway and reduced progress to a crawl. She tried not to think about the looming Mortlake Crematorium across the carriageway on the right. She needed no more reminders of mortality. Two blokes on the radio yammered about the latest Brexit controversy, so she turned it off. She needed to think.

After a few miles she passed the exit for Kempton Park Race Course. Her father had bet regularly on the horses. When she was young, she had asked why they always went to Kempton races and not Ascot. He had replied, "Not as many overbred twats and gits," conveniently forgetting that the title of Viscount Waleham was seven hundred years old, and the proper breeding of people, horses and dogs had been a preoccupation of his ancestors for most of that time.

A mile later she drove under the welcome blue sign announcing, "The SOUTH WEST M3." Traffic thinned, and the road opened out into the motorway proper. The Range Rover's big diesel strummed along, the climate control kept the temperature steady. Fiona lapsed into the tedium of the highway.

The exit to Kempton had summoned memories. Donald, the Viscount Waleham, had taken her and her older brother, Andrew, to the races often, until their mother's early death from cancer. Four years later Fee had returned home at the end of a school term to learn that Andrew had left abruptly for somewhere far away—Donald wouldn't say, but she had heard both Capetown and New Zealand rumoured. The last time she had seen Andrew was nearly twenty-five years ago, shortly after their father's death. Andrew had returned home to deal with the cremation and the inheritance legalities, and then had disappeared again. Because her father had opted for primogeniture, Andrew inherited the title and the estates. She had received an annuity worth about a hundred thousand pounds a year, but under her father's stipulation that she marry and remain married. Since then, her only contact with her brother had been through letters delivered via his solicitors, and a few telephone calls a year. Perhaps Andrew was still running from their father and, for all she knew, from her as well. Fee had no idea why he had exiled himself. She was fairly certain she had done nothing to harm him, but he had pushed her out to the very periphery of his life, and she missed him tremendously.

Ahead of her a shiny black Jaguar saloon trundled along a good ten miles an hour under the speed limit. It was too new to be Jacko's. She moved to the right to pass.

Why couldn't she be strong about Jacko? Or more to the point, why hadn't she been strong for herself and Jonny two years ago? If only they had thrown Jacko out on his ear and taken their lumps. Now the bastard had his claws in both of them.

She rolled under the A320 that led to the amusement park at Thorpe. She and David, her first husband, had spent many happy hours there with their children, Andy and Stella. She smiled— the visits were happy for David except for the roller coaster. He had tried to ride the monstrous steel serpent twice but had "lost his biscuits" both times he had encountered its famous inverted loop. The kids had never let him forget it. Ahead of her, flashing blue and yellow lights and a row of orange traffic cones indicated a road collision. She slowed and moved into line with the other motorists. Police in fluorescent yellow vests waved them past crumpled vehicles as paramedics tended to injured motorists. David had died at such a place, when a drunken sod rammed his police vehicle.

She always thought of David when she drove to Hampshire.

Jonny was kind and consoling in the aftermath, and a few considerate months later offered her marriage, saving her the ignominy of putting herself on the market. Or so she felt then— he'd never said a word about being gay.

She would always resent that he'd married her under false pretences. How could she not? She'd been angry at Jonny's duplicity and had struggled to comprehend how life with a gay husband—who was in love with a man she knew—could be at all fulfilling. She had thought the affair with Jacko would be the escape she needed. Of course Jonny knew—he had given his blessing at the beginning. She didn't believe Jonny was complicit in the videotape Jacko had shot.

Fiona opened her window and breathed deeply. The cold air sliced into her chest. Pieces of paper swirled in a miniature whirlwind around the cabin of the Range Rover, but she paid no mind. She was almost home.

The brief jolt of oxygen cleared her head. A blue sign ahead announced, "Fleet services." She moved to the left and took the exit road that snaked through fragrant rows of pines. She stopped at the edge of the large parking lot.

Quiet. She pressed the speed dial on her mobile. Peg's voice-mail answered. "It's me, Aunt Peg. I've stopped at Fleet for a pee and a coffee. Be home soon."

Half a large latte later, she decided. She didn't know why she and Jacko had been allowed to run away, but fear had immobilized her for two days. Something had to give, and she was damned if she was going to wait for the twisted bastard to call her.

After two warbles his voicemail kicked in. She kept her tone even.

"Jacko. Listen to me, you bastard toerag. You got me into

this godawful mess, and you're going to damn well help me get out of it. Tell me by Monday when you can meet next week"—she ran out of breath and gasped, filling her lungs—"or I'm bloody well going to come straight with Jonny about it, and you can deal with your own bloody consequences."

She felt better now.

Fifteen minutes later, Fiona exited the motorway. In the village of Overton, she turned on a narrow, sunken byway bounded by hedgerows. A mile later, she turned right at the drive that would take her through a pine wood to Waleham House's brilliant Capability Brown landscape. She gave a double blast on the horn as she passed Uncle Fritz's lodge. He was probably out mending fences or managing a work crew, but Fiona found comfort in the established ritual.

Just beyond, at the top of a small rise, Fiona pulled onto the verge. A short scramble through a copse of scented pines led her to the observation point that had been her favourite since she was a young girl. She stood on a round, flat stone, which looked natural but most likely had been situated there by Brown when he had sculpted the gardens in 1762. Expanses of lawn, yellow with winter, undulated before her, gracefully sloping down to several small dales, in which nestled cosy ponds enclosed by stands of leaf-bare plane trees and deep green conifers. On her right, the three-story red-brick and limestone edifice of Waleham House peered around a stand of larch, reflected in the glass of its artificial lake.

Fiona inhaled the woody scents and let her gaze drift over the scene once more. She was home. Why had she ever left?

ELEVEN

Wednesday afternoon, Camberwell

Joanna Christie lifted her bag to her chest, a defensive gesture. "Why are you here?"

Elaine stepped away from the black wrought-iron columns that marked the entrance to Datchelor House on Camberwell Grove. "Please, can we talk? Since I saw you Monday, I came across some information I'd like you to see."

Joanna looked both ways along the pavement. "I'm on my way home. I'm not sure I should be talking to you."

"I won't take much of your time, and this isn't about what happened to me." The statement contained a grain of truth. "We could go to your flat."

Joanna again scanned the street. "No, not my flat. There." She pointed to a Greek taverna two doors down.

Inside, Joanna embraced a smiling middle-aged woman. After a brief conversation in Greek, during which the woman assessed Elaine with a disapproving look, Joanna led the way to a small alcove off the back of the dining room. Old photos dotted the walls—a wedding group arrayed in front of a whitewashed church; a line of stern, black-dressed women under an olive tree; two young men with shotguns, each grasping a clutch of dead rabbits by the hind legs.

A waiter set a carafe of white wine and a plate of olives and dolmanthes on the blue-checked tablecloth. Joanna poured, then said, "My brother-in-law will join us in a moment." She forked an olive into her mouth and sat back.

"Your family owns this place?"

Joanna spit the olive pit into her hand and placed it on a plate. "My husband's family."

Elaine asked, "It looked like she didn't approve of me. What did you tell her?"

"That you're a nosy bitch of a cop my sister doesn't want to talk to." A burly, dark-haired man of about forty took a chair across the table from Elaine. "Is Joanna in trouble?"

"No, but I think she can help me with an enquiry. I'm DCI Hope." She flashed her warrant card. "What's your name?"

"If she's not in trouble, why are you harassing her? She says she doesn't want to talk to you."

"Who are you?" Elaine asked again.

"Cristo. I'm here to tell you to leave her alone. She cried after she saw you Monday."

"I'm not here to talk to you," Elaine said. She had an idea what was coming.

"I don't bloody care. Her husband was my brother, and she's now my responsibility."

Elaine ignored him. She faced Joanna and said, "I'm sorry if what I told you Monday upset you. But as I recall, you spoke to me first. And you haven't refused to speak to me now."

Joanna began to reply, but Cristo interrupted. "I don't care who spoke first. She was upset. I'm the head of the family, and I'm not going to let a nosy detective make life difficult for her because of some murder that happened months ago. That case is solved, so you keep away from her." He half-rose and pointed to the door.

Joanna placed her hand on his arm. "Cristo, I think—"

He ignored her and stood. "Get out, Hope."

Elaine sat back and appraised him. "Sit down and listen. I'm here about the murder in Kensington Monday night, and I'm not here to speak with you." She turned to Joanna. "We've come into some information. I have a list of estate agents and companies. I'm hoping you can tell us something about them."

"One last time, I told you to leave. If you don't, I'll file a complaint." Cristo moved to take Elaine's arm.

Elaine recoiled and stood. "Touch me and I'll charge you with assault and have you in cuffs. Not good for business or your family, right?"

Joanna spoke up. "Stop it, Cristo! I don't want you getting into trouble. DCI Hope, can you leave the list with me?"

"No, I can't do that." Elaine handed her card to Joanna. "I take it you're afraid of your boss. Or your brother. It's our job to protect you if you come forward. Let me know if you decide to cooperate." She started to walk away, but turned back to face Cristo. "One more thing. When a control freak like you gets aggressive, I have to wonder what you're hiding, what you're afraid of. Just makes me want to dig a little deeper."

TWELVE

Thursday morning, Greenwich Park

Elaine crouched low against the ancient plane tree, her body tucked into the fold of a huge root, her black hoodie pulled up over her mouth and nose to mask the telltale fog of her breath. She had risen at four AM to drive through the almost-deserted early morning streets, across Southwark Bridge, then east through south London. After parking her BMW, she had slipped silently through the stark, leafless trees of Greenwich Park to her observation point.

She gazed down the hill, past the humps of the Saxon burial mounds, to the Henry Moore *Knife Edge* sculpture looming out of the morning fog—a sacred megalith watching over Bronze Age ghosts. In the distance, hanging above the fog, sparkled the skyscrapers of Canary Wharf.

When she had asked DI Mehta for a meeting, he had dithered and stalled, but finally rang her back, saying they could have a conversation during his early morning run. Later, she had checked with several sources in the Met. From what she had gleaned, he was a cop who spent his days in front of a computer—a forensic accountant, investigating financial crimes. Not that it made him a bad cop—quite the contrary: his role was crucial to law enforcement. But he was hardly the sharp point of the spear.

She waited in the cold damp. According to her contacts, Mehta took fitness only seriously enough to pass the Met's annual fitness exam. Greenwich Park would be inconvenient to his office. And in this weather, he'd be on his treadmill, not outside. No, he didn't choose this place himself. Open ground, good vision, places to hide. They've given him a watcher.

Be still, Lainie. Footsteps coming up the hill from the right. The tree's blocking me. Wait. There she is.

In the grey predawn light, a short, dark woman in running clothes jogged past, moving towards the mounds and the monolith. Elaine pressed hard against the thick tree trunk. As the woman passed, she muttered something into the upheld collar of her tracksuit.

Elaine stayed frozen to the tree. Had the watcher made her? Elaine thought she had been screened by the tree, and the woman hadn't looked back. It was hard to tell. She decided that if the watcher came around again, she might reverse direction. *Need to move, Lainie.*

Once the watcher had disappeared into the fog, Elaine scooted back into the shadows and crawled to a spot behind a different large tree. She lay there prone, peering over the top of a large, sprawling root. Five minutes later, she again heard footsteps, this time from the left. She slowly lowered her head below the root. The footsteps stopped. The woman's voice again muttered something unintelligible. When the footsteps began again, they were moving away. Elaine lifted her head to look. The woman was halfway down the hill towards the huge monolith.

Why had she stopped? Was it because this location, in these trees, was an obvious observation point? Elaine knew she was screened. No point wondering. The watcher would probably find a place to hide, and Mehta would be along shortly.

As the watcher approached the sculpture for the second time, she veered from the path and disappeared into a small woody copse about a hundred yards to the east.

Elaine smiled to herself at the game. I know you know I know. The watcher had picked a perfect place to hide. Suzy Spy had gone to ground, waiting for the next move. Everyone would find out soon if Mehta's handlers had anticipated Plan B.

Five minutes later, Mehta's chubby figure jogged up the path and stopped beneath the huge bronze blade. Elaine slid from the root and slithered into the shadows of the grove. Once she was below the crest of the hill, she walked as fast as she could to her car and dialled Mehta's mobile number.

"This is DI Mehta, where—"

"Just listen." Elaine accelerated her BMW up Blackheath as she spoke into her Bluetooth. "I've got a cold, and the morning damp may be a bit much for me. I'll pick you up at the north end of the path, where it crosses The Avenue. I'll be there in less than a minute."

"But—"

"I know someone wants you to find out what I'm up to. If you're not there in thirty seconds, I'm driving away." She ended the call, downshifted to second gear, and accelerated through the left bend onto The Avenue. She pulled to a stop on the pavement and opened the passenger door as Mehta wheezed down the path into view. She spoke firmly. "Get in. Now."

Mehta bent over, his hands on his knees. Elaine looked in her rear-view mirror. The woman she had seen earlier was running down the pavement towards them. Mehta leaned against the car door, gulping for air.

"Get in the car this second, or I leave."

Mehta looked once at the woman running up the pavement, and chose to obey. Elaine accelerated away before he closed his door.

"What the hell?" Mehta slammed the door, then scrambled to fasten his seatbelt. His dark eyes flashed at her. "You could have killed me!"

"Give me your wire." When he protested, Elaine glanced in

the mirror again. The woman had disappeared into the fog. She slammed on the brakes. "Come on. I know you're wearing one. You had a watcher."

Mehta fished the small microphone and radio from inside his tracksuit. Elaine took it from him, removed the battery, and threw the lot onto the back seat.

"There now." She smiled at him. "Much friendlier, don't you think?"

"Where are we going?"

"A place where we can get tea and an excellent fry-up." She glanced at her passenger. "And talk without Auntie Met eavesdropping."

Mehta's mobile erupted into song, and he pulled it from his pocket. As soon as he swiped the screen to answer, Elaine slammed the brakes again. Mehta juggled the phone as he instinctively reached out to brace himself. Elaine pried it from his grip.

A woman's agitated voice blared from the phone. "Mehta! What the—"

Elaine interrupted. "This is DCI Hope. I'm a rotten driver, and DI Mehta is busy hanging on for dear life. You can speak with him after our chat. Perhaps in an hour or so. Goodbye." She pried off the cover, removed the battery, and pocketed the components in her hoodie. When she smiled at Mehta, he simply stared back at her, wide-eyed.

Twenty minutes later, they were seated in the cosy back room of a small café in Shooter's Hill. Elaine tucked into her fried eggs, sausage, and chips while she regarded the young DI across the table.

Mehta was short, with a smooth caramel complexion and chubby cheeks. He had panted for several minutes after he got in the car, and his tracksuit and trainers were brand new. She wagered to herself that he'd serve his time on the Met, maybe ten or fifteen years, then leave for a ridiculously high-paying consultancy position, advising businesses how to get away with those indiscretions he was now detecting. It was the way of the world, these days. He had gulped one cup of tea, poured himself another, and drained that. He hadn't spoken after their first brief exchange. Instead, he sat fuming, looking anywhere but at Elaine.

Elaine pushed her plate to the side and slurped her tea. When she finished, she said, "That was exciting, wasn't it? It got my blood moving, and yours too, I suspect. I've never had a friendly chat with a colleague begin quite so dramatically."

"You sit here, muddy, you've got leaves stuck to you. What the fuck were you doing? You really are a mad woman. I should report you to Professional Standards."

"Correct on all counts. But look at it from my point of view. I simply wanted to talk to you about corporate money laundering. When you said where you wanted to meet, and at such an ungodly hour, a creepy feeling came over me. A cold, damp, foggy feeling. It felt so wrong, mate."

Mehta scoffed. "I'm not your mate. My days are busy. The morning run is about my only quiet time."

Mehta lived in Barnet, on the other side of London. Presumably he had run all the way to Greenwich in his brand-new trainers. Elaine laughed. "Well, we're here, and it's much warmer than standing on those Saxon graves. So you can tell me what I need to know, and I'll tell you something you need to know."

Mehta studied Elaine's face. After several seconds, he appeared to decide. "Okay. I'll tell you what I can."

"Thank you. Can you go over the background once again? There are overseas crooks who need to stash their ill-gotten gains, and they choose London. Who are they?"

"These crooks, as you call them, are usually corrupt government officials from Eastern Europe. They accept bribes, or perhaps they divert skimmed contract funds into a sham bank account. After a while they've got a couple of million in readies, and they need to do something with it. If they try to launder it at home, they'll only keep a small percentage. Someone would notice and either turn them in for a reward or blackmail them. Or both. They need to buy something that holds value but doesn't raise red flags at home."

"So they go looking for real estate. Why London?"

"A few million quid for a house isn't such a big deal in London. Every day, a lot of high-end properties are bought or sold, both houses and flats. There are lots of large transactions."

"And lots of estate agents and lawyers who want to get rich quick?" Elaine asked.

"Not lots. Estate agencies are required by law to report suspicious offers, and most of them report fishy deals and walk away. But large commissions are tempting, so . . ."

"What about business properties? You know, office blocks, industrial estates, that kind of thing."

"And why exactly are you interested?"

Hence, the watcher. She asked, "Who is it? The Met? Operation Sterling?"

Mehta shook his head. "No. We don't go in for the thriller sort of thing."

"I didn't think it would be our lot. Must be the National Crime Agency."

Mehta didn't reply. Bingo. Elaine thought for a moment before continuing.

"My last homicide investigation was particularly nasty. A teenage girl was beaten to death, and another woman was disposed of in a particularly gruesome way. The killer was employed by a property company called IRG. It's run by an ethnic Serbian crime family. You may have heard of them, the Srecko brothers."

Mehta leaned back in his chair and studied Elaine. "I heard what happened. That you killed the suspect."

"IRG is involved with bogus offshore companies. They use sleazy, off-the-books lawyers and then murder them when they outlive their usefulness. They ran at least two brothels. They own business properties all over England. I thought you'd be interested. Why wouldn't they be laundering money through business properties?"

"Because Her Majesty's Revenue and Customs maintains constant vigilance in collecting as much tax as they can."

"That's no answer, and you know it."

Mehta placed his mug on the table. "Are you looking for revenge?"

"You think that's all there is to it? Revenge? You think I'm some kind of obsessed, damaged bitch out to settle a score?"

Mehta laughed outright. "From what happened this morning, that analysis gets my vote. But I don't care what you want. This is bigger than that. I don't want you barging around and fucking things up for us."

"For the Met? Or the NCA?" Elaine leaned forward. "I don't want to fuck up anything you're doing. All I want right now is for you to have a look at this list of shell companies and their directors. You don't have to say anything, but if there's a company, or a person's name, that you think it would be worth my while to have a look at, just put a tick mark by it. And if there's one you want me to stay away from, strike a line through it and I'll stay far away."

"You do know that Parliament's considering new money-laundering regulations to take effect later this year."

"They've been up to their arses in property scams for a decade or more, but that's not what I'm after in the end. I want justice for the murders they ordered and committed," Elaine replied.

"And if I do what you ask, you'll stay away and won't come asking again?"

She nodded and looked him in his eyes. "You have my word."

Mehta gauged her face from across the table and asked, "Do you have a pen?"

After studying each page for a few seconds, he spread them in front of him. With her pen, he drew a large X across each page. "Right. A psycho kid killed two women and nearly killed you. Now you're on a mission to fit the whole family into the frame." He shook his head and gazed out the window. "They told me you were impulsive. That what happened sent you over the edge, and now you're stark raving. Your behaviour this morning proved that to me. I've given you what you want. Now, take me to my car before I arrest you for kidnapping."

Elaine felt the blow deep in her gut. *Who are "they"? And that's what he thinks, does he? This chair-warming, key-tapping jackass who's never stared down a killer? Who's never seen a knife that wasn't next to his dinner plate?*

She gathered her papers, stood, and looked down at Mehta. "How the hell can you even conceive of what happened—or who I am?" She threw the pieces of his mobile on the table and started for the door. "Call a taxi."

THIRTEEN

Thursday morning, Kensington

"Good morning, people. I would say 'boys and girls,' but some-one informed me that phrase isn't appropriate for this nick." Costello stood by the status board and surveyed the incident room. "The evidence so far indicates there were three people in the room besides the victim. The shooter and two others. They think one of the others was a woman because the sole prints appear to be spike high heels." Bull glanced at Novak, who stood on the other side of the incident board, and then referred back to his notes from the crime scene report.

"She stood by the window, a couple of feet away. The other male stood about five feet to her right. Blowback patterns show the shooter stood between them, about three feet behind the victim. He fired directly into the back of the victim's skull, most likely with a large-bore tactical or sawn-off shotgun. One shot, no spent casing on site. The buckshot the CSIs retrieved was aught-aught. They're analyzing it to try to determine the manufacturer."

"How do you know the shooter was a he?" a detective asked.

Now for the interesting bit. "Could have been a woman, but we're going on male. From the negative images in the blood and brain matter, he wore a size eight, narrow width. From stride length, we estimate his height at five feet six to five feet eight. The splattering was intense, so all three unknown persons would have been well soaked in gore. Remember the window? We wondered why it was open. One of them, probably the woman, opened it and retched outside. We have smearing on the windowsill where she leaned over, female shoeprints in the blood on the floor, size four or maybe a half size larger. Only two clear steps, so height is perhaps five foot five. No finger or palm prints, but she left a puddle of vomit in the garden below. We also found what looks like dried urine on the floor inside that window. She had walked in it, so it's likely hers as well. Forensics is trying to extract DNA from the vomit, but as you may know, that's extremely unlikely given the acidity. They may have better luck from the dried urine, but it was mixed with the blood. Perhaps they can tease out something besides the victim's DNA. Two blonde hairs were recovered from the scene, one with the root bulb, which may provide some DNA. The reports won't be back for a while. Now, as to the victim—"

Novak spoke. "Thanks, DS Costello. I'll take it from here. Dr. Kumar estimates time of death between nine and eleven PM Monday evening. The victim was Eastern European, average height, dark hair longer than shoulder length. Interview the neighbours again. Focus on two men, one woman, loud noises or cars coming and going, late Monday or predawn Tuesday. I want CCTV from all cameras in a two-block perimeter. Questions?"

One of the DCs raised her hand. "How do we know he was Eastern European?"

"The usual dental work. Anything else? No? Good. Two things. One, DS Costello will brief you on today's actions. Two, nothing about this investigation is to go outside the team. I trust that is clear." He nodded at Costello.

Thursday morning, Highgate

Another shift in Accident and Emergency had taken its toll. Peter Willend leaned on the front of his locker, staring into the mirror fastened to the inner side of the door. A haggard, two day's growth of salt-and-pepper stubble accentuated his January pale skin. *Not much to look at,* he thought, especially in the white fluorescent light of the hospital locker room.

He turned from the mirror and peeled his scrub shirt over his head. He always faced the room when he changed clothes. The puckered, raised shrapnel slashes lining his upper arms and legs and the mosaic of burn scars on his back usually provoked quick turns of the head and downcast glances, even from people who knew him well. He wasn't ashamed; turning as he did was simply good manners. He had been away from the nose-clogging dust for over eight years, had moved to a new home on a lush green island, but still he carried Iraq everywhere.

Peter didn't face the locker again until he had pulled on his trainers, athletic pants, and San Antonio Spurs jersey. A dark hoodie completed his transition from trauma surgeon to anonymous London commuter. He contemplated the two pictures taped next to the mirror. One was of Diana and Liza, taken a decade ago, when they were all he had ever wanted. Diana's copper hair blazed in the Texas sun. Their daughter, Liza, grinning gap-toothed with eight-year-old pride, held up a frog she had caught in Bull Creek back home in Austin. They had been gone eight years now.

The other photo was one of Elaine he had taken at Nelson's Glory. She had just beaten him at a game of darts, and her huge brown eyes assessed him over a half-full glass of stout. At least she was still alive, but was she gone from his life too? He didn't know. So much love, so little time to give it.

Peter lifted the hood over his head and pushed through the exit door. It had become colder overnight, and the wind bit into the exposed skin at his throat. He shivered and pulled the hoodie's drawstring tighter. His breath gathered and hung in a cold cloud as he hunched his shoulders against the chill and waited under the bus shelter. He usually rode the bus to and from work. At this time of day, the bus ride to Crouch End took about a half hour. From there, it was a half-hour jog to his home in Highgate. It wasn't the most direct route, but it gave him exercise. He moved to the kerb as a bus sighed to a stop.

Peter's older sister, Kate, was in the kitchen when he arrived home. They had grown up on an army base in Texas, the children of an American soldier and a British mother. After their father died, Kate and Helen, their mother, had moved to the UK. Peter had gone to medical school in the States. The American army had taken him to Iraq.

"Morning." Kate's deep blue eyes inspected him as he picked up the coffee press. "Rough night?"

"Yeah. Thought you'd be gone by now."

"Working at home today. His BoJo-ness is still in Kent. New York on Wednesday." Kate worked for the Foreign Office.

She smiled at him around a mouthful of toast. "I ate your leftover chicken korma when I got in last night. It was delicious. You'll have to scavenge."

"No worry. I'll stop by the Khoury's shop and pick up a couple of kebabs and some falafel." He gave her a sidelong grin. "Or if you feel penitent, you could rustle something up for me to eat."

She chuckled. "Not a chance, Petey luv. You're the cook in the house. I made coffee and toast, and you don't want me to get any more ambitious than that, do you?"

He laughed and scrabbled his knife across a piece of charred bread, scattering fine black crumbs on his plate. "The coffee was excellent." He soothed the excoriated toast with a layer of jam.

"You're eating it, so your snide remark rings hollow." Kate

took a sip of coffee. "I saw the envelope from the med school in Austin. Did you leave it lying around for me to see?"

"Yep. You know they're getting serious when they skip the email and start using university letterhead. They've offered me an assistant professorship in the new emergency medicine department. Tenure track. I wanted to bounce it off you, and maybe Helen."

"Faculty pay might not be what you make now. But there's the lower cost of living and better hours." She hesitated. "You told them about the arrest, right?"

"Yeah. A couple of the committee members had concerns about hiring a doctor who'd been jailed for murder. You know how tetchy the university is about its image."

"Elaine could write a letter for you," Kate suggested. "Have you asked her?"

"No, I want to think about it. Whether I want the job, I mean."

Kate set down her toast and studied his face. "And whether you want to open up to her again."

Peter walked to the counter to refill his coffee cup. Two days' worth of Kate's dirty dishes were still in the sink. "I have never seen anyone as averse to domestic duties as you seem to be. Is it some kind of ideological imperative?" He set down his cup and turned on the hot water.

"Some things never change, little brother. Helen and I think you need to find a new focus. After what happened, your career won't go anywhere in London. Elaine isn't ready to start over with you. She's only been back from that cottage in Devon for what—two months?"

"Nine weeks."

"But who's counting, right? She's not ready. Look, you're forty-three years old, and you've fallen in love with two women in your life. Diana died. Elaine is only alive through your medical skill. Wherever you are, you'll wait for her. She'll let you know when she's ready."

"And you're sure of that, are you?" Peter was elbow-deep in suds, his eyes focused on a casserole dish.

Kate stood beside him at the kitchen sink. "I've always thought kitchen appliances are one of the great joys of the modern world. Stuff those things into this one here." She opened the dishwasher door and stepped back. "Then turn around and look at me."

Thank heaven for big sisters. Peter loaded the dishwasher and turned to Kate, smiling. "And now it's time for Sister Kate's Advice for the Lovelorn."

Kate leaned on the counter, her blonde hair obscuring her face. "It's time for a confession. I met Elaine at the cottage in Devon. We've spoken a couple of times since. You're a damn lucky man, Petey Willend."

Peter flopped in a kitchen chair, stunned. "You never said . . ." He felt his face flush with anger.

Kate held up her hand. "I had to play big sister. It was either Helen or me. You wouldn't talk about Elaine. One of us had to find out who she was, and we felt that a sister would be less intimidating than a mother."

"How the hell did you find her? It took me three months!" Understanding dawned. "Oh . . ."

"Right. It cost me four phone calls and a lunch at Le Gavroche. Lots of important people owe me favours. Or want them."

"Forever the diplomat spy, aren't you? Even with me." Peter closed his eyes and took three measured breaths. "I never thought it could happen again, but it did. We had so little time, before—" His throat closed. He took a gulp of coffee. "I love her. I have to wait for her. Mostly she pushes me away. Sometimes she agrees to meet, but she cancels."

"So you want to meet. You need to talk."

He exhaled. "Yeah. That night was hard on me too. I was covered in her blood. She flatlined. You think she doesn't understand what it did to me?"

She slid her chair closer and took his hand. "Her world has shattered. The rape ripped apart her core identity. Many women collapse into a shell after rape. It's anger and isolation, all mixed up. Elaine needs to rebuild her life, but she thinks the Met won't let her go back to investigation. So her professional persona is gone too. She has nothing to hang on to."

"You sound like a psychologist, not a diplomat."

Kate let his hand drop, and sat back in her chair. "There are more levels to what she's endured than you can begin to know. She's deeply scarred."

They sat silent, Kate sipping her coffee, Peter staring out the window.

Finally, Peter spoke. "Until Elaine, I'd always dealt with rape intellectually. I'd seen it as a doctor too many times. I saw the grief and fear, felt horrified, but I had to stay—not aloof, but clinical. My duty to patient care meant I had to follow the protocols, then hand off the deeper damage to a different professional. At least, I hoped someone professional was there to help."

Kate rose and set her coffee cup in the sink. "Elaine has nothing aside from the rage."

"I haven't told her about the job offer."

"You need to—the sooner, the better. She needs to know."

"She never talks to me about what happened. I tried a couple of times, but she closed up and rejected everything I said."

"She's not ready to open up yet. She will."

Peter shook his head. "In Devon she let me kiss her, hold her for a few minutes, and then she shut down. Pushed me away. It was like some invisible wall dropped down, and I can't break through it. We've only met once since then. Just a pint and darts at the pub. She started to loosen up, looked at me like she used to when . . . but she tensed up. I tried to hold her hand."

"And?"

"She went ballistic. Like I'd burn her if I touched her."

"It might be best if you took the job."

"Perhaps." He studied Kate's face. "I'm not sure I want to go back to Texas. It would take me away from her. And it's a long way from you and Helen."

"Helen and I will survive." Kate took his hand again. "Elaine will come to you. She told you that, right?"

"At the cottage. She said she would, after she's free."

"She told me the same. She's the kind of woman who keeps her promises."

FOURTEEN

Thursday morning, Kensington

"Here's the Jag." Bull reversed the video, then ran it forward in slow motion. The video was from the camera mounted high on the outer wall of the pub, angled downward to cover the benches and side entrance. Kerry and Wallace could be seen embracing outside the door. The frames caught the side of a dark car, but neither the number plates nor the driver were visible. The time stamp on the screen read 21:43.

Costello leaned over Bull's shoulder. "So that's your witness and her boyfriend?"

"Yeah, Kerry Pleasant, age nineteen, and Wallace Shaw, age twenty. The time fits with what she told me. Uniform interviewed him last night at the Sainsbury's where he works. They said he seemed a bit slow, but a nice, honest lad. He said he heard a loud bang, like a gunshot, when he was walking to meet Kerry. He doesn't have a watch, but if you take the time he clocked off work and how long it takes to walk from the supermarket, it fits. About 9:35 PM."

"So we have a time within what? Three or four minutes either way. I suppose we could have someone walk it with him, try to recreate it."

"If we catch him when he clocks off work, it might bring up something Kerry forgot to mention."

"I'll assign someone. Get a screen grab of the kids standing, then switch to the camera at the front entrance."

In moments the grainy, black-and-white view on the screen changed to the area on the terrace, between the front door and the street. At 21:43, the Jaguar moved across the frame, and although the entire side of the car was now visible, the number plates weren't. The inside of the car was too dark to determine anything about the driver, but Costello asked for a screen grab.

They kept watching, and just before 21:46, a woman entered the camera's field of view from the right side of the frame. She was blonde, medium height, slender, wore an overcoat. She appeared to be carrying an object in her right hand, but the dim light and poor resolution prevented a clear image of the object or her face. She stepped delicately, as if she were trying to keep each foot in contact with the cold concrete for the minimal time possible. She was only visible for about twelve seconds before she passed from view.

When the woman reached the middle of the frame, Costello ordered, "Freeze it, and zoom in on her, slowly." Bull stopped when the screen started to pixelate. Together, they inspected the frame. She had no shoes on. Her head was turned away from the camera. Bull pointed to what appeared to be a pattern of smudges, or mottling, across the front of the woman's coat. They tracked her until she moved out of frame, but never got a good look at her face.

Costello nodded. "Make a few prints of Barefoot Woman and the car. Is that as sharp as you can get it?"

"To get it any clearer, we'll need to let the forensic boffins work their magic. I'll send them the link."

Costello pulled up a chair and sat. "What about the intersection cameras. Any joy there?"

"No sign of the Jag at either Old Brompton Road or Fulham Road. There are a couple of side streets he could have turned on." He opened a map of South Kensington on the screen, and moved the mouse to a yellow dot. "This is the Onslow Arms.

The Jag could have proceeded north and turned on Onslow Square before it reached Old Brompton Road. Then it could have come out most anywhere, blocks away."

"Or gone to ground in the neighbourhood. Black Jag. Just like the white Transit we had to track in the Srecko case. Loads of 'em in London."

"Especially in Kensington and Chelsea." Bull shook his head and leaned back in his chair. "Hundreds, maybe. They made that body style for ten years. I looked it up. Guess what the favourite colours were."

Costello sniffed. "Black, dark blue, and dark green. Is it the murderer who's driving, or the other man? It could be someone visiting the neighbourhood or taking a shortcut."

"Then there's Barefoot Woman. Why is she walking?"

"If it's the murderer or the other man in the car, or both, there'll be blood in the carpets or on the seat. If she was the woman in the flat, why abandon her?"

Bull curled his lip. "If that's the case, somebody panicked. Makes no sense to leave her." He clicked the mouse, selecting the camera covering the intersection at Old Brompton Road, and began stepping the frames in fast-forward. At 21:51, he pointed at the screen. "And there she is."

Costello leaned forward. "Barefoot, without her coat. She hurries across the street, nearly flattened by that hatchback. Waves, gets into the taxi—there's the number plate. Contact that driver."

Bull jotted down the taxi's number plate. "Is DI Novak here?"

Costello shook his head. "Left after he warned us to keep schtum. Said he was going to Victoria Street. Something about the bean counters in financial. Haven't seen him since this morning, but I reckon this is worth a call. What about that other car? The second one your girl heard."

"Got it earlier. Blue Peugeot with French number plates.

Turned east on Fulham Road about 22:19. We're chasing it down."

"Any more CCTV?" Costello asked.

"The Fulham Road camera would have seen the house and cars, but the images were all snowy. The forensic techs are trying to clean it up."

Costello dialled a number on his mobile and switched it to speaker mode. Novak's voicemail answered immediately. "DS Costello and DC Bull. We've seen the Jag saloon and the woman on CCTV. Nothing yet on the car. We tracked the woman to Old Brompton Road and identified the taxi she took. We're contacting the driver." He rang off.

Bull exchanged glances with Costello. "Not exactly hands-on, is he? Not like Elaine—DCI Hope, I mean. She was always upfront with us. With Novak, it seems like he's holding something back. Like he doesn't trust us."

Costello shrugged. "Different styles. I haven't quite sussed him, but it's early days."

Thursday afternoon, Kensington

"Crossed Old Brompton in a hurry. She looked a mess, shivering, and no wonder—she was barefoot and had no coat, just a thin black dress. I handed her a fleece blanket, and she wrapped up in it."

Costello sat silent at the interview table. Across from him, the tall, thin taxi driver fidgeted with East London energy and impatience. His bald head reflected the harsh lights of the room. Costello consulted the notes a uniformed officer had sent him. "You told the PC that you took her to Mortlake. Was that to the station?"

"Yes. I told that to PC Wots-his-name. Biggs. He asked me all these questions, and now you have me all the way over here at Kensington nick, missing fares while you ask the same bloody things. Don't you rozzers talk to each other?"

"We asked you here to corroborate what PC Biggs passed on to us and to comment on what we've seen on the CCTV." Wright scoffed, so Costello adopted an even more conciliatory tone. "Doing so can often raise new questions and lines of enquiry. Or perhaps help you remember something new." He smiled at the taxi driver. "We don't want to have to call you back here some other time. Did you drop her at Mortlake Station?"

Wright huffed. "It's a waste of my time and yours, if you ask me, but—yes, at Mortlake Station, the eastbound platform."

"Thank you. How did she pay you?"

"A fifty. From a little purse she took out from her bra. There weren't much change from that, so she gave me another tenner and said that's for the blanket."

"And did you see if she boarded a train?"

Wright shook his head. "No. Can't see that from the street at Mortlake, can you? Not 'less you stop on the tracks. She were up the stairs to the platform as soon as she paid me."

"And you didn't see her again?"

"Didn't stick, did I? Had to go find another fare, or it was all the way back to town on me own. I turned right 'round and headed back to Hammersmith." He glanced at the clock on the wall. "I need to be going. Let me have a butcher's at this CCTV of yours, then I'm off."

Wright studied the grainy images on the computer monitor. "That's her. At first I thought she was a slapper and a bit rat-arsed. But she talked like a nob—educated-like. And she weren't drunk, just scared."

"Why did you think that, Mr. Wright?"

"Think what, that she was scared? The look in her eyes, I guess—rabbitty and twitchy. Her voice was shaky, but that coulda been the cold. No shoes, no coat. I felt that sorry for her, you know?"

"Did you talk with her at all?"

"No. Every time I looked back, at stops and the like, she were huddled up, staring out the window. I asked once if she needed help, but she didn't say nothin'. Only stared."

Costello frowned. "Until you arrived at Mortlake."

"Well, right. Until she thanked me for the blanket."

"What about her clothes? Did you notice anything in particular?"

"Other than no shoes, you mean? Nah. Black dress that looked a damn sight more expensive than the one my wife wears. Think she had a little pendant. Crystal or diamond or summat. That's about it.

"Nothing else, then?"

Wright frowned and shook his head. That was all Costello could get.

Back at his desk, Costello ran the video from the CCTV on the Mortlake Station platform. Barefoot Woman entered from the stairs to the street and stood against the wall, still wrapped in the blanket. There were no other passengers on the platform. About thirty seconds later, a train arrived, but she didn't board. As soon as the train pulled out, she exited back down the stairs and disappeared from the video record.

He entered an action to have an officer check the street cameras around Mortlake Station and for businesses with CCTV cameras. The wall clock indicated it was nearly six PM, and Novak hadn't authorized overtime. Besides, somewhere a pint was calling his name.

He pulled on his coat just as Novak entered the incident room. Costello called to him. "Sir, I'm glad I caught you. We've got Barefoot Woman on video and had the taxi driver in. He identified her and confirmed he took her to Mortlake Station. Only a glimpse of the Jag, though. No number plate."

Novak appeared distracted. "Ah. Well, it's nearly six. Perhaps in the morning?"

Costello couldn't help but be taken aback. "Well, sir, if you wish. It won't take long. I was a bit late back from lunch today, so I won't put in for overtime."

The DI didn't bother hiding his annoyance. "Very well. But be quick." Novak followed Costello to his desk. "Jag first. Show me the Jag."

He leaned in and watched as the sergeant found the link in his browser. "There, sir, at the corner of the frame. You can tell it's a Jag XJ, looks to me maybe eight, ten years old. The second car appears to have been a Peugeot—"

Novak interrupted. "Mmm. And the woman?"

Costello gritted his teeth. He advanced the video. "There, passing the pub, coat on, but walking gingerly."

"Pause." Novak leaned in close, studying the figure on the screen. "Mm-hmm." When he straightened, Costello advanced the video again.

"And here she is at Old Brompton Road. No coat now, and—"

"I can see, DS Costello. Stop. Back it up a few frames. Yes, there. Zoom in."

Costello clicked the magnifying glass until the Barefoot Woman's face nearly filled the window on the screen. Her features were almost indistinguishable. Novak again leaned in. This time, Costello caught a whiff of Scotch and, vaguely, a woman's perfume.

Novak walked towards his office. "Go home. We'll discuss it in the morning."

Costello rolled his eyes to the ceiling. Time to call Bull. A pint was in order.

FIFTEEN

Thursday morning, Hampshire

The huge chestnut thoroughbred stamped and snuffled, his breath steaming in the crisp January air. Fee clucked at him, then stroked the brush hard, working back from his withers and down over his barrel, following the lay of his coat. She'd already curried him—Peg had let his hair grow shaggy for the winter. This morning she intended only to curry and brush, and get a bit of horse therapy. Peg had taken him out for a gallop on the heath only yesterday, so today they would have a short lunge in the round pen.

"Trooper's missed you, Fee. We all have." Fritz's soft voice cracked. He was nearly eighty, and the morning was chilly, with enough fog to form slick condensation on exposed stone and metal.

Fee smiled at the straight-backed man walking towards her. He was fit, tall, with weathered skin and a full head of white hair. She always saw her grandfather in his slender face—Fritz was her bastard uncle from the old Viscount's brief dalliance with a German woman just before the Second World War.

Fritz continued. "I've set the local lads to work on the paddock fences. Peg's doing a fry-up. Why don't you go in for breakfast? I'll finish brushing him." He nodded at the long rein and training whip hanging on the barn wall. "You can lunge him after you're topped up with eggs and bacon."

She smiled. "And Peg's garlic chips." The smells of horse and hay in the barn filled her nose, but she could imagine the scrambled eggs, bacon, and potatoes waiting in the kitchen across the courtyard. The anticipation reminded her of when she was young, home from school on holiday and up early to ride the heath, with Peg in the kitchen, insisting she not leave before breakfast. "Are you coming in for brekkers?"

Fritz shook his head. "You go, lass. I'm meeting some lads from Oakley, come up to mend the stiles on Wayfarer's Walk. It's unending."

"Always busy. You haven't changed a whit." She handed Fritz the brush and stretched up to give him a peck on the cheek. "And I'll always love you."

Peg turned from the AGA cooker as Fee entered the kitchen from the boot room. "Chips are just ready. Wash up, girl."

"Will you inspect under my fingernails?" The water from the kitchen tap sprayed hot as needles on Fee's cold city skin.

"You've been in the barn." The corners of Peg's mouth rose. "Don't make me get out my hoof pick."

The women, two decades separated, shared a striking resemblance to Fee's mother, whose health had begun to fail shortly after Fee had turned eight. Peg had come to Waleham then, to look after the horses, dogs, and other animals. Andrew and Fee fell into that category too when they were home from boarding school. The kitchen routine from years past came naturally to both. Fee poured tea while Peg shuttled chips, eggs, and bacon onto plates and set them on the table. The aroma of slightly burnt toast wafted from a rack between them.

Peg spoke through a mouthful of eggs. "This seemed a bit short notice. Is one of Jonny's weekend conferences in the way?"

Fee dipped a chip in the ketchup and chewed. "He said he'd be here if he could."

"Do you remember that pony we called Ironsides? When you were nine or so?"

Fee searched her memory. "There were so many ponies. Which was he?"

"The little Welsh bay. The old bastard bought him for you as an apology for inflicting that hideous Dutch woman on us."

"That stone-cold child hater. Six months after Mum died, and he needed his leg over. The bastard never apologized to anyone. I got a bay pony. Andrew got a Yamaha dirt bike. Bribes."

Peg nodded. "I'd vetted Ironsides at his old trainer's. Sweet as treacle. Good horse, we thought. Nice and smooth past the first two poles, then he shied at the next. That horse wanted you off, and he was just waiting for a chance. He had you on his neck, then went down and almost rolled on you."

"Good thing he didn't, or I'd have been marmalade."

Peg laughed. "I told your father I'd never let you ride that pig again. Not after he'd shown he couldn't be trusted."

Which pig was she talking about? Jonny or Jacko? No, Jonny's just a liar. I'll live with that. Jacko's the pig.

"At least you can sell a horse on."

Peg asked, "Did I say something wrong, dear?"

"No, just thinking about Jonny is all." Fee poured tea and sat back. "I've never talked through it with you. Not face-to-face. I owe you."

Peg tucked a strand of silvered hair behind her ear. "I've known for a while. Walls do talk. I can't imagine." She had never married.

"When Jonny asked, I had no idea about his preference. But he doesn't sleep around."

"No? What do you call it?"

"He and Cranwell have been together for almost thirty years. If anything, I'm the intruder."

"You're his wife. And did he marry you out of the goodness of his heart?"

Fee scoffed. "He's always said it was for me and the kids. But it was a marriage of convenience."

"For him."

"It was convenient for both of us. The weeks were flying by, and I wanted to keep the money coming in."

Peg humphed. "Any chance he'll divorce you for Alec?"

"Three years, when they retire." She sighed. "Then I'm on the market again." *And that's the catch, isn't it?* "Maybe I could go to work in a shop. Get a tattoo and become a barista."

"We could open a barn, like we talked about when you were a girl," Peg joked. "I'll train the horses, and you can muck out the stalls." They laughed.

"I think that's exactly what the old bastard wanted to prevent. To save me from a life given to horses. Or from my bloody fucking hippie artist boyfriends."

"He did have a way with words."

Fee gathered the plates and carried them to the kitchen sink. "He also had a way of getting everything he wanted, even from the grave."

"So that's it, then."

"No." *I have to tell her, or I'll never respect myself.* "I'm having an affair. Jonny's known from the beginning. It was convenient. Exciting at first. Jacko made me feel twenty again. But then he changed. A little at a time. Now . . ." *Now he's sent me to prison.* "He might have gotten me in trouble. Legal trouble. Maybe criminal. I don't know yet."

She dried her hands on the tea towel and leaned against the counter. "When I look in the mirror, I'm staring at fifty. Almost fifty years, Peg. The first twenty-five at home and in school and under his thumb until he kicked off. The next twenty with a loving man and a family, thinking I was finally free of the old jackass. Now almost four of this shite with Jonny and—"

"A man who's using you?"

"I won't be fifty-three and hunting for another husband just to keep my inheritance. And I fucking refuse to be a pretty piece of arse any longer. I called him on the way down yesterday. All his bloody nonsense ends now."

"What about the gallery?"

"I've lost interest. I've decided to sell it. It's a damned millstone."

She bent and gave Peg a kiss on the crown of her head. "I think I'll go out and lunge Trooper. Horse therapy sounds like the ticket."

"Could be worse, dear."

Fee wasn't so sure. Halfway across the courtyard, her mobile buzzed. Jacko's name displayed on the screen. She let it ring until she was in the barn. Fritz had already left.

"Fiona." She'd lain in her bed and rehearsed this confrontation into the wee hours of the morning. It was time to grow up. To hell with being calm.

"You bitch. You go to Jonny, and his career is over. The Met doesn't look fondly on senior officers who cover up each other's fuck-ups, especially when they've been fucking each other for donkey's years. When he—"

"Shut up and listen, Jacko, or—"

"Or what? When he goes down, you're out on your tight little ass. And we'll go down too, for withholding evidence. Not coming forward. I'll—"

Her anger flared. "You'll what? You're in over your head, you bastard. I may go sit at the nick and have a chat with that Novak detective."

"And then it's prison for both of us."

"At most I might get a few months in Sutton Park open prison, but I figure you'll be on Her Majesty's guest list for quite some time. When your cellmate finds out you were a Crown Prosecutor, it'll be your ass on the line, not mine. So don't threaten me. Tuesday, Gionfriddo's, seven."

Silence. Fee counted the seconds up to five.

"You know it isn't me you have to worry about." Jacko sounded conciliatory. "I haven't told anyone who you are, but they can find out. Word of this to anyone, and they'll come looking."

"Whoever the hell they are, they'll come looking regardless." Her hand shook, scarcely able to hold her mobile to her ear. She urged herself to stay strong. "It was a warning to you, wasn't it? The poor sod getting his head blown off was as big a surprise to you as it was to me. So for some far-fetched reason, they have a use for you. He didn't expect me to be there. Why didn't he kill me?"

Again, silence. Finally, "Don't know why he didn't kill us both. Tuesday at seven."

"Be there. With answers." She sank to the cold cobblestones, her back against the barn wall.

Yes, Peg. It was worse.

SIXTEEN

Thursday evening, Westminster

Liz Barker giggled. "So what was it, Chanel? Bulgari? Revlon Charlie?"

Costello laughed. "How should I know? Ask your captive Royal Marine."

Bull grinned. "Right. Most of my squaddies carried their perfume in their combat kit, next to the grenades. I kept mine strapped to my leg beside my combat knife. Maybe it was his aftershave. He doesn't strike me as an afternoon delight sort of bloke."

"Could be a bit of a dark horse. He never commented on the Jag or the Peugeot. And his reaction to the woman's face—he had me keep zooming in. Then he stared a moment and walked away. Got no idea why he wants me in early tomorrow."

Bull held up his empty pint glass. "Not much to comment on, I suppose."

Costello shook his head. "Right, but keeping those tattoos from the team. That's bloody weird. Not good."

Bull stood and headed in the direction of the loo. "Same again? My shout."

Costello said, "A half for me."

When he was out of earshot, Liz said, "That's my guy, Simon. He only rents his beer. Now tell me. What tattoos?"

Costello picked up a napkin and began folding it. "Shouldn't have said that. Forget you heard it."

"Now, my friend, you know I'll twist it out of Bull, don't you?" She leaned towards Costello and gave him a conspirator's smile. "I promise it won't go past the three of us." She batted her big green eyes, then laughed.

He blushed and chuckled. When Liz teased, she made such an obvious joke of it, he had to laugh. He had a huge crush on Liz, but she and Bull were an item, and he had a strict personal rule. It was obvious she knew how he felt, but she always respected him. He sighed loudly through his nose. "It can't go any further. You'll weasel it out of Bull anyway. Might as well be me."

"Right. You have to tell me now, to protect your mate from his conniving, predatory girlfriend. So grass. What tattoo?"

Costello blushed again. "The victim had a tattoo that covered his whole back. Bull sent a photo from Kumar's autopsy. Novak recognized it—Serbian paramilitary. Called it an Arkan Tiger tattoo. Told us to keep it mum. He avoided telling the team about it. Never mentioned it. And it's not in the case notes. So . . ."

"So Novak doesn't want it known, and he's willing to destroy his career to keep it that way. If anyone higher up found out, Novak's balls would be on a plate." She frowned in thought. "And he told you to keep it to yourselves."

"Not let it outside the team." Costello swirled the final drops of beer in his glass, then downed it.

"Serbian. Any immediate connection to the Sreckos? God, I'd love to nail those bastards. Ever since that muscle-bound goon worked me over, I hurt when I bend down to pick something up. Can't do more than twenty-five crunches without my muscles cramping, and my nose is still bent. We never caught that fuck-ing creep."

"Bull worked that shite over good. He left a trail of blood

drops from your flat all the way out to the street. He's probably back in some hole a thousand miles from here."

"Yep. My Marine landed just in time. Speaking of whom . . ."

Bull set their pints on the table and looked from one to the other. He glared at Costello with a mixture of anger and disappointment. "I'm away five minutes, and she has you spilling your guts. Just couldn't resist her, could you?" He scoffed. "I would have told her in my own time and in my own way."

Liz smirked. "So, either Novak's bent, or someone higher up told him to conceal evidence from us cops. Cranwell? No, he's just a DCS. Hughes, maybe?"

Costello shook his head. "Not high enough. This would have had to come from somewhere way up. Only a commissioner could even consider it, and he'd need the support of the others. I can't imagine they'd do it on their own."

"MI5? Maybe the poor sod was an agent or a terrorist."

"But that means they were in on the murder. Blowing a thug's head off in a flat isn't their style." Costello looked from Liz to Bull. "And if it's them, they would have yanked the case from us by now and cautioned us under the Official Secrets Act."

"It's almost like a message," Bull said. "The murder, I mean."

"Maybe," Liz said. "If anyone outside got a sniff that critical evidence was being withheld, it would gut the team, maybe disgrace the whole Met. The tabloids would be all over it in an instant."

Bull finished his half-pint and set it hard on the table. "Could be anything, really. One thing I do know. If it's MI5 and we let this leak, we'll spend our lives standing security in a sausage factory."

"And where have I heard that before? Seems to me I heard Elaine say that to Jenkins right before he resigned." Liz drained her pint.

Costello laughed. "Does sound a bit like her, doesn't it?" His voice took on a serious tone. "I dunno what to do, but I'd hate for any of us to get caught in the middle of some scheme or other. Do you think the guv—Elaine, I mean—could maybe point the way for us?"

"She needs to know," Liz replied.

"Maybe she does." Bull looked at Liz and Costello in turn. "We'll need to be careful."

"I'm meeting with Novak early tomorrow, before the status meeting," Costello said. "I expect he'll have something to say to me about Barefoot Woman and the cars. Maybe we'll have a bit more to go on after I've heard him out. Liz, can you call Elaine? See if she can meet? But for God's sake, don't tell her anything. Not until we have more to go on."

Liz giggled again. "Barefoot Woman and the cars? Sounds like a rock band!"

Bull made a point of looking around the pub, then smiled at her gently. "Let's keep it down, sweetheart. You never know who's listening."

Liz pulled a face at him, then took a quieter tone. "This may not have anything to do with the Sreckos, but we still need to tell Elaine."

"I know Elaine's your mentor, and she's been a friend to both of us, but we need to protect ourselves and her. We don't want her barging in and confronting Novak unless she's fully armed. Right?"

Bull waited for her to nod in agreement before he continued. "Let's stow this talk for now. We have a plan. We'll get together at our flat tomorrow night."

Costello nodded his assent.

Thursday night, Bermondsey

Bull kept his eyes on the road as they crept through evening traffic. Taillights flared and blinked, scattered by the rain pounding the windscreen. Headlights reflected from the wet streets into his eyes, distorting his depth perception, making each oncoming vehicle seem closer than it really was. Liz stared out the passenger window.

They had been silent for fifteen minutes when Liz finally spoke. "No wonder you've been so quiet the last couple of days. How long did you think you could keep this to yourself?"

Bull shook his head. "Not long. But that's not the question, is it? What you mean is why didn't I tell you right away. I was between a rock and a hard place, luv. First, Novak says for Simon and me to keep mum about it. And then he went and made sure the team didn't know about the tattoos. We wondered what the hell was going on. And Simon didn't tell me he was going to bring it up tonight. Took me by surprise."

"Oh. Right," Liz replied. "So you were just going to let it go and say sod all to me? If there's a connection, Elaine and I need to know. We're the ones who paid the biggest price. Especially her. You owe it to us, Bull!"

Bull stopped the car and reversed into a parking space next to the kerb. "No, that's not it. But you know the rules. What your guv says is what goes."

"All I want is to talk about our days. It seems like we don't have as much to share."

Bull didn't respond. There was so much he wanted to share, but how to bring it all up? He didn't know how to talk about the moody silences that pocked those months while Liz was recovering from the assault. How often had he suggested going out to the cinema or a dance club, only to be told she didn't feel like it? How many times had he been rebuffed when he had only wanted to hold her? How many times had he reached out to her in the night, only to become the object of her startled rage?

He realized she was still recovering and that it could take a long time for her to overcome her PTSD. But he was confused, and his confidence had been shaken. He wanted to talk. Liz said she wanted to talk. But it was never at the same time. And he had been afraid that talking to Liz about this murder, with its apparent connections back to the Srecko case, might revive her old terrors.

They walked to the front door of their small apartment block in silence. After they were inside, he went to the kitchen and poured two glasses of fizzy water. He handed one to her and gestured to the sofa.

"Simon and I got a shout to Kensington, south of Queen's Gate. Turned out to be a posh house off the Fulham Road. By the time we got there, coppers were all over the place. Messiest crime scene I've ever seen, next to Elaine's, I mean. And Afghanistan."

"Who's the victim?"

"Dunno his name, but from tattoos, Novak said the guy was Serbian militia, from the war in Bosnia. That guy who assaulted you fought like he was military trained."

Liz's hands shook, spilling the water. Bull wrapped his huge arms around her. "I was afraid it would bring it all up again. I'm sorry, lover. I was caught in the middle."

Liz blew her nose. "I'll be okay. I need to come to terms with it." She blew her nose. "I have to tell Elaine. I can't deceive her."

"It needs to be you. When you call her, try not to tell her much, only that you need to talk. If she finds out anything and talks to Novak before we do, our careers are in the bin."

Liz snickered. "Not the bin. Remember what Elaine says. We'll be standing security in a sausage factory."

"We'd never have to worry where our next breakfast was coming from, would we?"

"Maybe lunch and dinner too. I've been wondering how soon I'll have my next banger." She looked Bull in the eyes and kissed him. Hard.

SEVENTEEN

Friday morning, Kensington

"Close the door." Novak indicated a chair. "What's the news?"

Costello pushed the door shut, took a seat, and referred to the overnight reports. "Forensics says there aren't enough epithelial cells in the urine to get a DNA result. They say she might have been wearing expensive silk knickers, and they may have filtered it. The only cells they found were the victim's blood and assorted other tissues. They might get something from the two strands of blonde hair."

"What about fast-tracking it?" Novak seemed to be studying a spot on the wall over Costello's right shoulder.

"They denied the fast-track request. They're swamped. It could take two weeks."

Novak scoffed. "The buckshot?"

"Same, sir—the metallurgy lab is backed up."

Novak stared at the wall without further comment. Costello shuffled the papers to the next item and continued. "A resident, La Veuve Berenice Claudette Dubuisson-D'Anjou, according to the desk sergeant's report, found a woman's black shoe behind one of the potted plants on her front stoop. Blahnik. Spiked heel. Forensics has it."

Novak smirked. "D'Anjou. The first sign the investigation's going pear-shaped. Does she drive a Peugeot?"

Costello detested puns, but he chuckled anyway. "I've assigned an action to check that today. La Veuve Dubuisson-D'Anjou turned up at the desk downstairs yesterday evening and handed a paper bag to the sergeant on duty. The bag contained the shoe, a handwritten and signed affidavit stating that she had found the shoe, and photos of the potted plant that concealed it, with inscribed arrows pointing to the exact location where she found it in front of her house."

"Damn. Really? How old is Verve-or-whatever-something-or-other-D'Anjou?"

Costello looked at the fine print on the report. "La Veuve means 'the widow.' It's a French family honorific, and she's seventy-five. The sergeant said her attitude reminded him of Aunt Violet on Downton, but her accent was all Isabelle Huppert. *Très formidable.*"

"Ah. Was the affidavit attested?"

"No, sir, but it says here she would do so if required."

"Why was she not interviewed during the house-to-house? Why didn't she come forward earlier?"

Costello again consulted his notes. "The affidavit states she and her companion were at the family pile outside Reims. They returned to London on the EuroStar yesterday about two PM. She found the shoe when she went out to water her plants. Then she heard about the murder, so she contacted her English solicitor. It seems she was unsure what the protocol should be in England."

Novak rolled his eyes. "She should call the bloody police, same as France. The name rings a bell, though."

"I thought so too, so I looked it up. It's a super-expensive brand of champagne. Around a thousand pounds a bottle." Costello hoped he could interview La Veuve. She sounded awesome. Perhaps he'd give the action to himself and Bull.

"Not fruit brandy?"

"No, sir. Pear brandy is made with a different kind of pear."

"Ah. You're a wellspring of useful information. Perhaps she'll provide refreshments when we interview her. Anything else, Sergeant?"

"Two things. I assigned a DC to review the CCTV cameras around the neighbourhood in the hope of finding where, or if, the dark Jag exited the area. No luck so far. And uniforms searched those private back gardens along Onslow Square that DC Bull mentioned, and interviewed the residents. They found nothing—no coat or shoe—and no one saw Barefoot Woman, or anyone else, enter or throw anything into the garden that night. *L'investigation fait en poire.*"

Novak stood and looked out his office window. "I'm not sensing much joy. And I'm not convinced the Barefoot Woman has anything to do with the murder. If she was a witness, why would the killer let her go? If she was an accomplice, it wouldn't make sense to abandon her, because doing so removes control over her. I have similar questions about the Jag driver. Peugeot driver too. Either or neither could be our killer. It all smacks of carelessness. No word on the Peugeot?"

"No, sir. We may hear from the French police today. I'm not sure what the delay's about. What if the Jag driver is the killer? If he was, and if the woman is his accomplice, it would explain the remark the witness heard about Jack being a coward."

"You're stringing *ifs* together, Sergeant. Forensics states there were four people present: the victim, the killer, another man, and a woman. Perhaps the woman in the room was the Barefoot Woman on the pavement. Perhaps not. Is the victim's blood on the shoe our French widow provided?"

"Forensics has it. And the presence of a shoeless woman—"

Novak held up his hand. "The crime scene report suggests that the woman stood in the wrong place to be the killer. The footprints and blowback pattern indicate that one of the other two men was the trigger man. Was the killer named Jack? What if they didn't all leave at the same time?"

"That's a good point, sir." Costello noted the question.

"Did they all come in the same car? Separate cars? Ask yourself if it makes sense for the killer to let the woman and the second man go. Perhaps he didn't, and we'll find them floating in Camden Canal tomorrow. Or maybe they're smoke up a chimney and we'll never find them. My point is that we may have the wrong end of this stick. Have you checked when the Peugeot and the Jag arrived on the scene? When and where they parked? Parking is devilishly difficult in South Kensington, what with permits and all. Did the woman walk to the house? Have you considered all that? What else are you missing?"

"I don't know, sir, but I'll assign actions." Costello wanted to ask what Novak was doing as senior investigating officer, if he was steering the investigation towards this kind of rabbit warren. SIOs were supposed to decide on clear lines of enquiry, and Costello thought they had one, even if they weren't making a lot of progress yet. But Novak had already criticized him once, and Costello had been around long enough to know better than to raise more objections. He kept his eyes on his notebook and jotted down Novak's questions.

"Thank you, DS Costello." Novak's mouth turned up in a half-smile. "You sound like you speak French. Or try to. Assign yourself to interview our French grand dame. You deserve her."

EIGHTEEN

Friday morning, Hendon

Elaine stared out her window, watching a train rumble east-ward. Liz's early morning call had taken her by surprise, but Elaine had agreed to meet after hearing Liz wanted some advice on a case. Liz had implied, but not stated outright, that her topic might interest Elaine as well. Simon and Bull would be there too. Interesting.

She turned back to her desk, which faced a glass door and wall. Unlike her previous office, this door didn't open onto a bustling major incident room. She couldn't hear the murmurs of a dozen white-shirted homicide detectives, holding their telephones between shoulder and ear. She couldn't watch them studying computer screens and tapping at keyboards, researching leads, entering the results of enquiries. She had no DC Evan Cromarty to work magic with his computers, no DS Paula Ford to organize the team's activities and keep things moving.

And no gut-driven purpose to turn her passion into a solid result. Those days were gone, at least for now. Her recent past was like a fragment of song that kept recurring in her mind. *What had Peter called it? An earworm—that was it.* He said he got them frequently, sometimes for days at a time, and that the only way he had found to get rid of it was to listen to the entire song, maybe even sing it aloud. Once he had finished the verses, it would fade.

I don't know the verses to my song.

Yesterday morning she had felt alive, active, effective. Technically, she hadn't kidnapped Mehta, of course. He had gotten in her car of his own accord, and up until the moment she walked out of the café, he had never asked to be let go, so she hadn't held him against his will.

But what was it he had said? She'd felt a warning flare go up in her brain, and then she'd let herself get pissed off at him, and it had passed. She had to think.

"DCI Hope? Elaine?"

Startled out of her reverie, she had to look twice to make sure who was standing in the door. "DCS Cranwell, what a surprise."

Detective Chief Superintendent Cranwell had been her superior for the twelve years she had worked in Murder Investigation. He had trusted her to take over her last murder investigation when DCI Benford, her immediate boss at the time, had suffered a heart attack while they were interviewing Peter.

As usual, Cranwell's tailored uniform was immaculate and fit his slender frame perfectly. His close-trimmed gray hair tapered to a neat, clipped line a half-inch above his collar. He reminded her of one of her professors at Durham, who Elaine had been sure was gay. She always thought Cranwell spoke as if he were afraid he might reveal something embarrassing. Why was he here?

"I was in the building and felt I must stop by to see how you're getting along. It's been almost four months since we spoke. How are you?"

"Settling in. The leg is stronger, but I'm not fighting fit yet."

"That's not what I heard. Word has it you got in a bit of a scrap earlier this week." He raised his eyebrows. "In the street, no less." He looked at Elaine askance and smiled as if he'd delivered the punchline to a sly joke.

"I'm sure the accounts of my scuffle are greatly exaggerated. I lost my balance and got tangled up with a bloke, is all. Bit of a misunderstanding." So, news of her little ruckus had made it to upper management, and Cranwell wasn't even in her chain of command anymore. Why had someone told him, and what else had he heard about?

Cranwell picked lint from his crisply pressed pants before he replied. "I'm sure the tale grew in the telling, then. Most tales . . ."

"Most tales," she echoed.

Both chuckled. Cranwell smiled self-consciously. Elaine needed to be wary. The chief superintendent was here for a reason. She waited.

Cranwell broke the awkward silence. "The Met's lawyers would tell me I shouldn't say this, but I will. We should have listened to you. Things might have turned out differently."

He shifted in the chair before continuing. "But that was then. What about now? Your work at the academy? It's important work, you know. We need experienced officers to share their wisdom. Your insights have a huge impact; they help us succeed in our service objectives."

Platitudes. Cranwell hadn't changed. Had he only stopped by to give a pep talk? He knew full well it was her lack of "wisdom" that had taken her out of the Serious and Major Crimes division and into the College of Policing.

She might as well let her feelings be known. "I know what I'm doing is useful, sir. But you know me. I've always preferred action to sitting, and I'm doing far too much sitting these days. We need experienced officers leading investigation teams too."

Cranwell nodded in agreement. "We certainly do." Their eyes met. "With all this terror unrest, and Brexit hubbub, and anti-immigrant feeling"—he diverted his gaze over her shoulder, out the window—"we need calm heads and steady hands. Off-the-books investigations are highly frowned upon these days."

And just like that, Cranwell had delivered the Met's official position. Elaine sat stunned, staring at Cranwell, but not seeing him as her mind followed his message. She could almost quote what Cranwell's superiors had told him. That DCI Elaine Hope is strictly back shelf and will be kept off the street. That, after a while, she will resign, out of either frustration or boredom. If she drags it on too long, a new psychological report will result in her enforced retirement. Either way, she'll have a suitable pension if she goes quietly.

With sudden clarity, she realized what it was Mehta had said that had bothered her. Cranwell had confirmed it. She was being watched. But followed? Surely not. Surely the Met wasn't wasting a detective's precious time following a half-mad malcontent. The emotional body blow took her breath for the second time this morning. She sat stunned, barely able to listen.

Am I really that much of a threat to them?

Cranwell half-rose from the chair. "Are you all right? Can I get you something?"

"No, sir. Thank you. I get a shooting pain from time to time. It passes."

"I see. There was something else. I've been asked to tell you informally that you've been requested to attend a meeting Monday afternoon. At Assistant Commissioner Collins's office at New Scotland Yard. They've requested that you wear your number-one dress uniform. I believe DCS Delaney and Commander Hughes will be there as well."

What the hell is this about? Have they already decided to retire me?

Cranwell continued. "I don't know more than that."

Like hell you don't. "Would it be about my leave? The shrink cleared me to come back. He said I was fit for this type of duty. What's it really about, sir?"

"That's all I was told, and I mustn't speculate." He leaned forward. "Please believe this, Elaine. I have always considered you to be a fine detective. One of the best I've had the good fortune to work with. So many detectives either don't have the gift of intuition or lack the ability to elicit loyalty from their team. You have both. I always thought you were a natural fit for the job."

It seemed to Elaine that he was studying her with an almost fatherly affection. *Saying goodbye?* She felt winded, hoarse. "Thank you, sir." She cleared her throat. "That means a great deal to me."

Cranwell's voice caught briefly before he continued. "Lately I've felt more and more that we often don't tell the people we respect how we feel. So I hope you don't think what I'm going to say is gratuitous. My hope for you is that you make the most of this research job as long as you need it." He gestured around the room. "The academy can be a calm harbour. Use it wisely. But take more care outside these walls. Rely on old friends. Rein in your emotions, and show some caution now and again."

He stood and held out his hand. His voice took on a solemn tone, as if he were speaking a benediction. "Elaine, you don't have to tell me anything, but I think I know why you're doing what you're doing. I will be your friend as much as my position allows. Please feel free to contact me if you think I can help."

His hand was warm and dry, and held a small piece of paper concealed in the palm. She slipped it from him as they parted. After he left, she went to the lavatory and locked herself in a toilet stall. She unfolded the scrap, which had been torn from a sheet of Met letterhead. The only writing on it was an unfamiliar telephone number. She memorized it and started to flush it, but instead placed it in the pocket of her jeans. With the painkillers fuzzing her brain, she'd code it into her smartphone first.

For minutes she sat, leaning against the partition of the toilet stall, sorting what she'd learned. *How much does Cranwell know about my—obsession? Yes, obsession's the right word. The therapist told me I might—would—become obsessed. If Cranwell suspects or knows I'm 'round the bend, who else does? Is he warning me? Baiting me? Who's* at the other end of that number? Someone in the Met is scared of me. They're tailing me. They want me out. Cranwell is scared of what they might do.

Okay, then. Come for me or kick me out. Either way, I bloody well won't go quietly.

NINETEEN

Friday night, Bermondsey

Simon Costello popped the cork from a fresh bottle of Rioja. "So I called the lady, and her haughty companion said she was ill with some kind of flu, and her doctor had told her to stay in bed for a few days. We arranged an appointment for Monday afternoon." He topped up Elaine's glass and handed it back. "I thought ladies' companions went out donkey's years ago, but apparently not."

Elaine took the glass and looked at the three young detectives sitting around Bull's kitchen table. *Simon should have pushed back. He knows to go for the immediate interview, not wait on the witness's convenience. It's a murder, for Christ's sake. But I wasn't there.* "Sounds like a thin excuse to me. Wasn't there a lady's companion in *Murder on the Orient Express*? That was set in the thirties, wasn't it? I think they were an anachronism even then."

Bull, Costello, and Liz were acting as though they expected shoes to fall from the ceiling at any moment. This get-together had nothing to do with advice for Liz. Something was up.

Elaine couldn't keep back a laugh. "Out with it. You surely have something meatier to talk about than Simon's infatuation with a French octogenarian." She swirled her wine. "Does this have anything to do with Novak's investigation?"

Costello raised his hands. "Please. She's seventy-five. That's so much more age appropriate. But it's a fair cop." He looked at Bull. "We need to talk to you about the Kensington murder."

Elaine sat back in her chair and crossed her legs, assessing the three younger detectives sitting on the sofa across from her. She asked, "Ask me, inform me, or warn me?"

Costello answered. "Little bit of all three. We think you may be interested."

Old friends. She didn't think Cranwell knew anything about this. He wouldn't have condoned it, and if for some unknown reason he had approved, he would be here. "I saw you and Bull on the news, in the background. Novak's your SIO, and you aren't going to him about whatever it is. Or you have and didn't get a good answer. So stop being coy. If he's bent, go see Professional Standards. If you want my opinion on something, I'll help you as best I can. If you're warning me, I'm all ears. I'm persona non grata these days, so you're taking a chance either way. It's about the Sreckos, right?"

Before Costello could answer, Bull cleared his throat. "Let me have it, if you don't mind. You're the DS, and you need some plausible deniability. I'm a green DC who doesn't know any better. Everybody's wine topped up?" He passed the bottle around. When everyone had settled, he began by holding his glass up to Elaine.

"You're our guv, no matter what team we're on. For better or worse, that's the way we all feel, especially after what happened. We're not sure what's going on, so we need some feedback. And you're connected to the case, for some reason."

Elaine started to interject but held up. Bull continued, "We need to make sure that you have good information so you can do what you need to do. That's why we're here.

"We don't know why we were added to Novak's team. From the first, it looked like they had plenty of detectives. Novak was in charge, and we knew sod all about him. He seemed smart, but he was aloof. Just his style I guess. Then he assigned Simon to run the incident room and me to liaise with Forensics. Nothing too much out of the ordinary, but it felt wrong, like he was singling us out."

Elaine looked from one to the other. "Perhaps he felt that since you and Simon had worked together before, you'd coordinate better."

"Could be. I was the only detective at the autopsy. Exhibits bloke, photographer, and me. Novak was busy, I guess. When Kumar—"

"Sorry to interrupt, Bull. Novak didn't attend the autopsy? His first murder in what—two years?" Elaine needed to confirm. This wasn't unheard of—the SIO wasn't required to be there, but it was odd. Had she been SIO, she certainly would have wanted to be able to question Kumar firsthand.

"No, but something turned up, so I called him. The victim had tattoos covering his back and coming up over his shoulder. I took photos and sent them to Novak. He knew what they were."

Bull pulled out his phone, swiped the screen several times, and handed it to Elaine. "That's them. The double-headed eagle is the Serbian coat of arms. The script says 'Made in Serbia.' The tiger head is interesting. It's the symbol of the Arkan Tigers."

Elaine had seen photos of the Serbian eagle before. "I remember the Bosnian conflict. The ethnic Serbs tried to kill, well, everybody else who lived in Bosnia but them. But Arkan Tigers? A military unit?"

Bull nodded. "Sort of. Paramilitary. The regular army was run by criminals. You remember the war crime trials. But the paramilitary units were lower-level criminals, bullies really, who were getting off on being important for once in their lives and being able to do anything they wanted. A little shite named Arkan was the commander. Did whatever Milosevic or whoever told him to do. Go burn a village? No worries, done in a flash. Kill the men and boys, and rape the women? Helluva good time."

Elaine remembered now. "So those were the Arkan Tigers."

"Yep. Novak called them 'Tigrovi.' My sergeant in Ghanners had been one of the peacekeepers in Bosnia and Kosovo. He told stories about the Tigers and how they'd slaughtered and raped their way through the Balkans."

"Royal Marine campfire tales, eh?" As soon as the words left her lips, Elaine regretted saying it. "Sorry, Bull. It just slipped out."

The huge detective glanced at Liz, then continued. "Sarge needed to tell us about what he had experienced, how it was similar to what we were seeing in Sangin—that's a village in Helmand Province in Afghanistan. Deadliest place in the world, some newspaper said. It needed cleaning out, and 40 Commando drew the short straw." He drained his glass. "For our fucking sins. Sarge and a couple of my other squaddies had been in Bosnia, back in the nineties, trying to keep the Christians from killing Muslims. Ten years after and we're in Ghanners killing Taliban, and they're killing both us and each other. Crazy shit, you know?"

Elaine couldn't imagine what Bull had gone through. Or Peter, for that matter. Religious war. Onward Christian soldiers and Taliban fighters. In the name of Jesus, Allahu Akbar. Perverse interpretations of God's Word had always proven to be an effective mass motivator. Evil madness. The powerful would spew self-righteous muck about how God's on their side, rile up some dim-witted bullies, and turn them loose. Next thing you know, the war's been going on for centuries, and everyone's confused about whose side is which and who started it. Even the right-minded clerics can't make it stop, and all the best, most disciplined professional soldiers can really do is maintain some shaky form of status quo. It was enough to put a person off religion altogether.

Elaine pulled her mind back to the present. "You can justify any sin if God's on your side, can't you? So where does this lead us? Why did you need to tell me about the tattoo?"

"Because Novak told us not to."

Simon chimed in. "Not exactly, but close. After the second morning briefing, he took us aside and asked if we had talked with you. When we said no, he said to keep it to ourselves and not speculate. He said if you approached us about it, to tell you to talk to him."

Elaine looked at each of them. What had she done to gain such loyalty from these fellows? They were risking disciplinary action by telling her this. Her voice grew stern. "Do either of you realize you've disobeyed an order from your SIO? At best, that's insubordination. It wouldn't look good on your record—not at all. Novak could haul you up before Professional Standards. A tribunal could put you both back in uniform. Simon, they could break you back down to constable and you'd never see sergeant again, if that's what they wanted."

Simon and Bull glanced at each other. They were aware of the consequences. Now that she'd spoken the necessary words, she had to prove she was worth her salt, worthy of such devotion. That she'd protect them. "Well?"

Simon spoke first. "Guv, I think he wanted us to tell you. And even if he didn't want it, I don't think he'd break us. He's withholding the tattoos from the team. I think he may have deleted the pictures from the investigation files."

"What? Withheld evidence from his own murder team? Tell me more."

Simon and Bull told Elaine about their misgivings regarding Novak. That he hadn't worn a scene suit and how he seemed to disappear at odd times during the day. That Simon had smelled Scotch on his breath and a woman's perfume after one of those absences. And how, when they appeared to have a clear line of enquiry, he had diverted resources to other, less likely avenues. When they had finished, Elaine sorted through it in her mind.

"Who's Novak's boss?" she asked.

Bull answered. "Cranwell, then Hughes. Up the chain to Collins, I—"

Simon interjected. "But I don't think he talks to Cranwell. I've seen him drinking with Hughes, at the Monk. Funny too, now I think of it. I saw them there when Novak was at NCA. Might be nothing, but there you are." He smirked. "Perhaps they were friends in a more innocent time."

Elaine laughed out loud. "Okay, boys and girls. This is all interesting, but not the stuff of reality. You suspect Novak because something's odd. Granted, it looks like he's hiding evidence. There could be dozens of reasons, and yes, it could be part of a larger plan. You have no solid facts, only your own interpretations. You want me to barge in and set things right, but in all likelihood, there's nothing wrong except your suspicions." She set down her wine and leaned forward. "I can't interfere with another officer's investigation. You know it's just not done. Novak's got a good reputation, a solid record. I'd look a complete arse if I jumped in, and it would be the end of your careers in murder too."

Bull shrugged. "So you want us to do nothing."

"That's not what I said. I think you need to keep your eyes and ears open, and do your job. If you see something you can't explain, something odd and not proper procedure, come back to me, and we'll have another chat. Another thing. Cromarty gave me a crash course in navigating Companies House. I used your murder house as a test case, looking for connections with the Sreckos. It turned up some interesting information. Nothing concrete, but a few correlations. I'll let you know if I find anything." She looked from face to face. "Are we good, then?"

"Right, guv." Costello and Bull nodded. But Liz sat brooding, staring at the wall.

Elaine waved her hand. "Yoohoo! Are we good, Liz?"

"I don't know, guv. I'm worried it could start all over again."

"Look. You're busy working burglaries in Croydon, so you're not connected to this. Right? Simon, can you bring me up to speed on what else you have? I'll keep it to myself."

For a half hour Elaine listened to Simon and Bull describe every scrap of evidence they had—the layout of the crime scene, the position of the killer, Barefoot Woman. They discussed the dark Jag, the Peugeot, and the shoe La Veuve found. All the while Elaine wondered about Novak and why Simon and Bull had been made part of the team. And what she was getting herself into.

★ ★ ★

Jenkins washed down the bite of apple with a sip from his water bottle and placed both in his backpack. As he zipped it, he wondered whether Hope still hated him after all these months. She'd filed insubordination and misconduct charges against him, and had driven him out of the Met. He laughed. He'd deserved it.

The last time he'd seen Hope, she was lying face down across a low table, naked, covered in blood. As her unconscious body reflexively gasped for breath, he had turned her head, inserted his finger in her mouth, and cleared blood and broken teeth from her airway so she could breathe easier. Then he'd scarpered out the back door to avoid meeting her belated backup coming in the front.

And now, here she was, walking calmly out of the apartment block of those same tardy backups. She'd been in there a good hour and a half. Jenkins always had a bit of trouble reconciling Hope's loyalty to the babies who had failed to protect her. She was an Amazon warrior, tall, lean, confident. Costello barely weighed ten stone and talked like a schoolteacher. Bull was a huge, decorated, battle-tested Marine, but he licked Hope's shoes like a dog who'd peed the carpet. And Liz—she was just a green girl, wasn't she? They all hated Jenkins, but he'd been the only one there when Elaine needed help. He'd made sure she lived, and they didn't even know it.

When the lights of Hope's blue BMW flashed on, he twisted the key of his black Saab. Its turbocharged six-cylinder engine rumbled to life, sending sensual pulses through the driver's seat. He watched Hope exit the parking lot and accelerate away. After a three-second pause, he pulled out behind her. Hope always drove as fast as traffic allowed, which he liked, as it gave him the sensation of racing her. He loved taking his old Porsche Boxster to track days at Brands Hatch race course and burning the shine off the stockbrokers in their Caymans and Carreras. He'd seen how she handled her Bimmer, and reckoned she might stick with him in a street race.

Hope pulled into a Chinese takeaway. She looked to be headed home, and he had enough to report for the evening, so he tapped a speed-dial number on his mobile.

As usual, his wife's soft voice set his heart right. "On your way home? It's salmon tonight and some nice curried vegetables."

"Music to my ears, Roxy, my love. About half an hour."

Jenkins considered that Hope was alright, for the mannish sort of woman she was. Strong, smart, and reasonably bad-assed in a scuffle. She'd topped that sick bastard Nilo even after he'd nearly killed her. The tall detective was clearly someone to reckon with, but she'd be no contest for a man who was ready for her and knew what he was doing. He hoped it never came to that.

TWENTY

Friday night, Brentford

It was well past Scratch's usual dinner time when Elaine arrived home, so he was more insistent than usual that she feed him immediately. The large tabby weaved a path back and forth between her feet as she walked to the kitchen, nearly tripping her, his loud purrs interspersed with angry chatter. For the first time in weeks, Elaine had an appetite. While Scratch was making short work of his tuna, she tucked into her garlic shrimp and a good Czech pilsner.

Afterwards, she sat cross-legged on her bed, contemplating the pinboard on the wall. Anton's image stared back at her, but his impact on her had diminished, her attention diverted to the dark silhouette six inches to its right. *What's going on with this case? Think through it, Lainie.*

She went to the kitchen cupboard and retrieved a glass and a bottle of whisky. She bunched pillows against her headboard to support her back and sat cross-legged again. *No. I can't sit here. Those pictures are too distracting.*

She pulled the duvet from her bed, picked up the bottle and glass, and went out on her veranda. The shock of the cold air was immediately energizing. She sat at the small table, drank a whisky in one gulp, and pulled the duvet tightly around her.

The lights of the narrow boats lined up along Brentford Marina reflected off the surface of the canal, shimmering on the dark water. Traffic hummed on the A4 a half mile to the north.

Forget Anton, Lainie. He's the end, not the beginning. Not the here and now. What did you learn tonight? Put it together.

Three days ago a suspicious death had been reported in an empty house in Kensington. A poor sod's head had been ploughed with a shotgun in front of at least two witnesses.

Within a couple of hours, the Met had pulled together an ad hoc murder investigation team and assigned Novak to the case. Why? The Met wouldn't assign an ad hoc murder team to a DI who hadn't been part of a murder investigation in over two years. It wasn't like there was no one else. Was this case related to one Novak had been working on at the National Crime Agency?

The temperature on her veranda was dropping. Elaine poured another two fingers of whisky and again drank it in one gulp. She pulled her feet under her and wrapped herself back into the duvet.

Bull and Simon were assigned to Novak's team within an hour after the victim had been discovered. Did that mean something had touched the Srecko case? Then Novak had warned them away from her. Was that his backhanded way of telling them there was a connection?

The previously unidentified victim was an ex-paramilitary thug. The Sreckos fit the profile of ex-soldiers turned to crime. Coincidence? Elaine despised coincidence. There must be some connection to the Sreckos and their real estate dealings. When she'd pressed Mehta about that, he hadn't denied it outright, but he'd prevaricated. What else did he know?

She couldn't put her finger on it yet, but the picture was bigger than the Sreckos, more convoluted than she had first imagined.

Her own police force—that black silhouette—was stalking her. As difficult as that was for Elaine to comprehend, Mehta and Cranwell had confirmed it. She didn't know why they would need to do that. What were they afraid of? She searched her memory for anything she knew about the Sreckos that could compromise the police, and she came up empty.

Was someone in the Met protecting the Sreckos because they were paid informants? The Met's regulations stipulated multiple layers of control over snouts because many jurors viewed paying for evidence as too corrupting, and sometimes discounted testimony from informants. This made the need for corroboration so strong that it made no sense to rely on informants for much beyond intelligence gathering. Elaine agreed with this view, although once or twice she had slipped fifty quid to the right person when that was her only option for getting information.

She considered Anton. He would never be an informant, and would never let someone control him. He'd certainly want to control a cop. Was that what this was about? But who was on which side?

She gripped the whisky glass tighter. Mehta's disdain, Cranwell's warnings, Novak's apparent subversion. Was the whole bloody world against her? If her off-the-books detective work was interfering with an investigation, why didn't someone just say so? She'd gladly tell them what little she knew, get in line, and join the hunt. She had been thinking, researching, tailing for two months—all to no avail. The possible connection between the Lights Out London real estate fiddles Mehta had talked about and the Sreckos' dodgy real estate company had given her a glimmer of hope. Now all this confusion.

Christ, it's getting colder. She took a last deep breath of the freezing air, picked up the bottle and glass, and went inside. In the bedroom, she turned her attention to the pinboard. *Useless. Fucking useless. What the hell have I been doing?* She pulled the note cards off, ripped them in half with sharp jerks, and dropped them in a waste bin. When all the cards were gone, Anton still stared down at her. Why did she keep that monster in her room?

She yanked his photo from the board but stopped short of tearing it apart. Instead, she placed it in the envelope containing other photos she had taken.

She was being followed, but who'd ordered it? She had no fucking clue what Novak was up to, but was he, or Cranwell, or whoever, trying to tell her something? Was someone in Anton's pocket? And was it someone on her old team?

DS Paula Ford had run the incident room and had been privy to all the plans and actions. Elaine had worked with her for years and had no doubts of her loyalty. Costello? Bull? Liz Barker, God forbid? They could be risking their careers by coming to her now. She didn't, or couldn't, believe the traitor to be any of her former team.

If the traitor wasn't one of her detectives, then it could only be someone higher up. Someone who knew the line of enquiry, who had knowledge of the evidence, and was privy to her plans.

She focused on the black silhouette. Someone higher up. Cranwell oversaw murder investigation teams. Mehta was a forensic accountant in Financial Crimes. He hadn't been involved in the Srecko case, but who had briefed him, wired him, assigned a watcher? They had to be high enough up to be able to cross divisional boundaries. She wrote names on three note cards, pinned them to the board, and stood back to take them in.

DCS Alec Cranwell had been her immediate superior when she'd been in Murder Investigation. Commander Jonathan Hughes had been, and still was, Cranwell's immediate superior. John O'Rourke had been the Crown Prosecutor assigned to their unit, and he most likely still was.

After some thought, she realized there was another, more sinister and malicious possibility. DC Jenkins had been involved in her last case, but she had removed him and brought him up on charges of insubordination, sexual harassment, and incompetence, which had ended his career in the Met. He had resigned from the service rather than go before a Professional Standards tribunal. After he resigned, she had seen him lurking in the crowd at an office fire in which evidence had been destroyed. Why had he been there if he had left the service?

She pulled out another note card and wrote a name: Ex-DC Arvel Jenkins. Could he lead her to the traitor?

Four names. Why hadn't she thought to narrow it down sooner instead of trying to boil the ocean? Had her obsession overcome everything she knew about the detection process?

Who should I start with? Simon said he'd seen Novak meeting Hughes. Now there's a thought. He had said that he thought Novak and Hughes knew each other before, but it was still a connection. She added another card with Novak's name and stretched a piece of yarn from there to Hughes.

Her mobile warbled. Before Elaine could say her name, a woman's voice asked, "DCI Hope?"

"Yes. Joanna?" This was completely unexpected.

"Can we meet, talk? Tomorrow?"

"Of course. Pick a place and time."

"There's a pub, the Clarendon Arms on Camberwell New Road. Around three?"

"Certainly. I'll be there at three. Can I ask—"

Joanna had rung off. There was no point ringing her back. Best to be patient. Elaine saved Joanna's number in her contacts list and turned her attention back to the pinboard.

Five names. Where to start? She knew where to find Cranwell, Hughes, O'Rourke, and Novak. Jenkins could be in Leeds or Dublin or Montevideo, for all she knew.

Cranwell. Why had he warned her? It could be out of friendship, but—no, something else was at play. She had looked up the phone number he had given her on a reverse lookup site, but with no result. That meant it was probably a prepaid "burner" phone, useful because they couldn't be traced to an owner, cheap enough to be thrown away if necessary. She could find out more about the number and its call history if she needed to. She wrote

"What about the burner?" on a note card and pinned it below Cranwell's.

Hughes and Cranwell had risen through the ranks together. Hughes's higher rank made him more difficult to reach on her own initiative.

Experience told her that O'Rourke had plenty of character flaws she, or others, could exploit. She'd look over his recent cases. Had he decided not to prosecute supposedly solid charges? Had he proposed light sentences against the advice of police? What was his personal life like? She'd start in the morning, working from home.

Would she have enough time to follow this up and work at the Police College as well? She had come back early from her compassionate leave. Perhaps she needed more time off. If she could get it, she'd be free of her obligations to the Met for a while.

She had the beginnings of a new plan. She'd begin researching O'Rourke on Saturday morning, then meet with Joanna Christie in the afternoon. The meeting at New Scotland Yard on Monday.

A feeling of relief coursed through her. It was after ten; perhaps she could sleep. Elaine slid under the duvet and gazed at the ceiling, her arm crooked over her forehead. Scratch hopped onto the bed and draped himself over her lower legs. She had plenty to do.

TWENTY-ONE

Saturday morning, Kensington

Novak marched to the front of the squad room and pointed at a photo Costello was tacking to the situation board. "Europol identified our victim from fingerprints. Dragan Bosko, age forty-four. Convictions in the Czech Republic and Hungary for auto theft, credit card theft, and various assaults. Wanted in Denmark and Sweden for drug trafficking and suspected people trafficking. No record in the UK."

He nodded at Costello, who took up the thread. "We think Bosko is the father of Zoltan Bosko, who was seventeen when he worked in the UK as a dogsbody for IRG Ltd., a company run by Anton Srecko. We believe the younger Bosko assisted the suspect in the Sheila Watson murder investigation, nine, ten months ago. He disappeared about the same time the case was cleared."

An older DC spoke up. "When DCI Hope was assaulted, Sarge? Nilo Srecko?"

"Right. Eventually we got a match for Nilo's DNA off the victim's bra, which we found in a nearby building."

Bull raised his hand. "So this Dragan bloke comes here to find his son, who he hasn't heard from. He discovers he's dead and goes looking for revenge. He gets too close to whoever did it, and they top him. The Sreckos again?"

Novak answered. "Don't think so. Boxe-Berkshire Ltd. has been in business for over a century. Financial Crimes told me there's no relationship between the Sreckos and the murder flat. Not even as clients."

"But guv, there's a connec—"

"Leave it to Financial Crimes, Bull, and focus on your own breakfast. What can you tell us about the cars? You've had that on your plate all week. Too tough to chew?"

Laughs erupted, then faded as Bull stood, bristling. He gathered his notes and walked to the front.

"The Peugeot is owned by Jean-Paul Duclerq, a retired French politician, seventy years old, lives on an estate outside Reims. Began as a conservative and became more right wing, finally forced out. Now he's an advisor to the National Front. I called a friend in the Gendarmerie. Duclerq has been housebound for the last two years, paraplegic from some bogus medical treatment. He couldn't have been the driver. So who was driving, and why were they on that street?"

Novak spoke. "Police Nationale might be more helpful. Our liaison info is online. Don't spend much time on it."

"I was thinking there could be a connection with that French widow who found the shoe. Her house is two doors down from the murder scene."

Novak nodded at Costello. "DS Costello can follow that up directly with the lady on Monday. What about the Jag?"

"We're checking every Jag sedan that CCTV picked up on Fulham Road and Old Brompton Road that night and all that are registered in a five-mile radius. Nothing yet."

"Forensics?"

"No DNA from the vomit, due to alcohol and acid," Bull replied. "No epithelial cells in the urine, so no DNA there either. The shoe the French lady found had been washed, but blood was present in the crevices. We should have results by tomorrow."

"Rain?" Novak asked.

"They found traces of detergent."

Novak nodded. "Right. Get back to it." He walked to his office and closed the door.

Bull had just sat down at his desk when his phone signalled he had received a text message from Costello.

<Jag Queens Gate x Brom cams 2125 who u see>

Bull called up the east-facing CCTV camera that covered the north-west corner of the intersection at Queen's Gate and Old Brompton Road. He hadn't watched it before—one of the uniforms had reviewed the video, noting number plates and identifying vehicle owners. He forwarded the video until the time showed 21:24, then advanced the frames slowly. At 21:25:17, a dark-coloured Jaguar saloon entered the intersection from Queen's Gate on the north side, driving south. He stopped the video and advanced it one frame at a time. The driver's profile looked familiar. Bull rewound and watched, then zoomed the frame and played it yet again. This time he could just discern the outline of a head on the passenger side, but there were too many shadows to tell much else.

He switched to the west-facing camera, which was positioned on the south-east corner of the intersection. When he zoomed in on the Jag this time, he could see the light-coloured profile of a person in the driver's seat.

So a dark-coloured Jag saloon with a driver and a passenger had crossed Old Brompton Road, heading in the direction of the murder scene. He opened the database file containing the number-plate identifications and scrolled to the location and time. When he saw the name, he nodded. He'd been right about the driver looking familiar.

John Gilbey O'Rourke. The home address indicated a flat in Notting Hill. John O'Rourke, also known as Jacko, lawyer with the Crown Prosecution Service. Brilliant attorney, womanizer, drinker, generally disliked by the coppers who worked with him. Months ago, when they had all been stationed in the Empress State Building, Bull had watched Jacko hit on DCI Hope mercilessly and had watched her dismantle him in return. The guv had far too much self-respect to be attracted to someone like Jacko.

Jacko—Jack? Driving towards the crime scene, at about the right time, with what could be a blonde passenger. Did he leave the area with the same passenger? Bull looked at the database once again, this time using the number plate as the search criteria. The next entry for Jacko's Jag indicated that at 21:44 it had turned from Cranley Gardens onto Evelyn Gardens. Bull called up that camera, which was mounted above street level, high atop St. Yeghiche's Church. Bull watched the Jag approach. The number plate was fully visible. As the car got closer to the corner, the camera angle became too steep to see anything of the windscreen. By the time Jacko turned west on Evelyn Gardens, the viewing angle was almost straight down.

Bull reversed the video and watched the car approach. When he zoomed in, reflections of street lights blocked his view through the windscreen. He couldn't tell if there was a passenger. He sat back in his chair. Barefoot Woman wouldn't have been in the car because at that time she was passing in front of the Onslow Arms pub.

There were no other sightings recorded in the database, most likely because the officers had been instructed to look at cameras within a three- or four-block radius of the crime scene, and Evelyn Gardens was right at the edge of the area of interest.

Where was Jacko going? Home? The route to Notting Hill was fairly direct if he'd just driven north. But Jacko headed south and west. Was he drunk? Confused? Was he trying to avoid CCTV cameras?

He pulled out his phone and texted Costello.

<How jacko get to nttng hl?>

He pressed "Send" and waited. Seconds later came the reply.

<Will put eyes on>

Bull sent another text.

<21 mins not acctd for>
<Recd>

Costello rose and disappeared into Novak's office. Bull returned to the list of CCTV files from forensics. A new file had popped up at the bottom of the list, with the description "Peugeot occupants? Partially recovered from damaged pvt CCTV." Bull remembered a video from a security camera mounted on one of the houses near the murder scene. The camera was malfunctioning, and the video was of extremely poor quality. Forensics must have been able to recover something. He opened the file.

Grainy images appeared, mixed with white static snow and large square pixelation. The beginning time stamp in the lower right corner showed 21:01:34. A car, probably the Peugeot, moved into the frame and parked at the kerb. Snow and pixelation obscured the image for a moment. When it cleared, Bull could discern two figures on the steps of the house two doors down from the murder scene—La Veuve's house. A caption, "Gap of 32:52," appeared, followed by a section that began at 21:34:26. Bull watched as the time counter ticked by. Snow and pixelation obscured the image for seconds at a time. Bull peered closely at the screen. He could just make out the Peugeot, but the image was too poor to determine if the Jag was parked close by.

Then, just after 22:35, the image cleared somewhat. Bull saw a single figure emerge from La Veuve's house and get into the Peugeot. The car pulled into the street and drove away, but the snow and pixilation obscured the image thereafter.

Two went in, one came out. Could the killer have been the blurry figure he saw leave? He checked the house-to-house file that Costello's team had compiled. The address between the murder scene and La Veuve's was vacant. He called up Google Earth on his computer and inspected the back gardens of the terraced homes. It was difficult to tell, but it appeared to him that most of the gardens had walls separating them. They needed to check.

Costello wasn't at his desk, so Bull texted him.

<Two ppl arrvd Peug, one left need fllw up>

There was no immediate answer. A half hour later, Bull was catching up on his reports when Costello dropped a folder on his desk and walked away. Bull opened it. The only item inside was an advertisement for Marks & Spencer that appeared to have been torn from a newspaper. When he studied the advertisement more closely, he saw the words "Scarsdale 1 pm" had been written in the margin in light pencil.

The Scarsdale Tavern was around the corner from the nick. If Costello was scared enough to resort to spy craft, the Scarsdale was a poor choice for a meeting ground. Officers from the nick often went there for lunch. He thought a minute, then erased the writing and pencilled "Onslow 1" over it. Why not meet on the ground around the crime scene? He stuffed some blank sheets of paper into the folder, rose, and dropped the folder in Costello's inbox on his way to the loo.

He was washing his hands when Costello entered and walked to a urinal. Bull kept washing until Costello joined him at the next basin.

Costello kept his voice at a whisper. "Onslow. I'll bring the key."

"Right." Bull walked out, wondering what the hell was going on.

TWENTY-TWO

Saturday afternoon, Kensington

"Novak wanted to what?" Bull pulled a face. "It looks like Jacko's got a passenger with him. The timing is right. It's the first ident we've got except for the victim. We still need to do more digging, and Novak wants us to just ring Jacko up and ask what he was doing there? Not exactly procedure."

The two detectives sat at a table in the back room of the Onslow Arms. Kerry had brought them chips and half-pints, then left them alone and closed the door.

Costello took off his eyeglasses and began cleaning them with a napkin. He appeared shaken. "He gave me a right bollocking when I suggested we bring Jacko in for questioning. Said it wasn't my job to think about lines of enquiry. That he was the senior bloody investigating officer, and if I wanted to keep the stripes on my bloody epaulette, I should damn well remember that."

Bull picked up a chip, frowning. "Elaine wasn't above handing out a bollocking when we cocked it up, but she'd at least listen to us. Ask us what we thought." He doused the chip with malt vinegar, dusted it with black pepper, and popped it into his mouth.

"I was on a team with her for years, and I usually thought

that when she asked us for our opinion, she already knew what we'd say."

Bull nodded. "You should know the answer before you ask. She kept us focused." He turned to Costello. "So what do you think? Will Novak warn Jacko?"

"Dunno," Costello said. "Whether he does or not, we need to confirm how Jacko left the neighbourhood. Where'd he go? Was Barefoot Woman his passenger?"

"You'd think Novak would want to exclude Jacko as soon as possible. But we can't do that on just his word. He was in the area. He had opportunity. It's up to Jacko to identify who was with him, and we'll check it out. It would give him an alibi."

Costello drained his beer. "We're not there yet. All we know is that he's a loose end we need to tie off. We don't need to ask why he'd kill. Now, motive might become relevant if we can place him at the scene. In this case it's method, opportunity, then motive."

"What about the Peugeot? Two in, one out. Could be murderer and victim. We haven't seen anyone arrive at the house on CCTV. We don't have a good look, given the wonky camera. We've looked back a whole day with what we have, but no luck."

"I'll bring it up when I talk to the French woman. It's reasonable to approach her as if she knows the Peugeot bloke. Duclerq. Do we say anything to Elaine?" Costello asked.

Bull thought for a moment. "I don't think we should ask her now. You heard her last night. She'd tear us new arse holes if we go back to her so soon. Even if something seems odd, we honestly don't know enough to evaluate it properly. Maybe we think about it. See what happens in the next day or so. Then look at it again."

"If Jacko's story smells like old socks, we let her know. And I think we need to have another look at the murder scene." Costello fished in his pocket for the house key. "Got it."

The house was less than a half-minute walk from the pub. A rising wind chased low, leaden clouds towards the northeast, flapped the hems of their raincoats, and tousled Costello's red hair. Thunder cracked.

Novak had not yet released the house back to the owners, so they ducked under the blue and white police tape and let themselves in the front door.

The forensic team had scraped the solid matter from the walls and floor, but dark brown stains and splatters still marred floor and walls in the corner where the body had been found. Blue tape outlined the position of the body, and small taped arrows pointed to the places where the killer and witnesses had stood. Silhouettes of the victim's lower legs and the killer's shoe prints, stood in stark white against the smeared reddish-brown bloodstains.

Bull began to describe the murder. "So, the victim knelt there, killer there. Woman there." He moved a few feet to some tape marks. "Man here. Jacko, you think?"

"Let's talk about that later. Okay. Woman pisses herself. Before—or after? Urine would have mixed with the victim's blood. We need to check with forensics to see if they could tell." Costello pulled out his notebook and pencil, made a note, and moved to the spot where the woman had stood.

"Boom. Gore everywhere."

Costello took two steps back. "Woman staggers back against wall, smearing the blood on the floor."

"Man runs. That moment—or later?"

"Woman spins, there's the swirl mark in the blood from her shoe. Throws open the window and chucks her supper into the flowers."

Bull turned to Costello. "Now, that's odd. Why did she open the window? Why not just spew on the floor?"

"Why indeed?" Costello's mouth puckered into a thoughtful frown. "She didn't want to mess the floor. I think it was reflex."

"Oh, come on. All that gore and she's worried about making a mess?"

"Bull, look in front of you—she spewed out the window, not on the floor. I think it's what I said—it was reflex. Rigid training when she was a child, perhaps. Mummy—or no, a girl's school or a governess—telling her that ladies don't make messes. Maybe Barefoot Woman is upper middle class or top shelf."

"That would be in line with the shoe your French verve found. Wasn't it a designer shoe?"

Costello smiled at Bull and tutted. "You'll have to do better than that if you ever want to breathe the thin air of the executive ranks, my friend. It's Veuve and Blahnik." He accentuated the foreign vowel sounds.

Bull didn't laugh. "I'll keep that in mind if I'm ever in line for commander."

Costello turned and looked at the wide archway that led from the room to the atrium that separated the main rooms of the ground floor. "We don't have it on CCTV, but we're pretty sure the man called Jack and Barefoot Woman arrived and left by the front door. At least Kerry and her boyfriend's evidence seems to show they left that way. Did the killer leave the same way?"

"We don't know. There were three sets of tracks in the blood, but we couldn't track the killer beyond the corridor. Do we know if the back door was open or locked when the first coppers arrived?"

"Something to check."

The kitchen door of the house opened onto a small porch, where Bull and Costello stood and surveyed the walled back garden. Paving stones covered the ground between the walls, except for flower borders along the back of the house.

Costello bent and walked along the wall, studying the paving. Finally he shook his head and said, "You're nearly twice my size. Give me a leg up."

Bull cupped his hands and lifted Costello high enough to see over the wall.

"Aha." Something had interested Costello.

"What?"

"Storage sheds along each wall. Easy to get here through the back gardens. Use the shed roofs."

Lightning flashed and a large raindrop splatted on Bull's bald head. Thunder clapped and the pace of the raindrops increased. "Time to go, Simon."

"Yup. We get no police medal for being struck by lightning."

They locked the house and scurried back to the pub just as a heavy rain began. Kerry saw them enter and held up two fingers.

Bull grinned. "You read my mind. Two dark. The room?" She nodded.

A few minutes later, she set two pints of stout on the table in the back room. Bull held up his glass. "To London's best barmaid."

Kerry giggled and gave a small curtsey. "Chips, Detective Bull? Crisps?"

"Not now, Kerry. But thanks, luv."

When they were alone, Bull said, "So, what about Jacko?"

"It's no coincidence. The woman Kerry heard could have been shouting 'Jacko,' not 'Jack.' Far more likely than not, given the timing."

"The passenger. I couldn't tell much from the CCTV."

"Only so many ways out of that neighbourhood," Costello replied. "CCTV had to have caught him somewhere. We'll suss it out."

"We don't tell Novak about the Peugeot."

Costello looked aghast. "What the fuck? We have to tell Novak. We've got to report it."

"I've got a tenner that says he'll steer us away from it."

"You opened it with your computer. It has a time stamp. Someone else will look at it and maybe wonder why you didn't report it."

Bull shrugged. "I couldn't make out what it was. Couldn't see properly."

"No. Don't play that game. Novak wasn't born yesterday. Wait." Costello furrowed his brow and tapped his finger on the table. "You put it in a report and file it. Let's see if it disappears."

"Good point. I suppose it's not so surprising you passed the sergeant exam." Bull drained his glass and leaned forward. "Question is, though, what about Elaine? I vote we tell her about the Bosko identification."

"That's what I think too," Costello replied. "It wouldn't be right to keep it from her. I'll call and see if she can meet this weekend. What about Liz?"

"We bloody well better bring Liz into it. I'd like to keep my balls attached right where they are."

Saturday afternoon, Camberwell

"I serve food part-time at the taverna, and my shift starts at four, so I need to get back, or Cristo will ask where I've been." Joanna glanced nervously through the window at the street. "I don't want to have to lie to him."

Elaine didn't grow up in a rigid extended family. "It's hard for me to fathom personally. The way I see it, you're an adult, you support yourself. You deserve more respect."

Joanna scoffed. "People give respect in different ways, don't they? I'm a widow, so he thinks I'm weak. Like it's my fault. But it's not just me: it's all us women who work outside the family businesses—the taverna and the construction company. I deal with it." She looked at the clock over the bar. "Anyway, meeting you the other day was a wake-up call. I told Cristo it was you who upset me so much, but it's not that. Things at work have changed. Strange people have been showing up. Hard, crass men from America and Europe. Holding meetings. Talking in whispers. I'm . . . uncomfortable."

Elaine took a sip of her cider. *Let her come to you, Lainie.* "I can imagine. How do I fit in?"

"What you said, about the police coming to me for evidence. Then at the taverna you mentioned the murder you're looking into. If there's something illegal going on, if it's tied to that murder, I don't want to be suspected."

"Have you talked to anyone else about this? Cristo?"

Joanna took a deep breath and shook her head. "Never him. He'd just use it to make me feel small, like I couldn't cope. I talked to the priest, though. He said I should talk to you." She looked up at Elaine. "You said you wanted me to look at something. A list."

Elaine took a sheet of paper and a biro from her bag and placed them in front of Joanna. She didn't want to scare Joanna off by asking for too much too soon. "I know you're short on time," she said. "For now, could you look at this list of companies and people's names, and just put a tick by those ones IRG does business with, maybe two ticks by the ones who you suspect are shady? Or who meet most often with Anton? It would help get me started."

Joanna pulled the paper closer and pursed her lips. "This is quite a few names." Her hand moved down the page, occasionally flicking the biro. When she reached the bottom of the second column, she slid the paper back to Elaine. "There. I suppose you'll have questions."

Elaine glanced at the page, which contained numerous tick marks, then at the time display on her mobile. "Thank you. I don't want to make you late. But yes, I'm sure I'll have some questions." She smiled at Joanna. "Perhaps we shouldn't leave together, just in case someone you know is passing by. Why don't you go first?"

After Joanna had gone, Elaine examined the list. Only about half of the sixty-plus entries were actual names from her research—she'd invented the rest. She opened her laptop and compared Joanna's responses with the master list. Joanna had ticked most of the real names, and only one of the fake ones, so she was confident Joanna was being truthful. Later she'd dig to see if any of the names were mentioned in Jacko's court cases. One never knew when gold would turn up.

She had gathered her things to leave, when her mobile rang. "Hope."

"Novak. You've been in touch with my team. We need to talk."

"Aren't you a charmer? Not even a hello. I don't know we have anything to talk about. Bull and Costello are old friends. We get together from time to time."

"Don't give me the piss about old times' sake. Tomorrow works for me."

Hadn't he ever learned to be nice when he wanted something? Put the rude git off, Lainie. "If you know anything about me, you know I don't respond to bullying. I don't see a reason to meet, and I'm sure as hell not going to ruin my Sunday. Give me a bell later in the week. Maybe I'll have time then. And pleased to meet you too, DI Novak."

She ended the call. He'd be back.

Sunday afternoon, Brentford

Elaine stood just inside the door to her veranda, watching a narrow boat move slowly up the Grand Union Canal past the docks of Brentford Marina. Bull, Costello, and Liz had left only a half hour ago, after updating her on the case. *Think it through. What have I learned?*

The identity of the victim was exciting because it pointed to a possible tie between the murder and her own investigation. Why wouldn't Novak allow his team to follow up the connection between the victim and the Srecko family? Understanding the victim's lifestyle and connections was a key tenet of any murder investigation. Giving up such a basic line of enquiry was so unusual, it could be seen almost as a dereliction of duty. If she were leading the investigation, she'd have been leaning over Anton Srecko's desk within an hour. What was Novak's game?

Had Dragan Bosko been executed because he threatened to expose the Srecko operation? The premise made sense and pointed to a real connection. But connecting Bosko's headless corpse to Anton Srecko would need a long and difficult investigation, one Elaine couldn't hope to carry out on her own. *It's meaningful, but not practical. Move on.*

They had identified the owner of the Peugeot, who was French. Given the timing, Bosko was likely the missing passenger. Either that, or the missing passenger stayed in the house and Bosko had arrived some other way. Resident or guest? Costello would follow that up when he met with the French woman.

Bull's witness heard a woman screaming for someone named Jack. Jacko had driven through the area. Was Barefoot Woman his passenger? If Novak wouldn't bring Jacko in for a formal interview, would he direct his team to follow it up? She doubted it.

So, four people converge on a location in South Kensington. Three leave—Jacko by car, Barefoot Woman on foot, and the murderer probably by car, but in truth, unknown. The victim was connected to a family that owned a real estate company. The murder flat was located in an area of increasing foreign ownership, and it was for sale. One person in the murder party appears to have had a key.

Elaine picked up her phone and texted Costello.

<Follow up on Boxe-Berkshire>

She went into the kitchen to refill her tea. She had no sooner returned to the bedroom than Costello replied.

<Understood will do>

She smiled to herself. Sergeant rank was just a stepping-stone for Costello. She turned her attention to the large pinboard on her wall. Four names, any of whom might have betrayed her: Hughes, Cranwell, Jacko, and Jenkins. Jacko was the least disciplined of that lot, so finding a weakness to exploit would be easier with him.

Jacko's involvement in the current murder case might be purely circumstantial, but given the timing and the witness's evidence, it was a good bet he was in the thick of it. She'd logged into the Crown Prosecution Service calendar site and downloaded his court schedule. She'd start obs on him Tuesday, after his last case finished at the Criminal Court.

Tomorrow, she was due at New Scotland Yard. She looked at her dress uniform, hanging at the side of her wardrobe, still in the plastic bag from the cleaners. What was the meeting about? It couldn't be disciplinary because she hadn't been presented with a list of particulars, and she hadn't been instructed to bring her Police Federation representative. It wasn't termination. There was a separate process for that. Would the tribunal suggest retirement? She laughed. They could suggest until hell froze over.

TWENTY-THREE

Monday afternoon, New Scotland Yard

Elaine's chair was too low for her long legs, and its straight back forced her to sit rigidly upright. Her damaged right leg ached within a minute after she took her seat.

The conference room at New Scotland Yard was hot, almost stifling. She hadn't worn her number-one dress uniform in over a year. The starched collar of her white shirt and the clip of her chequered cravat itched and cut at her neck. She longed to dig her finger between the collar and the skin of her throat and tug. She wanted to stretch her neck like a tortoise reaching for a carrot, but she knew that when she relaxed, it would itch all the more. Neither behaviour would impress the three senior officers who sat behind the table in front of her. At least the prescribed bowler with its chequered band and crown-and-star badge fit her head properly. But what the hell was she here for?

Commander Delaney spoke first. "Good afternoon, DCI Hope. I believe you know Commander Hughes."

Elaine smiled politely at Hughes. "Sir." He had commanded her division when she had been in Murder Investigation. She noticed he had lost weight in the months since she had seen him last.

"And this is Assistant Commissioner Collins."

"Good afternoon, Assistant Commissioner," she said.

AC Collins was in charge of Crime Operations Directorate. As such he was Hughes's immediate superior. The tall, burly officer acknowledged Elaine with only a rigid nod. *So that's the way this will go. They follow me, assign watchers, and haul me before this—what? What's this about?*

Delaney, Elaine's immediate superior in the police college, shuffled several sheets of paper, glancing at each before finally perusing one. "DCI Hope. We're here to discuss two incidents that have come to our attention. The first occurred six days ago with a civilian outside the Cave of Bacchus pub. Do you recall being there?"

"I would like to ask a question before I answer. Is this a Professional Standards tribunal? If so, I have a right to be informed, and if I am up on a complaint, I'm allowed to have the facts in hand before I'm called. Either way, I have the right to have my Police Federation representative present. The same applies if this is a fitness hearing."

"It is neither, DCI Hope," Delaney replied. "We are informally ascertaining the facts about two incidents that have been brought to our attention. One involves a member of the public, and the other involves another police officer."

She had wondered when Mehta would whinge about the abduction. "With all respect, sir, it seems formal to me. I have a right to know why I'm here and what might be the consequences of this informal fact-finding meeting."

The three senior officers exchanged glances.

Collins scowled. "Now see here, Hope—"

Hughes interjected. "If I may, sir." He looked her directly in the eyes. "DCI Hope, among the three of us, I am probably the most familiar with your record of bravery and excellent results. DCS Cranwell has been your champion for years, ever since you were assigned to Benford's team as a sergeant. We were all deeply saddened by your injuries. I have never known an officer to endure such a horrific assault and be able to return to duty so quickly."

She replied, "Thank you, sir. I'm not sure what to say."

Hughes continued. "We're aware of the after-hours investigations you've been conducting. That in itself is cause for concern, but the incidents with the civilian and DI Mehta raised alarm bells. We're concerned that you may have returned to duty too soon. You still have just over six months of compassionate leave available."

"Hold on, Hughes." AC Collins's gruff voice fit his hard eyes and bushy eyebrows. "We don't need a lone wolf right now, Hope. Frankly, your behaviour appears a bit obsessive. We need to know how to deal with these incidents and prevent a recurrence."

Obsessive. The bastard. Doing it for the good of the force. The image of the Met demanded they find a reasonable way to sweep the complaints under the rug of compassion. It didn't sound bad. Six more months without the constraint of showing up at the office every day might be what she needed. Freedom to move.

She again gave him a polite smile. "I'm sure you consulted the police psychologists about what constitutes obsessive behaviour, sir. What you just said makes this either a fitness hearing or a Professional Standards tribunal." Collins's jaw muscles clenched. Elaine continued, "Which means I should have been warned to bring my Police Federation representative. Without my representative present, any results that I don't agree with from this little party are moot."

"This little party? How dare—"

Elaine interrupted. "Very well. I don't know what to call it, but you're correct, sir. It's not a party. About the incident outside the Cave of Bacchus: I had a minor altercation with a man who was leaving the pub with some friends."

Collins waved the sheet of paper in his hand. "A bit more than that, wouldn't you say? He's threatened to file a complaint against you." He referred to his notes. "He states that he merely jostled you while exiting the pub, but you attacked him, injured his shoulder, and threw him across the pavement."

The little scumbag had threatened to file a complaint, probably thinking he'd get a quick monetary settlement of some kind. He clearly didn't know how the Met operated.

"He's a liar. I was provoked and acted in self-defence." She looked directly at Collins, then scanned the other two officers. "He can file a complaint against me. I'll file an assault charge against him. He's correct that he jostled me. He knocked me off balance. He then took hold of my clothing and forcibly slammed me against a concrete wall, pinning me there with his weight. I merely broke his hold, got control of him, and pushed him away. I then identified myself as a police officer."

"So it's your word against his."

"It sounds like you don't believe me, sir. Perhaps the CCTV would change your mind, if you take the time to view it."

"Steady, DCI Hope. I have watched it several times. And in my opinion, it leaves much room for debate. You appear to be spoiling for a fight."

"You've never seen me fight, have you? I don't believe I exceeded Principle Six, sir. I was under threat. You didn't see the look on his face or smell the whisky on his breath. I used only enough force to defend myself from him and possibly his mates. And I stopped when order was restored."

"How dare you lecture me on Peel's Principles. But since you brought them up, had you considered Principle Two— maintaining public approval of our actions? This bloke felt threatened too. He didn't know you were a police officer. So you took him down in front of onlookers who watched you wrench his shoulder out of its socket. Only then did you identify yourself. That is what I'm concerned about. Police officers out of control. Look what's happening in America these days. Violence by police officers is undermining their relationship with the communities they police. Police in Great Britain operate with consent of the public, not through fear. You appear to be right on the edge, DCI Hope. If you are unable to control violent impulses—"

"Out of its socket? Control my violent impulses? What is this kangaroo court all about then?" She jumped to her feet. "He was drunk! You didn't smell his breath, see his face, sir. You didn't feel his hands on you. At that moment, he was ready to beat me. He wanted some rough, and he meant to dish it out."

She pointed her finger at Collins. "And you're damn right I'm on the edge. I was on the goddamn edge of dying, and where the fuck was my backup? Who was it who decided I could wait? Wait for what? Do what? Sit on my fucking hands while someone was being assaulted? Murdered? Which lame excuse for a gold commander made that decision?" She spun around and strode to the back of the office, clenching and unclenching her hands. *Oh, Jesus Christ, Lainie, you've lost it now. Get control, get control.* She stopped and closed her eyes.

Elaine gasped five or six deep breaths into her lungs, then faced the three shocked senior officers. She gripped the back of her chair to stop her hands from trembling, regaining just enough self-control to not shout. "But I would say I restrained myself adequately in this case. Ask yourself what you would have done." She leaned forward and fixed her gaze on Collins. "I killed the previous man who touched me with violence. Have you ever killed anyone, sir?"

She looked from face to face. Delaney and Hughes wouldn't hold eye contact with her. Collins stared back at her, his eyes wide, his jaw working, clearly at a loss for words.

They don't know what to do with me, do they? That's why I'm here. I'm a hero and a crazed, out-of-control bitch, and they don't know how to deal with me.

After a few seconds, Hughes's calm voice broke the silence. "I cannot begin to comprehend your situation, DCI Hope. As a man, I have no basis, or right, to judge your response."

He closed the folder on the desk in front of him. "I don't

need to hear anything more. My opinion is that DCI Hope should be encouraged to take the rest of her leave, if she chooses to use it."

Collins jerked his gaze from Elaine and nodded. Delaney glanced at Hughes and also nodded.

Tears welled in Elaine's eyes. Her voice had calmed. "I'll begin my leave tomorrow, if that's acceptable, sir. Good day to you, gentlemen."

TWENTY-FOUR

Monday afternoon, Kensington

The woman who opened the door at La Veuve's house was short, with the muscular physique of a gymnast. Her brown hair was bobbed just below her ears. She glanced at Costello's warrant card, beckoned with two fingers for him to enter, then said, "Wait here while I see if Madame is ready to receive you."

Costello didn't reply. He watched the woman disappear through a pair of stained-glass double doors. He estimated her age at forty. She had not offered her name.

The entry hall of La Veuve's house had seen better days. White paint peeled in the corners and along the edge of the ceiling. Like stone steps in an old castle, the marble tiles in the centre of the floor had worn more than those on the edge, creating a concavity. Cast iron tables, one on each side of the hall, were crammed with pots of aspidistra, spider plants, and dumb canes, plus twenty or thirty other plants Costello couldn't identify.

The pots sat on newspapers that had been spread across the tables. Costello twisted his neck to read headlines. *Le Minute Hebdo*, a French newspaper, sported a headline that read, *"Le complot de l'immigration pour masquer le crime d'etat parfait."* He translated it aloud, slowly. "The immigration—*complot*, that's 'conspiracy'—masks, hides, the perfect state crime." He remembered now. *Le Minute* was a far-right-wing weekly newspaper that supported nationalist politicians and a multitude of anti-government conspiracy theories.

The newspapers were wet. Pencil-thin tubes of a drip irrigation system ran along the baseboards and up the wall behind each table. Occasional hissing sounds and spurts of mist explained the humid fug of compost and mould that lent to the air of decay. Costello felt every breath required effort. He was about to step back outside into the fresh air when the woman returned. "Madame will see you now in the sitting room." She stood aside to hold one of the doors open.

As he passed, Costello asked, "What's your name, mademoiselle?"

"Mon nom n'est pas important."

French? Her English has a trace of Geordie. Two steps past the door, Costello stopped and turned so quickly the woman nearly ran into him. He held up his warrant card again. "This is a murder investigation. I decide what is important. Now . . ."

The woman's blue eyes flashed. "Lydia. Lydia Anstey."

"You're British."

"So?" She shouldered past him. "This way."

La Veuve's sitting room had the same humidity and odour of compost as the entry hall. Potted plants abounded, sitting atop almost every available surface. In the centre of the room, an elderly woman dressed in a black pants suit sat in a wheelchair. Her thick white hair swept back from her deeply lined forehead and curled elegantly behind each ear. Her only jewellery was a brooch pinned to the left breast of her jacket. It appeared to be a gold and enamel family crest. A small, brown, long-haired dog growled at Costello from her lap.

Lydia Anstey indicated a chair, then moved to the side. A portable oxygen tank with a breathing mask stood on the floor next to her.

The older woman regarded Costello sternly. "You are . . . ?"

"Detective Sergeant Costello, Metropolitan Police. For the record, what is your name?"

"Madame Claudette Dubuisson-D'Anjou." Her breathing seemed forced, with a definite wheeze. So she really had been ill, as she'd said.

"Last Thursday you came to the station with a shoe you found. You stated that you found it behind a potted plant on your front stoop. When exactly did you find it?"

"I included that in my affidavit."

"It's procedure, Madame. We have to verify. When did you find it?"

"We returned to the house from La France about three in the afternoon. We went outside to check the plants perhaps an hour later. That is when I found the shoe." Her breath rattled, and she gave a wet cough.

"I will try to get this over with as quickly as possible, Madame. When you checked the plants, did you notice any blood on the front porch or on the cast iron railings?"

"No."

"What did you do with the shoe after you found it?"

"It was dirty, so I gave it to Lydia to clean."

"And then?"

Lydia interjected. "I noticed the blood. That's about when we heard the news, the murder. Can we hurry this up? Madame isn't well."

Costello nodded. "Madame. Do you know someone named Jean-Paul Duclerq?"

La Veuve sat straighter. "I thought this was about the shoe."

"Please answer."

"I've known so many people. There are many men named Jean-Paul. Perhaps—" She stared past him. "I don't know."

"Your family estate and the champagne caves are outside Reims, correct?"

She gave a slight shrug and stared at the wall past Costello's shoulder.

"Madame, I know where your family home is located. Jean-Paul Duclerq lives on an estate not three miles from yours. Your families have been close for decades, if not centuries."

"Ah, my mind wanders sometimes."

"I accept that as yes, then. Do you know his son, René Duclerq?"

"I have met so many people. *J'ai oublié beaucoup d'entre eux.*"

"I appreciate that, but I ask again, do you know his son, René Duclerq?"

"Didn't he die?"

"No, madame. He's alive. Did he visit you recently?"

"I've had no"—a coughing fit seized her—"visitors since my return." She extended her hand towards Lydia. *"Ma fille, oxygene."*

Lydia fixed the oxygen mask over La Veuve's face and turned a valve on the tank. The old woman closed her eyes and began taking deep breaths.

Costello made a show of consulting his notebook. "Oh, my mistake. Do you know if he visited this house while you were in France?"

Lydia advanced towards Costello, her face reddening with anger. "Can't you see she's ill? She's nearly ninety years old, and she isn't well. You need to go. Now! Leave this house!"

"If your employer has respiratory problems, why does she live in London? Surely she can afford to live in a warm, dry climate? Provence perhaps?"

"That's none of your concern. Leave." She took another step forward.

Costello stood, calmly closed his notebook, and placed his pen in the inner pocket of his suit. He looked past Lydia at La Veuve, whose eyes were open, staring at him over the plastic mask, her breath rasping.

"Madame, if you must live in such a cold, damp place, surely you should consider plants that don't require mouldy compost and constant moisture. Cacti, perhaps?"

Lydia advanced until her face was inches from Costello's. She growled. "Get out now. You are not welcome here. If she takes a turn for the worse, I'll definitely file a complaint."

Costello didn't retreat. "Have you or Madame spoken to another policeman about the murder?"

"No. Get out."

"Have you met with another policeman recently? Late last week perhaps?"

She clenched and unclenched her fists. "Get out!"

Costello smiled and moved to the door. "I can find my own way out, thanks."

Once on the pavement, he dialled Bull. "Met with La Veuve."

"Is she as formidable as you imagined?"

"No. She tries to be, but she's old and certainly ill, needs oxygen. She confirmed the affidavit, but when I pressed her on Duclerq, she said she couldn't remember, claimed senility. Said the Duclerq kid was dead. My arse. I know bloody well he's in London, or was."

"The Duclerq kid?"

"Sorry. Son of the guy who owns the Peugeot." He paused. "There's more, but I don't want to stand out here talking. Your place, tonight?"

"Okay. Liz is on obs tonight, so I dunno when she'll be in. I've got news too. Bring Chinese. Something with prawns."

"Right. Give me a shout when you get home. I've got a bit of research to do."

TWENTY-FIVE

Monday afternoon, Brentford

It took almost an hour for Elaine to drive home from New Scotland Yard. She stopped twice along the way when tears obscured her vision. By the time she had parked her car and climbed the stairs to her flat, her tears had stopped, and her hands had ceased trembling. She opened a pilsner and stretched on her sofa.

Enough tears. Think of the positive, Lainie.

What next? She still had her warrant card. Going "on the sick" didn't suspend her powers as a police officer. Hughes had mentioned her after-hours investigation. All her days were now after-hours. She had freedom to do what she wanted, when she wanted. Freedom. A two-edged sword. She had been cut loose, with no hope of support from the Met or protection if she got herself into trouble.

She closed her eyes. *Everything comes with a price.*

She opened her eyes to a dark room and the insistent warble of her mobile. How long had she been asleep? She fished her phone out of her pocket. The time showed 8:07 PM. Peter's name was displayed. *Christ. What could he want?* She swiped the green button and answered. "Hope."

"You answered that very same way the first time I ever called you." Peter's voice was warm and positive.

"Habit." *Shit, Lainie. Lighten up.* "And how did you reply?"

"That I was full of it. Was then, still am."

She shook her head. "An eternal optimist."

"About things that truly matter."

He still believes I truly matter? I'm so fucked up. "To what do I owe this call?"

He was silent for several breaths. "Right to business, then. I've had something come up. I'm off the next two days, so I thought maybe tomorrow or Wednesday we could get together for a chat, if you're free."

"And what subject warrants such mystery?"

"Darts at Nelson's Glory, loser buys the beer."

And an arm around my shoulder. In a crowd of people. "I'm not ready. You should know that." As soon as she said it, she cursed herself. How could he know that? They hadn't spoken in weeks. He'd always been respectful of limits, and now she'd cut his legs out from under him without knowing what he wanted. "Sorry, Peter. You didn't deserve that."

"No, I didn't." His voice lost warmth. "And you should know I'll behave. Like I said, something's come up, and I want to talk it over with you face-to-face, not on the phone."

"It's that important?" She didn't need this distraction, not now. What could he possibly want that he couldn't tell her over the phone? "It's not a good time. Something's come up at my end too, and I don't know how busy I'll be the rest of the week. Why can't you tell me now?"

"I'd feel better if—"

"It's hard for me to get to sleep at the best of times. I don't want to lie awake wondering what could be so important. Tell me now."

"—if we could have a real conversation." Silence. When he continued, his voice sounded harder, resolved. "All right then, have it your way, like always. I've been offered a teaching post at the new med school in Austin. Community involvement, good hours, pro bono work."

"And you've accepted."

"I wanted to talk through what it means, face-to-face. You deserve that, and—"

"When?"

"—and I deserve that. Term starts in June. I need to confirm with the university by the end of this month."

"You're . . ." *He hasn't formally accepted.* She cleared her throat. "So you wanted to tell me goodbye?"

"No."

"When would you leave?"

"In a few weeks. Give myself time to settle in."

"Please understand. The way I am now, I can't be good for either of us. But remember what I told you."

"I do, every day. I talked with Kate about you. About us."

Sister and brother. "And?"

"She said you're a woman who keeps her promises. That I'm a damn lucky man." He gave a sardonic laugh. "Kate knows what she's talking about—most of the time."

"Peter, please understand."

"No, you understand that I have to say this. I can't comprehend what you've been going through. But remember that I was there too. When I saw you on the table . . ." He stopped, his voice breaking.

"Peter, you know I'll always be grateful for what you did, and—"

"What the fuck?"

"—and I—"

"Grateful? You're grateful? I don't believe you said that. I don't need or even want your fucking gratitude. I was up to my goddamn elbows in the blood of the woman I love! I watched you flatline! What the hell do you think that did to me? Have you ever wondered that?"

"Peter, I . . ." The sound of his breath pulsed in her ears, her heart pounded in her chest.

"I'm goddamn sick and tired of holding all this in, Elaine.

Sick and tired of lying awake at night, wondering how you are. Yeah, I lie awake too. Ever since Diana and Liza died, I've gotten bloody good at nightmares, and now I have nightmares about you dying too. And I'm sick and tired of being rejected by the woman I love. Sick of being so bloody understanding when you won't even give me the chance to talk about it and get it off my chest. Jesus bloody Christ. I don't think you give a rat's ass about me."

Before she could speak, Peter continued. "Have you ever thought that if you could allow yourself to give, if you could just open up to someone who cares about you, what a difference it could make? I'm not a therapist. I'm a man who loves you. Body and soul, Elaine. I can listen. I can learn. I can be there for you on those nights you can't sleep. Even if it's only on the other end of a phone."

What can I do? I need to be able to give everything, and right now I can't. "Let's get together before you leave. Okay? It's all I can promise right now." *Oh, Jesus, that was weak.*

The sound of his breathing slowed. When he spoke, he sounded exhausted. "I don't believe you. You know I love you." He ended the call.

The line had gone silent, but she said, "I know you do, Peter."

All he had asked for was one meeting at Nelson's Glory. Two honest pints, a game of darts, and time to tell her about his job and what it meant for them.

You couldn't even give him that, Lainie. "Peter, I'm grateful." *Nothing but fucking words. What have I become? Am I as hollow as that?*

A few weeks before he leaves—weeks to find the peace that would let her love him. In a few weeks would she be able to grasp a kitchen knife without retching? Would she be able to stand in a crowded lift without her skin crawling? Or walk into her darkened bedroom without her heart leaping into her throat?

For months now, the hot voice of her rage had insisted peace would come only through vengeance, but lately she'd begun to understand wrath could bring no peace, only casualties.

Elaine ran her fingers through her short-cropped hair. As she stared upward from the sofa, the ceiling appeared to descend lower with each breath she took. She twisted herself right, then left. The sitting room walls crept inward towards her, pulsing in time with her still-pounding heart. She rolled off the sofa and crawled to the French door. It stuck—again, dammit—but she yanked it open and staggered onto her terrace.

Below her, the trees lining the Grand Union Canal whipped to and fro in the north wind, the susurrus rising and falling with the gusts that carried the scent of water to her nostrils. Elaine clung to the frigid steel rail and gasped as the crisp air pierced her lungs. Her knees weakened, and she slumped to the cold concrete, her back to the railing. After a few breaths, the drumming rhythm in her chest slowed.

Peter. Refuge. Trust. The three words melded in her mind and heart. She hadn't been seeking refuge in his bedroom that first time, when he had revealed his scars to her, trusting her not to pity, not to recoil. She had wanted truth, and he'd opened his grief to her, exposing his life's love and joy, sorrow and guilt. He had allowed her to draw her own conclusions.

Now, she might never again hear him play piano and sing the ridiculous Cole Porter tunes he loved. Or lie silently with him on his bed, her head on his chest, moonlight streaming through the huge window, the distant lights of Canary Wharf glittering, until passion again enveloped them.

Throughout her career she had been driven to find the truth that would condemn killers. She had done her best and had desired nothing more than to be allowed to solve murders for the rest of her life.

What did she want now that the refuge of her work was gone? Would peace and Peter be enough? Which should come first? Could she give up and move to Austin, where she could bask in the sun almost year-round? But what would she do there? Stay at home? Volunteer? Go fucking shopping every day? She'd go mad.

Her thoughts stopped short. This was madness. How could she think he even wanted her there? He'd only said he wanted to talk about what his move meant to them. He hadn't asked.

He certainly wouldn't ask her to join him until she opened up to him. Was she willing to make the choice? To go with him, she would have to give up her search, admit that the traitor and revenge on Anton didn't matter as much as a future with a loving man. A forked road. She wondered what was at the end of each path. Wondered what it truly was she was looking for.

What else had he said? That he was hurt too. She'd never acknowledged that. Hadn't given it much thought beyond an empty expression of gratitude. She was a heartless bitch who didn't deserve his love. She had no right to it.

And Liz and Bull had been so loyal. To acknowledge their pain and sacrifice now, to say the words she should have spoken long ago, would just seem an afterthought. As sincere as a two-quid thank-you card. A gesture as empty as she must really be. Would doing nothing be better than that?

Elaine pulled herself to her feet. Tomorrow she would tail Jacko after he finished in court, so she needed to get to sleep. Back inside, she stripped and turned on the hot water, wondering who she would see in her dreams tonight—and if she was beyond salvation.

TWENTY-SIX

Tuesday evening, Shepherd's Bush

Elaine stood inside an organic greengrocer on the Uxbridge Road, munching an apple. Darkness had fallen, and Jack O'Rourke sat at a table in the brightly lit front window of the restaurant across the street. For ten minutes he'd done nothing but gulp red wine and glance at his mobile every thirty seconds.

She'd eaten at Ristorante Gionfriddo once, with a pretentious date who had waxed poetic in Scottish-burred Italian over the *pappardelle al ragu di cinghiale con pecorino*. Elaine had finally silenced him by asking why he fussed over wild pig stew with cheese and noodles. She told him it was likely the boar had grown up on a farm in Kent; that its grunts had never echoed through a Tuscan forest. The pretentious Scottish foodie hadn't asked her out again.

Before her rape and injuries, Jacko had regularly asked her to his apartment for Tuscan-grilled steaks, Montepulciano wine, and a bit of relaxation, which he promised would include a full-body massage. His enticements, in themselves, were attractive, but not Jacko. She'd had her fill of bores.

A voice startled Elaine from her thoughts just as a black cab arrived at the taxi rank near the restaurant.

"Excuse me, ma'am. May I help you find something? Mm?"

A greengrocer in a white apron stood next to her, gesturing at a tray of Spanish plums.

She flashed her warrant card and returned her attention to the restaurant. "DCI Hope. Sorry, I'm not sure how long I'll be here. I doubt for—"

She froze as she saw Jonathan Hughes pay the taxi driver and enter Gionfriddo's. Seconds later he took a seat at Jacko's table.

The greengrocer craned his neck to see over the plums, studying the street outside, clearly trying to identify what she found so interesting. "It appears you're on 'obs,' as they say on the crime shows. I understand, DCI, um, Hope. But you've been rooted here for twenty minutes, gnawing that apple and staring out the window. Mm? Just that it's a bit, um, unsettling for the clients, as you might understand. Myself included."

"Would it help if I bought something?"

The little man smiled and wiped his hands on his white apron. "We have some nice mandarins, just in this morning." He indicated a display of the small oranges. "Perhaps some of those would suit you? The aubergines are especially nice also."

Elaine glanced across the street. Hughes and Jacko appeared deep in conversation. She picked out a few mandarins and two of the small, purple aubergines and paid the grocer. By the time she returned to the window, three middle-aged women had commandeered her observation point.

Two women peered over the plums, eyebrows raised, their attention on the street, while the third assessed Elaine.

"You're a 'tective?"

Elaine gritted her teeth and forced a smile. "Detective Chief Inspector Elaine Hope."

"Oooo. Chief Inspector." The woman tipped her head towards her friend but kept her eyes on Elaine's face. "She's important, Rose. Dressed in blue jeans and a donkey jacket. Must be undercover, then. Are you watching summat we should know about? Should we go out the back way? Be extra careful?"

Her friend Rose peered out the window over the plums, unsteady on her tiptoes. "Is it those two men having a row on the pavement there 'cross the street? In fronta Johnfreeda's?"

Hughes and Jacko stood outside the door of the restaurant, arguing. As Elaine watched, Hughes jabbed his finger into Jacko's chest, forcing the larger man to take a step back. Jacko's response was to laugh. He returned to the restaurant and took his seat at the window table. Hughes watched for a moment, then entered a taxi.

Jacko dialled his mobile. While speaking, he motioned for a waiter, who brought a second wine glass and placed it across the table from him.

The argument she'd just witnessed could have been a disagreement over a case, which happened from time to time. But that was something they would have kept behind closed doors. She couldn't imagine either of them jeopardizing a case by discussing it in public.

"That was personal," she muttered, without realizing she'd spoken aloud.

"Oh, it certainly looked that way," the greengrocer said. "It's a wonder they didn't come to blows. Getting close to seven, ma'am. I'm closing."

She smiled sheepishly and handed him a fiver. "Sorry, just thinking aloud. Thanks for your patience. No chance I could wait here?"

"Sorry, luv." He nodded towards the door. "The missus will have tea ready."

Elaine debated whether to give up for the evening, but she was curious whom the second wine glass was for. So she stepped outside into the shadow of the shop doorway and pressed against the wall. Jacko appeared busy with his smart phone. A few minutes after seven, a slender blonde woman alighted from a black cab, entered Gionfriddo's, and took the seat across from Jacko.

Elaine clicked a photo. She felt the woman was vaguely

familiar, but couldn't put a name to her face. More to the point, could she be Barefoot Woman? Possibly, but word was that Jacko had several girlfriends. Still, she was blonde, elegant.

The blonde took a huge gulp of red wine and began speaking to Jacko. Click. As Elaine watched, the woman's face became more animated. If only she could hear what the woman was saying. Click. The conversation appeared to flow back and forth. First the woman appeared to rant, then Jacko would reply. With each exchange they became more animated. Click. The maître d' now stood at the table, gesturing. Click. The woman stared out the window. Jacko threw several bills on the table and, with a word to the maître d', left the restaurant. Click.

First you argue with a senior police officer, then have a spat with your girlfriend. This just isn't your night, Jacko. But who is she?

The woman didn't leave immediately. After checking to make sure Jacko was out of sight, Elaine dashed across the street and strolled past the restaurant, casually looking inside, as if she were considering a meal. When she passed, the woman looked up.

Elaine almost stopped in her tracks and stared, but her trade-craft took over and she continued her stroll past the window. *I've met her.* Once she was out of view, she leaned against the wall. The woman wasn't a cop—Elaine would have remembered if she were. A reporter?

An image came to her mind of the woman, kids, and a big hairy dog. The photo on Hughes's office wall. His wife? Bloody hell. Hughes had introduced her to the team at some awards do or other, maybe two years back. Her name began with "F." Felicia? Faith? Damn painkillers. Fuzz in the brain. *Fiona. Right, Fiona. Okay, here we go.*

Elaine turned to enter the restaurant and almost collided with Fiona, who was leaving.

"So sorry. Clumsy of me. I—don't I know you? Fiona Hughes, isn't it?"

"No worries. Sorry, you're mistaken." Fiona brushed past without a glance and continued up the street.

Elaine caught up after a few steps. "Please, my name's Hope. Elaine Hope. I was a DCI in your husband's division. I'd like to talk to you about something. It shouldn't take long."

Fiona stopped and stared up at Elaine, her eyes wide. "DCI Hope, you say? Show me your warrant."

Elaine opened her warrant card. "DCI Elaine Hope. I used to be in Murder Investigation, but not anymore."

"Not anymore?" Fiona's forehead creased in thought. "Hope. Now I remember. Jonny pointed you out once."

Elaine noticed a quiver in Fiona's voice. She held her hand out as if to push Elaine away, and looked all around, past Elaine and up and down the street. "You're alone. What do you want with me?"

Does she think I'm here to arrest her? Elaine said, "This is un-official. A personal matter. I want to talk to you about Jack O'Rourke. It looks like you know him."

"You? Talk about Jacko?" She looked up at Elaine's face. "Right. Like I believe that." Fiona stepped around Elaine and backed up the pavement. "Stay away from me. I've got nothing to say to you."

Elaine watched as Fiona hurried towards the taxi rank. After a few steps, she glanced over her shoulder. Elaine waited a few seconds, then followed. She kept about ten yards distance between them.

Fiona turned. "Don't follow me. Leave me alone."

"I'll let you go, luv." Elaine pointed. "But I need a taxi too." She allowed the distance between them to grow. As Elaine watched, a dark-coloured van turned off a side street just ahead and crept slowly up the street, hard against the kerb.

Fucking kerb crawlers. They think she's a prostitute. In this part of town, though? She increased her pace as the van stopped a few yards ahead of Fiona, who swerved away from the street.

The van window rolled down, and Elaine heard muffled words. Fiona screamed as the sliding door of the van opened and a man emerged.

Elaine felt in her pocket for the metal bulk of the asp she carried. She yelled, "Hey, scrote! Police! Leave her alone!"

The attacker stopped. Elaine advanced on him, holding her warrant card in her left hand while flicking her asp open to its full two-foot length.

The man on the pavement froze, undecided for a moment, before flinging himself back into the van. The door banged shut, and the van accelerated away. Elaine stepped off the pavement to read the number plate, but it was obscured.

Fiona stood in the shadow of a shop door, her shoulders heaving as she sobbed. Elaine waited until the sobs had slowed before she spoke. "Come on. You'd best not be alone after what happened. Where were you planning to go just now?"

Fiona took a deep breath. "Home." She was trembling.

Elaine considered. "Me too. My flat's only ten minutes from here. You need to get off the street. I'll drive you home after you're feeling a bit more yourself."

"No, I don't—"

"I could take you to your place. Is your husband at home?"

"No—I mean, yes, probably." Fiona shook her head. "I don't want him to see me like this."

She knows he's not at home. Elaine smiled. "No worries. You can freshen up a bit at mine. I have a cat. Is that a problem?"

Fiona looked puzzled. "No, no problem with cats. But maybe we should go back to the restaurant."

"We could. But after, you'd still need to get home. Those bastards took a huge risk and almost pulled it off. They could return. Better for you to get away from here. Somewhere they can't follow."

Fiona glanced up and down the street. "No. I suppose you're right. I'd feel better if I was with someone."

Elaine opened the taxi door and spoke. "Brentford, please, driver. Near the locks." She climbed in after Fiona. "In twenty minutes we'll have our shoes off and be sipping a cheeky little red. There may be some crisps and cheese in the pantry too."

Tuesday night, Shepherd's Bush

Jenkins left the cover of the building and sprinted down the side street to his black Saab. Fifteen seconds later the Saab's engine burbled to life, and he sped away from the kerb. He reached the corner just as the two women entered a taxi. He waited, then pulled into the Uxbridge Road traffic fifty yards behind them. Now he could think.

He'd been watching Jacko off and on for the last month. What a life the guy led—court appearances almost daily, Saturday nights at the illegal casino above the Soho bodega. On separate evenings, Jenkins had seen him with different women, but he'd never seen Blondie before. He'd taken some photos and sent them to a friend to see if she could help with the ID.

It had been a rough night for Jacko. He'd argued with Hughes. It could have been a professional disagreement, but Jenkins didn't think so. This looked personal. Then Blondie showed up, and his date turned to shite immediately. Tough luck, boy-o.

Jenkins had noticed the van driving past Gionfriddo's just after Blondie arrived. It came around twice, going slowly, the last time just as Jacko left. Then Hope had shown up. Damn, that woman got around. Why the hell was she here? He'd taken more photos of Blondie as she left the restaurant with Hope. He was uploading them when the shit hit the fan and Hope attacked. He laughed. Those buggers had cleared off quick. A pissed-off six-foot-tall Amazon with an asp is a fearful sight.

Hope's taxi had turned right onto Kew Bridge Road, when a dark shape sped past Jenkins's Saab. The van slid into the gap just behind the taxi. Hope's building was two minutes away now.

Jenkins searched his memory. The entrance to Hope's block of flats was a recessed, sloping drive that led to the parking spaces under the building. It was protected by an electronically controlled gate. He couldn't remember seeing a separate pedestrian entrance, but there'd have to be one, wouldn't there?

They arrived. The taxi circled a small roundabout and parked across the gated entrance. There was a pedestrian door, and he watched as the two women entered. The van slowed as its occupants assessed the situation, then accelerated away. Hope and Blondie were safe for now, so Jenkins followed. Thirty minutes later, his quarry pulled into the forecourt of a house in Saint John's Wood.

Jenkins called up 192.com on his tablet and keyed the address into the property report section. The current resident showed to be someone named Baker Anstey. The name was familiar. He'd have to do some research.

Identifying the blonde would be harder. He dialled a number. "Hi, Charlie. It's Jenks. Did you get the photos?"

"You want instant service, don't you?" Charlie's voice rasped. "You think janitors rate that high? Haven't had a chance for an ident yet. *Shetland*'s on TV and you wouldn't want me to miss any clues, would you? I'll get to it once yummy DI Perez has solved the case. Won't be long."

Jenkins laughed. "Right, then. I'm heading home. Ring me when you've made up your mind."

Charlie Young was a retired Met detective sergeant, and one of the original members of the "super-recognizers," a squad made up of detectives known for their preternatural ability to recognize faces. If she'd ever seen the woman before, in any context, she'd remember her.

TWENTY-SEVEN

Tuesday night, Bermondsey

"What news?" Costello opened a container of rice and spooned it onto a plate. "Turn up something from the CCTV?"

"We were busy." Bull set two open bottles of Belhaven ale on the table and opened another container. "Ah. Prawns in garlic sauce. Good man. We expanded the CCTV search for Jacko's route home. He didn't pop out of the neighbourhood until he was way to the west, almost to Brompton Cemetery. Then he went home like a shot. No passenger. But—" He dug in the container with his chopsticks, finally retrieving a bite of prawn and water chestnut.

"Don't you use a plate? Or a bowl?" Costello chided. "But what?"

"Don't you start with that. Not all of us are upper-middle-class boarding school products." Bull chewed another bite, leaned back on the sofa, and placed his feet on the coffee table. "Besides, it's my night off. Liz is on obs, watching for burglars at some warehouse or other."

Costello frowned at Bull's shoes and moved his plate to the other end of the table. "Point taken. But what?"

"I backtracked from where we first picked Jacko up." Bull opened a small tablet computer and set it on the table where

Costello could see it. He tapped an icon. "Looks like he came from a hotel further north on Queen's Gate. This is from a number-plate camera that's set to cover the approaches to the Museum of Natural History. About a hundred yards across the street from the hotel." He tapped the screen. "Here's the Jag pulling up at the hotel. A valet gets out, then here's our lawyer exiting the hotel with—"

Costello pulled the tablet closer. "I'll be buggered. A blonde in a light-coloured coat. Blurry, but she looks like the right height and all. Why didn't the screener catch this earlier?"

"Dunno. You can't see the number plate, so I guess they passed over it and didn't send us the link. Do you recognize her?"

"Not enough to put a name on her." He squinted at the screen and shook his head. "Classy blondes abound in this part of town, especially at night. See if you can get it enhanced, and send it to the super-recognizers."

"Well, I wouldn't know about this part of town. And I've already requested. They're busy. I plan to visit the hotel tomorrow to see what I can find out." Bull took another bite of garlic prawns. "Tell me about your visit to the Verve."

Costello chuckled. "We already had her report about the shoe, and it was at the lab. I was more interested in the Peugeot and finding some connection there. So I did some research."

He pulled out his notebook and flipped through pages. "Remember the Peugeot is owned by that paraplegic French aristocrat?"

Bull answered, "Duclerq. And?"

"His son, René, is a French commercial representative. Based in London. No apparent criminal ties, but he goes to casinos. Hangs out with some shady characters."

"Hard to avoid if you're a gambler. I take it you pressed her about him."

"Yep. As soon as I did, La Veuve's memory got shaky. Next thing I know, she's coughing like crazy and asking for her oxygen. Her companion, a woman named Lydia Anstey, got upset and demanded I leave."

"Sounds like a reasonable thing for her to do."

"Yes, but I decided to wind the Anstey woman up a bit before I left. She got fucking livid. Aggressive. In my face." Costello held his hand three inches from his nose. "She was this close. Thought she was gonna slap me. I left then."

"Who is this Lydia Anstey? The name rings a bell."

"I thought so too. She's British, about forty, short and fit. Looks like she lifts weights or at least works out. Arrogant, with a temper. Surly attitude. Not exactly a winning personality. I looked her up after I left."

"Politics. That's where I've heard the name Anstey."

Costello nodded. "Baker Anstey. He was a Tory MP until the party kicked him out for his racial conspiracy rants. He claimed Tony Blair was an ordained priest of a Nigerian Satanist cult. Then he put it about that Cameron was a closet Muslim, whatever that is. He made his money in real estate. Lydia's his daughter. And there's more." He took a bite of beef and broccoli and looked smug.

"What do I have to do, put you in a hammerlock? What more?"

Costello finished chewing. "Remember I said La Veuve needed oxygen? Well, when she asked the Anstey woman for her mask, she said *ma fille*. That means—"

"You know I don't speak French."

"It's what she'd say if Lydia Anstey was her daughter."

Bull considered the news. No connections between Anstey and the murder leapt out at him, but they'd hardly begun to dig. Still, it was interesting. "So, we've got a murder possibly witnessed by a CPS lawyer and his classy girlfriend. We've got a French aristocrat who lives two doors down from the murder scene, with a possible connection to a car that possibly carried the murderer and his victim. And we have a woman who may be the French aristocrat's daughter but is definitely connected to a conspiracy crank." He laughed. "Not a barrister in England who couldn't cast reasonable doubt on that string of possibles."

Costello laughed. "It gets better." He reached into his coat pocket and extracted a small, blue cloth bag, closed with a gold drawstring. "After I looked up Lydia Anstey, I called up my sister, who works in fashion. Together, we went looking for this."

Bull put down his food container and leaned forward. "That's not from the Chinese takeaway."

"Hardly. She took me to a small establishment on Elizabeth Street. Very exclusive. They help wealthy patrons craft their own perfumes and colognes. They asked me to describe the scent I wanted, then they waved various pieces of paper under my nose for me to test. After a while they were able to point me at a shop that sells this delightful little whiff." Costello opened the bag and took out a tiny gilt bottle. "A normal size bottle costs two hundred and fifty quid. This wee dram cost me ten. It's what a rich woman would carry in her tiny purse if she needed a top-up. Hold out your arm."

Bull did so. Costello rolled his eyes and twisted Bull's hand palm up. He coaxed the miniature glass stopper from the bottle and used it to dab a bit of liquid on Bull's wrist. "Now, just let it sit for a moment before you take whiff."

Bull wrinkled his nose. "I can already smell it. It's familiar." He sniffed his wrist. "I'll be damned. That's what Novak smelled like after he was gone all that afternoon."

"And that's what Lydia Anstey was wearing this afternoon."

Tuesday night, Brentford

Elaine sat at the end of her deep green leather sofa, her legs folded under her. Fiona perched stiffly at the other end, feet flat on the floor, swirling her wine glass. They hadn't spoken much in the taxi or after arriving.

After Elaine had closed the electric gate to the building,

she'd looked back and noticed a dark van passing. It had turned left on the High Street and sped away. The number plate was unreadable, so she figured it was the same one. They had her flat pegged now, but she decided not to say anything. A panicked Fiona wouldn't be very helpful.

Elaine spoke. "I worked with Jacko on several cases when I was in Murder Investigation. How did you meet him?"

Fiona stared a few moments before responding. "We'd always moved in the same police crowd, the lot of us," She drained her glass. "David, my first husband, introduced me. Mostly couples, but Jonny, Jacko, Alec Cranwell, some other singles. I thought Jacko was harmless at first. You know, jokes, double entendre, that sort of thing. He did it to all the women."

Elaine laughed. "Don't I know it? He chatted me up once or twice. Trying for a notch on his dick. I made my thinking on that clear."

"I think David made his thoughts clear, at some point, because Jacko stopped doing it and stayed away." She held out her glass. "Is there enough red for another?"

"Lots." Elaine retrieved the bottle and poured. She remembered now. When David died, Fiona's picture was in the papers and on TV. The grieving police widow. "Then you married Jonny?"

"Have you ever been married?"

"Never had the time, being a cop." Elaine shook her head. "Most of the men I've known can't deal with it."

"Most."

"There's one. Was one. Before all this happened." She pointed vaguely at her face.

"He dumped you." Fiona scoffed.

"No, he didn't. We're . . . I'm . . . working through some stuff. I choose not to see him."

"How does he take that?"

Elaine sighed. "He wants to be with me, but he just got a job offer in the States."

"Is he solid? Do you think he's a good man?"

Elaine thought for a moment. "Yeah. The best that's ever shown interest. I think he wants me to go with him to Texas. He said he'd wait."

"Then I'd say it's more than interest. But you have things to do. If he truly loves you, he can help. Don't be a fool."

Is that what I'm doing? Elaine poured more wine. "So Jacko came sniffing around after David died."

"You're looking to fit Jacko up for something." Fiona studied Elaine. "Do you think Jacko was responsible for what happened to you?"

"You and I may have a common interest. You didn't look all that happy with him."

"Why would I want revenge on Jacko?" Fiona asked.

"I thought those thugs in the van were just kerb crawlers. But that's not right, is it? I saw your reaction. They called you by name, didn't they?" When Fiona didn't reply, she continued, "They wanted you specifically."

"No, they didn't." Fiona pulled her mobile from her pocket and glanced at the screen. "It's late. I'm calling a taxi."

"You're stuck in the middle of something. You're afraid of me because I'm a cop. You're afraid of something else too. What have you done, Fiona?"

"Nothing. I've done nothing."

Elaine willed softness into her voice. "Then you have nothing to fear from me. I'll drive you. You shouldn't be alone. Is Hughes home?"

"What do you want with me? Why are you so bloody interested?" Fiona's voice rose. "I can manage myself." As she began to dial, her mobile slipped from her hand and clattered across the coffee table.

Elaine retrieved it. "How did they know where you were?"

"Give me my phone." Fiona held out a shaky hand.

"Think. If they know who you are and where you would be tonight, they probably know where you live. Do you really want to be alone? Why don't you call Hughes? He can arrange protection."

"I said I'll be fine. Phone. Please." Fiona's hand continued to tremble. When Elaine didn't give her the phone, she walked to the French doors and looked out into the night.

"Is Hughes home?"

"No. He's in York."

"Fiona. I think that van followed us here. I don't know if they're still out there, but what would they do if you leave alone in a taxi?" She placed the phone on the coffee table. "I don't know why you're afraid of me. I know you're in trouble, and I care about your safety. This flat is as safe as your house. Safer. It's got coded gates and a security guard downstairs. Stay here. Call Hughes, tell him what happened."

"I need to work through this on my own." Fiona started as gust of wind swirled against the French doors, hissing and rattling.

"You say you want that, but could you have handled what happened tonight? Alone? It's a good thing I was there. Let me help you." Silence. "I may be a cop, but I'm a cop who the Met has abandoned. Now, tell me why you're in trouble."

Fiona turned, a quizzical look on her face. "Abandoned? What do you mean?"

"I don't have to report we met, what we say. No case, no team. I'm on leave."

"Jonny and Alec were devastated by what happened to you. Tell me why you said they abandoned you."

Patience, Lainie. Give to get. "I'm an embarrassment. A detective who ignored procedure, got raped, and killed the suspect. Most of the chief officers want me to go away because they don't know what to do with me. Maybe they think I'm a tragic hero." She laughed. "Or at least tragic. Your husband may be one of them. He talked AC Collins into putting me back on compassionate leave when I think Collins wanted to retire me, or red-card me, or worse. The executives are hoping I'll fade away."

"Jonny stood up to Collins? That's a first. Collins is a bully. It's one of the few things Jonny rants about."

"Collins was pushing my buttons, and I almost melted down. Your Jonny interjected and defused the situation. Came up with a solution that wouldn't leave them facing a Police Federation lawsuit. The funny part is that it was the outcome I was hoping for. They've cut me loose, so now I can investigate what I want. I'm a woman on a mission, and I refuse to fade away. It might be helpful and safer to have a friend like me."

"If he stood up to Collins, I'd say Jonny's on your side." Fiona looked through the doors and shivered, her arms crossed over her chest. "It's not so much what I've done. It's what I haven't done."

"You and Jacko witnessed a murder. In an empty flat in South Kensington. That's why those men tried to abduct you. You saw the killer. He's the one who cornered you outside the restaurant."

Fiona dropped her arms to her side and sat back down in the armchair, her face turned away from Elaine. "How did you know?"

"Complex story, that. He called you by name?"

"Not by name. Jacko said he hadn't told them my name. It was his voice. I never saw his face. He wore a balaclava, that night. He held a shotgun under my nose and said, 'So sorry, lovely lady.' I thought they were the last words I'd ever hear." Fiona turned to face her. "Are you going to arrest me?"

"For what? What did you do?"

Fiona shook her head. "Just . . . Jacko said . . . I was just there. Peed myself. Saw something I never imagined I'd see. Spewed out the window."

"Then why do you think I'd arrest you?"

"Jacko said I'd be arrested because I hadn't gone straight to you lot. Said we needed to stay low. I told him it was idiotic, but he insisted I'd go to prison for withholding evidence.

Obstructing the police." Fiona's eyebrows arched in a question. "Are you saying he's wrong?"

"You haven't broken any laws by not coming forward. It's a different story if you lie to us, but no law says you have to come forward."

"Then I'm not sure if I will. If they don't know who I am and they haven't followed me, I'm probably safe for now."

"Probably safe? That's unlikely. If they really threaten Jacko, he'll squeal your name to the heavens. I recommend that you come forward. The police may not be inclined to protect you if you refuse." Elaine paused to let that thought sink in. "Jonny would tell you the same."

"Yep. But it's up to me. Please take me home. I live in Mortlake. Near the Chiswick Bridge."

Tuesday night, Purley

Jenkins had just reached Purley when his mobile rang. He pulled over and answered. "Sing to me, Charlie. Dulcet tones, luv."

Charlie wheezed a rheumy cough. "Not much chance of that, Jenks. Two packs of fags a day for forty years has seen to that. Three guesses who you've caught with the O'Rourke jackass."

Jenkins laughed. "Quiz night with Charlie? Right then, Princess Di."

"Aristocratic enough, but not alive enough."

"An aristocrat? Hmm. Grace Kelly?"

"Too aristocratic, closer in the looks department. Still not alive enough, sad to say."

"Rosamund Pike."

"Alive, but dead common."

"Nothing common about her in my book, luv. Alright, who is our mystery blonde? Chop-chop. Roxy's waiting."

"Married life calls, eh? Never saw much use in marriage, myself, which explains a lot. I've seen your blonde with her husband. She's Lady Fiona Paternoster, daughter of the late and little-lamented Donald Paternoster, the Viscount Waleham. Married to Commander Jonathan Hughes."

"Blow me over. Didn't see that coming."

"Something to ponder. I thought it was beyond interesting, so I called an old friend who likes to reminisce. But it can wait. You want to get home to your supper and a leg over Roxy."

Jenkins snorted a laugh. "You know me too well, Lady Charles. Tell me about Lady Fiona."

"Hippie life at university. Sex, drugs, rock 'n' roll. Flipping her finger in her father's face. The old goat kicked off, and she had to do some growing up. Married a copper, had a bairn who's the image of his father. She lived a solid, middle-class life till a drink-driving git rammed hubby's car at a collision scene."

"And Hughes snapped up the grieving widow."

"Mmm-hmm. Fairly quickly. Hubby had been in the ground a year or so."

"Something to be said for middle-aged lookers, I guess."

"Ooh, hardly, luv. You don't know?"

"Don't know what?"

"Hughes is gay. And it's known only to the initiated, but he and Cranwell have been an item for years."

"Fuck me." Jenkins ended the call and sat stunned. Hughes and Cranwell? This required serious thought. Nothing in his mission brief had mentioned that situation. He'd stayed away from Hughes after the initial operational meetings; doing so was good tradecraft. Seeing him with Jacko had been a little too close for comfort. But sleeping with Cranwell?

Either Hughes was a numpty with absolutely no awareness, or he was playing both sides of a dangerous game.

TWENTY-EIGHT

Tuesday night, Brentford

Elaine stopped her BMW just outside her parking garage and let the electric gate close behind her. She inspected the road in both directions. When she didn't see any sign of the dark van, she turned west on Brentford High Street.

Fiona sat forward, her fingers on the door handle. "What are you doing? Where are you taking me? This isn't the way to Mortlake."

"It's one way to Mortlake, and I need to make sure we aren't being followed. If we are, I don't want to lead them straight to your door. I'll twist around and double back a few times. Caution is a good thing, don't you agree? Why don't you tell me about your house? Will I just drop you at the kerb, or do you have a drive?"

Fiona appeared to relax, but she left her hand on the door. "We live on a close. There's a wrought-iron gate that I can open remotely."

"What's the street like?"

"What's it like? Just a street."

Elaine checked her mirrors and turned right. "I mean is it busy or quiet? Wide or narrow? Secluded or open?"

"Oh. Long and narrow. Not much traffic this time of night.

Just local residential. There are a few blocks of flats. A pub around the corner."

"How many houses behind the gate?"

"Seven. We're number five."

Elaine turned up a close and stopped at the end. "Long and narrow is good. There'll be a nice line of sight." After a half minute, she exited the close and wound back to the main road. "I'm taking the back way to Mortlake, loop around to the south and come through Richmond."

"That will take awhile," Fiona replied. After a few minutes she asked, "So what's Jacko done to you?"

Elaine smiled. "Dunno. As we say in the job, I need to eliminate him from my enquiries."

Fiona laughed. "Good luck with that. I need to pee."

"Bound to be someplace up ahead in Isleworth. Needs to be the right place, though."

"You said he hit on you. What did he say?"

"Nothing that interested me. He said he found my interrogation techniques to be erotic. He wanted to sit across the table from me and let me have my way with him. Wanted me to verbally abuse him."

"No, he didn't say that."

"He did, in several different ways. I guess he thought it was an intriguing icebreaker." She glanced at Fiona. "I wondered at the time if he wanted me to be his dominatrix."

Fiona gave a sharp laugh. "Wouldn't surprise me. Across the table. Did he offer to cook dinner for you?"

It was Elaine's turn to laugh. "How did you know? He went on and on about what a good cook he was, and why didn't I stop at his place to unwind. Seemed every time he offered steak, with an Italian red and a massage."

"It was cooking with me too."

Elaine waited for more, but when she looked, Fiona was staring out the window.

Two miles later they passed a sushi bar with a sign in front that said, "Parking at rear." Elaine drove past for a couple of hundred yards, then turned into in a small parking lot. She watched traffic for a few moments before she reversed direction.

"Where are we going?" Fiona twisted in her seat to look behind them. "Is someone following us?"

"Not that I've seen. We passed a sushi place with off-street parking. They'll have a loo, and we can sit in private."

The interior decor of the restaurant was red, black, and plastic. Fiona made straight for the loo. Elaine followed. "We go together. Take no chances."

A few minutes later, they sat at a table in a corner that had a view of both the front and rear entrances.

Elaine studied the selection of sushi on her plate. "I never took him up on it. Jacko, I mean. At first it was funny. I teased him, just to see how far he'd go. I don't think he realized what an ass he made out of himself."

When Fiona didn't reply, she continued. "I haven't run into him since I was raped." She wiped her hands on a paper napkin. "I'm going to check the parking lot. Won't take a minute."

Elaine slipped out the back door and into the shadows along the back wall of the restaurant. On her right, the roofs of residences were visible over a high boxwood hedge. Trees overshadowed the lined parking spaces along the back wall of the lot. When they had arrived, there had been three cars in the lot—two blue and one silver.

Now, those cars had been replaced by four new ones. Besides her and Fiona, there were only three other sets of customers in the restaurant, so there was possibly one extra vehicle not accounted for. She crossed to the shadow of the trees and moved along the row of cars. The first had a child seat, which corresponded to the young couple with a toddler who had entered while they were there. The next two had no occupants, but she detected movement in the fourth, and last.

Elaine retrieved her asp from her coat pocket. Staying low, she moved between two other cars so she could approach from behind. When she was ten feet away, the car started and the reversing lights came on. She stood as the car reversed from the space.

The driver's window opened and a young woman spoke. "Best be more careful, lady. I didn't see you back there. Might've knocked you over if I'd been in a hurry."

Elaine gave a small wave as the car drove away. "I'll watch out next time. Thanks."

Back inside, Fiona sat leaning against the wall, her elbow on the table, chewing her thumbnail, apparently lost in thought. One knee bounced nervously.

"Looks all clear out there. No dark van. Why don't we get on to your place?"

"He groomed me. Isn't that what they call it? Grooming?"

Elaine sat. That's a term we use. I suspect Jacko's quite good at it."

"Did he groom you?"

Elaine thought for a moment, remembering when she had first met Jacko, then said, "He tried. He picked days when I was fagged out, exhausted. Came over all sympathetic, wanting to talk. If I was having a hard time building a solid case, he'd offer to go over it with me, give advice. Most of the Crownies do that. It's part of their job. He rarely wanted to meet in the office, though. I fell for it once."

Fiona looked up. "How?"

"I was at my office late, working on some evidence. He showed up, gave me some good pointers, actually. Then he said why don't we continue at The Swan. We went and had a pint, I said I was hungry. He offered to cook for me at his place."

The restaurant manager appeared next to the table. "Thanks, ladies, but it's closing time."

Elaine paid the bill. When they were back on the A310, Fiona asked, "Did you go?"

"No. I'd like to say warning bells went off, but the real reason is I was too tired. Told him I needed to feed Scratch and I'd just grab a salad at home. Left him there."

"I thought you said he wanted you to abuse him."

Elaine laughed. "That was later, after his offers of wine and steak and massage didn't work. The creep never really gave up."

"I didn't realize he was grooming me until it was too late."

Elaine checked her mirror and signalled a lane change. "What do you mean, 'too late'? You couldn't tell him to fuck off?"

"I'd been married to Jonny for three years. We knew Jacko. Same parties, friends, that sort of thing. You know how it is when your husband's married to the job."

"Not really."

"Oh, sorry. Most of the women in our circle thought Jacko was sexy. He's bit of a rogue, and the game was exciting. Every now and then he'd pick one of us off. A one-night stand here and there. I didn't think of him as a predator. He was just a randy lawyer who got lucky once in a while."

"I get that. The job's a marriage destroyer."

Fiona stared straight ahead. "I think back, and I realize he knew whose husband was working twenty-four/seven. Whose marriage was in the toilet. He flirted with me. At first I was determined to keep my marriage with Jonny going."

She went silent. When Elaine glanced at her, she was met by Fiona's blue eyes, studying her face.

"What?"

Fiona reached out and touched Elaine's shoulder. "I'm not surprised he tried it on with you. You're a beautiful woman."

"No. I was a challenge to him, is all."

"Yes, you are." Fiona withdrew her hand. "You and I, we're not so far apart. I don't think any two women our age are far apart, once we start talking about things that matter."

Elaine slowed for the roundabout at the A315. "Almost there. On the home stretch."

"He started complimenting me. My hair. My style. Wanted my advice on buying art for his flat. One night at a party, Jonny and I had a row. The next day Jacko sent me flowers and a note saying it wasn't my fault given Jonny . . ."

Fiona stopped and took a deep breath. "Jonny and I started to fall apart. Maybe my resolve was shaken. Maybe I . . ."

Elaine stopped for a red light. *This is coming hard for her. An abuser? I wouldn't have pegged him for that.*

"Jonny's gay. He told me two years after we married. His partner is . . . they've been together for almost thirty years. Almost since they joined the force." Fiona fished a tissue from her purse and blew her nose.

"Jacko knew," Fiona continued. "He said he couldn't comprehend my loneliness, but if I ever needed a kind ear, then he had two. And he knew something else, but I didn't find out until later."

"What was that?"

"Don't you have a light inside this thing? A mirror?" Fiona rummaged in her purse and extracted some lipstick.

Elaine pointed at the sun visor. Fiona flipped it down and slid aside the small cover of the vanity mirror. She studied herself in the light. "I should have known."

"Some cars are diff—"

Fiona scoffed. "Not that. He was blackmailing Jonny."

"What? Jonny's a shit for doing what he did to you, but that's not blackmail material. Neither is being gay." She stopped. "What else?"

Fiona gave a huge sigh. "I'm not sure exactly. I think years ago Jonny covered up something his lover did. Or didn't do. Something about evidence. A murderer got off."

Crap. That was blackmail material. Even if it had been years ago, it could cause all kinds of havoc, possibly cost both of them their careers and pensions. "Don't tell me any more about that."

"I don't know any more."

"Hold on. You're the price?"

Fiona shook her head. "At first it was an affair. Jonny was paying him money, but I didn't know that. The threats started after I learned what a shit Jacko is and tried to end it."

A few turns later they pulled up to a gate. Fiona pushed a button on her electronic fob to open it, and indicated a parking space at the end of the close.

"I should come in with you?" Elaine asked.

"No, I'll—"

"Yes. There's no point taking a chance." Elaine opened the glove box and retrieved a heavy, cylindrical torch. "I don't like the idea of you sleeping here tonight. I'll stay with you."

"Come inside, but I've decided to go to the family pile in Hampshire for a few days. My aunt and uncle are there."

Elaine considered. An estate in Hampshire was safer than being alone here. "Okay, we'll check the house together, top to bottom. Then I'll see you off and make sure you're not followed."

"Are you going to grass on me?"

"Not right away. You need to make the right decision. But remember—I'm a cop."

TWENTY-NINE

Wednesday night, Brentford

"I have to tell you again. Some would call this meeting insubordination." Elaine looked across her kitchen table at Costello and Bull, who had arrived a few minutes earlier with a bottle of Argentinean Malbec for her and beers for themselves.

"We haven't forgotten, guv." Costello pried the cap from an ale and handed the opener to Bull. "And it could be more than that, if someone wanted to construe."

Elaine studied the label on the wine bottle. "This isn't your standard Spanish plonk. Beer and wine glasses are in the cupboard, Bull. Bring the corkscrew from the drawer by the sink, please. We'll be civilized drinkers tonight."

The cork squeaked as Elaine twisted it. "Coppers are paid to construe." She watched the levers rise as the screw penetrated the bottle. "Like I'm doing now. I ask myself, if this isn't garden-variety insubordination, what is it? What more?" The cork groaned before emitting a pop of submission. She poured half a glass.

Costello began. "Remember the French lady who brought in the shoe? I interviewed her Monday. She appears to be in poor health, but it was hard to tell if she was taking the piss with me or if she was truly ill."

"Avoidance."

"That's it. Especially when I pressed her on the Peugeot driver and the connection with the Duclerq family."

"The guy who owns the Peugeot?"

"His son. She was downright evasive about whether she knew them. Claimed senility. Hell, the families have been neighbours for centuries. Definitely some smoke there, guv."

Elaine swirled the deep red wine, sniffed, and took a sip. The strong fruitiness and acidity were balanced perfectly. "She's what—seventy-something? Could be true."

"Don't think so. She knew what she was doing. I pushed as hard as I dared. We have to tread carefully. Don't want to be accused of being uncompassionate."

Elaine snorted. "Certainly not. Delicate feelings must be respected, especially during murder investigations. What else?"

"Remember Novak's disappearances and his afternoon delight?"

"That's speculation."

It was Costello's turn to snort. "Not so sure now. I met La Veuve's companion, and what an angry little piece of work she is. Name of Lydia Anstey. I may have been a bit provocative and accidentally tread on those delicate feelings. She was ready to smack me, got in my face, this close." He held his thumb and forefinger a few inches apart.

"And?"

"She was wearing the same perfume I smelled on Novak. I rang up my sister afterward and we went to find it. Here it is." He laid the small blue bag on the table.

Elaine picked it up and read the logo. "Never heard of it. May I?" She retrieved the minute flask and sniffed. "Not something I'd wear. Expensive?"

"That little drop you have in your hand runs ten quid. Full bottle over two-fifty."

"I can afford this flat partly by avoiding that kind of

extravagance. So this Anstey female bathes in it. At least she wears it in the afternoon. Thousands of women in London might. It hardly narrows the scope of the investigation."

"That's just it, guv. Thousands of women don't. It's popular on the Continent but hasn't taken off here. Only one shop in Britain sells it, a small place in Elizabeth Street. They say they sell fewer than fifty bottles a year." He lifted an eyebrow at Elaine, who cackled.

"And they keep a list of their customers."

"Who are almost exclusively rich males. One John Novak figured prominently. He dresses like a toff, but I'd wager he's hardly rich."

"What do you make of it?" Elaine asked.

"It's interesting. Novak's investigating a murder the Veuve household voluntarily got involved in. I think he's boinking the Anstey harpy. Maybe she told him about the shoe during pillow talk. Maybe he said they needed to turn it in to avoid scrutiny. He could be materially involved."

"Or not. It seems all you have for your work in this whole investigation is a string of possibilities. Maybe this, maybe that. You're spending more time worrying about Novak than you are focusing on the case. Your perfume"—she waved her hand in the air—"thing or whatever may not be relevant to the investigation." She downed the remnants of her wine and scowled at Costello, who avoided her gaze.

"But this is." Bull shifted in his chair to more directly face Elaine. "We've been after that dark-coloured Jag. There are near sixty Jags registered in a four-block radius, and we tracked down all of them. Nothing. Now we're most interested in one that came from outside the neighbourhood. It belongs to an old friend of yours—I shouldn't say 'friend.'"

Costello laughed weakly. "We've seen you rip his ego to shreds more than once."

Elaine looked from one to the other. "At least now you're

focusing on something pertinent. I've sent dozens of blokes away crying. I can't guess who you mean."

Bull grinned and nodded. "Watching you take ponces down a few notches has been instructive and entertaining, ma'am." He took a long draught of beer and leaned forward, his elbows on the table. "John Gilbey O'Rourke. Jacko, your favourite Crownie."

Elaine looked away. She took a sip of wine, and waited several breaths before she turned back to Bull. "More like an annoying rash that resists treatment. What do you have on him?"

"He's in the frame for being the third man. He arrived within the times we estimate for the murder. He left by a twisty route that didn't take him straight home, clearly avoiding traffic cameras. And he had a passenger, a blonde woman we haven't identified yet, but who we think is Barefoot Woman."

Elaine poured a half-glass of wine and sipped. "She didn't leave the scene with him?"

"Not that we can tell. It looks like he arrived with her and left without her, but we're not completely sure. Glare on the windscreen, fuzzy CCTV images. But just before the murder, one of the ANPR cameras caught them getting into a car and leaving a hotel on Queen's Gate, right on time."

"Do you have a video?"

Bull exchanged a glance with Costello. "Not a good one." He opened his tablet computer, tapped the screen a few times, and set it in front of Elaine. She leaned forward and watched.

In the grainy video, the dark Jaguar stopped at the hotel. The valet left the driver door open and sprinted around the car to open the passenger door. Even without enhancing the image, Elaine would have bet a hundred quid the tall, bulky man who slid behind the wheel was Jacko. The blonde, sleek and elegant as the car itself, slipped into the awaiting seat and gathered her coat as the valet shut the door.

Elaine picked up the men's empty beer bottles and dropped

them in the bin. When she turned back to the table, Bull and Costello were exchanging questioning looks. She asked, "Do you have an ID yet?"

Costello replied, "We've checked with the hotel staff to see if anyone could ID her. They said she meets O'Rourke there every couple of weeks, but they've never learned her name."

Elaine nodded. "He pays for discretion."

"Something's up, guv. Do you recognize her?" Bull asked.

They evidently had read something in her face while she watched the video. "It would be in his name, wouldn't it? The reservation. You could use the super-recognizers."

"Long queue for their attention these days. We'll find out who she is before long."

"Bound to be somebody who knows the dirty on Jacko's love life." She rose from the table. "It's late and I'm ready to get some kip. I'll ask around and let you know if I find anything."

Costello remained seated. "But guv, do you know something? Who is she?"

It had only just turned eight PM. Bull and Costello appeared perplexed—and surprised enough that neither rose to go. She smiled and repeated, "I said I'll let you know if I find anything. Good night, my friends."

THIRTY

Wednesday night, Brentford

Elaine dragged her duvet from the bed and retreated to her veranda. She decided against taking wine with her. Wrapped warmly in the chair, she watched the lights of the narrow boats moored in the canal basin and reviewed what she had just learned.

She'd deceived them, and they knew it. That alone was enough to turn her stomach. But what could she have done at the moment? If she were their senior investigating officer, Fiona would have already been interviewed. But then, if she were the SIO, she wouldn't have encountered Fiona.

Should she have come clean with them after she saw the video? She'd hesitated because she had doubts about Novak. He wasn't trustworthy, so she wasn't about to put Fiona at risk by revealing she was the witness. Not yet. Everything she'd heard about Novak from Bull and Costello was speculation, but they were sound thinkers, and she gave credence to their suspicions. She chuckled. They were probably discussing her right now, asking themselves if their trusted old guv had lied. She'd clear it up later—they'd understand her decision to compartmentalize intelligence. And besides, she'd taken them to task for bringing her suspicions based on unfounded assumptions.

And what about Fiona? She'd saved the silly woman from almost certain death at the hands of those thugs. She should let Fiona know it was now only a matter of time before she was discovered, and that they were both faced with tough choices. Fiona had to turn herself in, preferably to her husband. If she didn't, then Elaine would be forced to identify her to Bull and Costello.

She dialled, and Fiona's voicemail answered. "Something's happened. Call me as soon as you get this."

The kitchen was a helluva lot warmer than the veranda, and she was hungry. She retrieved a half-eaten steak from the fridge and popped it into the microwave. It was probably dried out, but it would do for tonight, if she slathered it with HP sauce. No sooner were the sauce, a plate, and cutlery on the table than her mobile warbled. The number on the display was unfamiliar, so she hesitated before answering. "Hope."

"DCI Hope. This is Jonathan Hughes. Do you have a few minutes?"

Her heart pounded. *Careful, Lainie.* "Just a moment, sir. Be right with you." What the hell could Hughes want? Had Fiona come clean? There was nothing for it but to listen and brazen it out. She took a deep breath and counted down the seconds with the microwave, to let her emotions subside, then retrieved the now-steaming beef.

"Sorry, sir. Dinner in the oven. How may I help you?"

"And I'm sorry for interrupting your meal." Hughes hesitated. "Seems I'm full of apologies. First, I apologize for the way the meeting with AC Collins went. I know it was extremely hard on you, and I truly feel wretched for putting you through that. But I couldn't see any other way to extend your compassionate leave. It was the outcome I was hoping for."

What did he mean, the outcome he was hoping for? Who the hell was he to play with her emotions—her life—like that for his own purposes? What the fuck did he want?

Hughes hesitated before continuing. "I hope it was what you wanted as well.

"Sir." She waited.

"Well, then, I'll get to the point. I have a proposal for you, and I'd like to present it to you in person. Can we meet in about an hour?"

She saw no point in making it easy on him. "So you didn't want me on leave. Whether we meet depends on the proposal."

"DCS Cranwell said you could be exasperating." He exhaled before continuing. "I'm in charge of a special investigation focused on corruption within law enforcement, and I want—need—your help. I've wanted you on board for some weeks, but circumstances made that difficult. I can explain more fully once we meet."

"I'll have conditions." As powerful as Hughes was, she needed to retain control.

"Such as?"

"We can discuss them once I know what you need. Where are you?"

"At my office. New Scotland Yard."

"Who will be there?"

"Myself and perhaps another person."

"I'll ring you right back." Some wine was left in the bottle. Elaine emptied it into her glass and swirled. Sheets of the deep red liquid clung to the side of the glass, then sagged back to the surface. She took a sip, cut a bite of steak, and chewed.

What was going on? Jacko was having an affair with . . . no, *affair* wasn't the right word. He was fucking Hughes wife. Jacko had a gambling habit. She'd seen him meet Hughes and argue publicly. He'd met with Fiona and argued. She had quite possibly saved Fiona's life. Bull and Costello suspected Jacko and one of his girlfriends of being a witness to a murder. Elaine was certain Barefoot Woman was Fiona. What tangled webs. Which of those strands is part of Hughes's investigation? Who was Hughes investigating? Novak?

And could she trust Hughes? Probably not. He was high in the chain of command that had let her down—no, abandoned her—and then afterward made supportive and compassionate noises to assuage his sense of guilt. Never mind what he'd done to Fiona. The man was a snake.

Weeks, Hughes had said. Why now? She'd be a perfect scapegoat. If his investigation went pear-shaped, guess who'd be blamed—the damaged, outcast, rogue detective they could say had fucked up. Or mishandled evidence. Or even better, roughed up a suspect. They'd find something and then disavow all connections with her. In the end, senior officers would retire to their all-male clubs with cigars and nice pensions, and shake their heads at one another about the woman who'd ballsed it up for them.

It could be a trap in so many ways. Would a dark van intercept her on the way to his office? It was a possibility, but she doubted it. She stood at the French doors and looked out.

But if it wasn't a trap? Why her? Bull and Costello? Could she use Hughes to get the answers she sought? A quid pro quo? So many questions. If she refused, she might never know the answers. She picked up her mobile and dialled. A familiar voice answered.

"Guv." Bull's voice grated, with an edge that implied he wasn't pleased to hear from her. Traffic sounds in the background told her he wasn't home yet.

"I know I acted strangely tonight, but I had reasons. I'll make it up to you and Costello. Something's come up, and I need a favour. The kind of favour that only you of all my friends are capable of delivering. Can we meet at your flat? In, say, forty-five minutes?"

"Friends."

She sighed. "I hope so, Bull. I'll explain when I get there, if you'll listen. Can we meet?"

"Liz will be there. Costello?"

"I'll ring him. I can't leave Liz out. But time is short. Forty-five minutes, then?"

"We'll put the kettle on."

Like Bull, Costello was wary, but he agreed to meet.

When she rang Hughes, he picked up immediately. "I'll be longer than an hour getting there, perhaps as long as two. Make sure we're passed through security."

"We? Who are you bringing with you?"

"Never mind who. This is my first condition."

THIRTY-ONE

Wednesday night, Bermondsey

"When you saw that video it was like someone had slapped you, guv. You knew something, but you weren't telling us." Costello leaned against the wall, facing Elaine across the small sitting room of the flat. Bull and Liz eyed her from the sofa to her right. Waiting.

"That's exactly what I felt like. Staggered anyway. I needed time. I'd been watching Jacko, but until then I didn't know you were interested in him too."

"Novak wants us to interview him informally," Costello replied. "Just ring him and ask. Not create a fuss."

Something in his tone told her that he was more concerned about Novak's activities than what they'd learned about Jacko. "There you go again, letting Novak distract you from the case. An interview is an interview. You know the routine, both of you. Jacko's weak. He lives to feed his ego, so crack that. Show up at his office unannounced. Make sure his colleagues see you. Let him know you're watching him. Then do your mea culpas with Novak. The case comes first. Crack the case and you'll find the truth about Novak."

Costello replied, "Still digging. Boxe-Berkshire is an old name in real estate, but the true ownership isn't easy to suss out.

Only a couple of named people, who are on the boards of other companies. I'm thinking it's a shell. We have a specialist in Companies House working on it. Maybe we'll know in the next day or two."

"I've done some digging too. There may be crossover between Boxe-Berkshire and IRG. I may know more soon."

"What about Barefoot Woman, guv?" Bull glanced at Costello, then Liz. "Seeing her on the video jolted you more than anything."

"I know her. Until you told me about Jacko I had no reason to connect her to your case. But now . . . there are connections. I got a call after you left tonight."

Costello shrugged himself away from the wall and took a step towards Elaine. "We've been looking for Barefoot Woman for days. If you know and you're not saying . . ."

Elaine waited a beat. "If what? Calm down, DS Costello. Don't get tetchy—just listen. There's—"

"There's what? More you haven't told us? If you were any old witness, I'd—"

"Shut up, Simon!" Liz leapt to her feet. "After everything she's done, you go off on her like that?"

Costello turned to face Liz, who stood scarcely six inches from him, her upturned face almost as red as her hair. Elaine interjected.

"Sit down, both of you. I need your help. We don't have much time." She raised her eyebrows at Liz and turned her hand palm down. Liz returned to her place next to Bull.

Costello scowled, and said, "Sorry, guv. When I was a DC, I was used to not knowing everything that was going on. This is my first case as a sergeant, and I feel like it's going to be my last. I know I can't trust Novak, and now you've withheld something we should know. I'm tired of secrecy." He ran his fingers through his curly red hair. "Liz is right. You've never steered us wrong. What do you need?"

Elaine studied his face before she continued. "That's better. After the two of you left tonight, I got a call from Hughes. He asked me to join a corruption investigation. Said he'd wanted me on board for some time, but he needed me back on leave first."

"What did you tell him?" Bull asked.

"That I had to think about it. If I did, I'd have conditions."

"You don't trust him," Liz said.

"Not even when I can see both his hands and his feet. After what these two told me tonight, and with the video, I think his investigation has crossed over into the murder case. Here's why . . . don't interrupt. Just listen."

Five minutes later, Bull and Liz sat with dumbfounded expressions. Costello stared at a spot on the ceiling. Elaine could tell his brain was in high gear, sorting and digesting the implications of what she had told them.

"Tea, Bull?" Elaine held up her cup. "Milk, no sugar . . . you know that—sorry."

Costello came out of his trance when Bull returned with the tea. "Here's what I think you said, guv. First, there was a conspiracy within the Met that delayed backup and resulted in the assault on you. When backup finally arrived, they found one of your attackers unconscious and trussed up on the pavement outside. You say you didn't do that, couldn't have done because he'd left before you were raped. Inside the house there were shoe prints in the blood on the floor that neither you nor Nilo Srecko, the other attacker, could have made. You were unconscious, Nilo was dead with a knife you'd rammed into his throat, so you didn't know this other person was even there. There's evidence he—or she—cleared blood and broken teeth from your mouth, possibly saving your life. And the footprints left the house through the back door and down the alleyway."

"Right," Elaine said. "And this other person must have been watching for some time. Was already there when I arrived, or knew I was going there. Maybe followed me. Maybe was told not to interfere. How else could it have happened?"

Costello shrugged. "Whoever it was, or whoever was in charge of them, wanted you and your investigation out of the picture. You followed Jacko last night because you wanted something you could use to screw information out of him."

Elaine laughed. "Poor choice of words, but yes. I started with him because he was the sleaziest. Other top choices were Cranwell and Hughes."

Bull picked up the thread. "Last night Hughes met Jacko. They argued. Then Jacko met the blonde. Must have been a shock to find out she was Hughes's wife. Tonight you discover that she and Jacko may be the two we're looking for. No wonder you had to think about it."

Elaine smiled. "Then Hughes calls. Why do you think he'd want me on the team? Think back."

Costello burst out laughing. "Of course! He must have assigned Bull and me to Novak's team. For some reason he couldn't get you on board right away, but he had to keep at it, because he wants you to be our control."

Elaine nodded. "That's what I suspect. Thing is, I have my own agenda. Bull, I want you with me when I go see him tonight. I need your Marine's eyes and ears and maybe muscle if things get nasty. Costello, you and Liz find a spot on the Victoria Embankment where you can keep eyes on the vehicle entrance and Richmond Terrace. A couple out for a romantic stroll along the Thames. Plenty of benches. Watch for anything suspicious. You all have your communicators? Yes? Earpieces everyone."

Liz asked, "So I'm back on the team, chief?"

"Wouldn't have it any other way. I need someone outside the investigation to help keep an eye on Novak, or whoever. Someone Novak doesn't know about. It's one of my conditions."

Liz pumped her fist in the air. "Excellent! But in the interest of disclosure, who is she? The blonde. I think you need to tell us."

"Of course you have a right to know. I told her I wouldn't grass her up, that coming forward was her decision. So I need an assurance from you that you won't use what I tell you until I say it's okay or until you absolutely need to. Can I have that from you?"

Costello and Bull exchanged glances before Costello spoke. "Won't be the first time we've trusted you, ma'am. We'll let you decide."

"Thanks. She's been attacked once, and I don't think it will be the last time. She's left town for the country. I'll have another talk with her, try to get her to come in. Her name's Lady Fiona Paternoster. She's married to Commander Jonathan Hughes."

THIRTY-TWO

Wednesday night, New Scotland Yard

"Not completely unexpected." Hughes's blue eyes shifted from Bull to Elaine. "Did you think you'd need a bodyguard? That I planned to abduct you, DCI Hope?"

Elaine took a chair across the desk from Hughes. He leaned back in his brown leather chair and continued, "With everything you've been through, I can hardly blame you."

"Time will heal what I've been through, sir. It's the why that nags me."

"The why?"

"Why I got no backup. Why I had to respond alone."

"You were told to wait. Command policies dictate that—"

"I heard a woman screaming in fear for her life and wouldn't you know it, nary a policy manual in sight. What a pity. Actions count. A great American naval commander once said that the difference between a good officer and a bad one is about ten seconds. Sir."

Hughes nodded at Bull. "Bull and Barker were on their way. Late, but . . ."

Bull growled a protest, but Elaine held up her hand. "They were on their own as much as I was, and they were on their way out of loyalty to me. Not because the Met directed them to be there, or even knew where the hell they were. Or that DC Barker had been savagely assaulted herself and was only alive because Bull saved her. Someone betrayed me. I need to know who."

Hughes spun his chair around and stared silently at a group of photos on his office wall, as if he were weighing a decision. Elaine followed his gaze. A country house, Fiona, dogs, and kids on the lawn.

"So I'm correct," she said.

"How many conditions are there?"

Elaine shrugged. "Depends. I can't proceed blind, and my trust level needs topping up. To consider your proposal, I need something from you. Surely you understand."

"Financial Crimes has been running a long-term investigation into money laundering and real estate for about four years. Not just criminal organizations, but legitimate businesses, politicians, even some foreign government ministries. Growing their cash reserves at our expense. Then some murders started popping up that appeared linked to the money."

"The Srecko family."

"Before I go any further, Elaine—it wasn't me making the decisions. It was someone in the National Crime Agency. We only knew them by code name. We got directives."

Elaine scoffed. "Everyone's blameless, no one's responsible. What about the Sreckos?"

"They were involved with the money laundering, but we didn't know how deeply. We were instructed to place an agent in their organization. One we could trust. One from outside who had been building his legend for years."

"And then the Watson girl was murdered, and you assigned our team to the investigation."

"Right. You and Benford arrested the American."

"Then I took over the team and let Willend go. I started sniffing around the Sreckos, and the NCA didn't like that."

"Alec and I tried to manage it. Manage you. You're not easily managed, Elaine."

"So it's my fault? You botched it. Why didn't you come to me directly?"

Hughes made a wry face and held up his hand. "We tried to steer you clear of the family without compromising your investigation. Either investigation."

"Who was the gold commander that night?"

Hughes shook his head. "No. We need to move on."

"It's a condition, sir. Who was the gold commander?"

"No, DCI Hope. That night's gold commander made the decision he needed to make. He had limited options, and he had to make a snap judgement."

It was unlikely Hughes would give her any more tonight. She'd save it for later. "Right. What's your proposal? You said corruption."

"A sad old story, really. Crooked money needs a place to hide. Casinos and real estate are excellent washing machines. On the other side, police, prosecutors, magistrates are just people, and some of them get in over their heads at the card tables. Or get involved in seamy love affairs. They make some bad decisions, and the next thing you know, they're ripe for blackmail and extortion. The legal system, maybe even the country's economy, gets undermined. Our investigation will target corrupt cops and other law enforcement staff. We'll identify them, weed them out, and bring them to justice. We call it Operation Spectra. I want you to join my team. Give me your eyes and ears and brain until we bring this in."

Elaine wanted more—what Hughes said sounded a bit vague. But he wasn't going to give her more detail until she was on board. "And for me?"

"You may get your spear back. Your attitude these last few months hasn't won you many allies in this building. Alec Cranwell and I are about the only friends you have." He glanced at

Bull. "Apart from your old team, I mean. Play nice and there's a chance you can get back into Serious Crimes. Maybe go after Anton Srecko."

"If I don't?"

"I find someone else and you go back to the college, for as long as you last there."

"All right then, I'm in. When do I start?"

"Right now. I need to say, prepare yourself for a bit of a shock." Hughes pressed a button on his desk. A door opened, and in walked a person Elaine only saw in her nightmares. A person she thought she would never see again. DC Arvel Jenkins.

Chairs scraped and clattered as both Elaine and Bull jumped to their feet. She couldn't help shouting. "Jenkins! This son of a bitch! What the hell?" She felt more than saw Bull at her side as she faced Jenkins.

Hughes stepped from behind his desk, moving in front of Jenkins. "Steady, Elaine, Bull. I know this is unexpected, but—"

Elaine stopped inches in front of Hughes. "You're bloody well right it is. What's that sorry excuse for a copper doing here?"

Jenkins placed his hand on Hughes shoulder and stepped up to face Elaine and Bull.

Bull growled. "Not an inch closer, bastard."

Jenkins looked up silently at Bull's face, then turned to Elaine. "DCI Hope. I apologize for the trouble I caused to you and to your team. Especially to you and DC Barker. All I can say is whatever I did was in the line of duty."

"Line of duty? Harassing female colleagues is line of duty?" She couldn't hold back. "Gross insubordination is line of duty? Foul sexual innuendo is line of duty? No line of duty I've ever heard of. If I'd—"

"DCI Hope!" Hughes nearly shouted to gain Elaine's attention. "DC Jenkins is the agent I spoke of. He was building a legend—"

"Oh, he's a legend alright!" Elaine pointed an accusing finger at Jenkins. "I know I'll never forget him. A legend how to be a lousy, lazy bastard of a—"

"Silence!" Hughes ran his hand through his hair. "Listen for a change, Hope! If you ever want to see the inside of an incident room again, you'll shut up and listen. Now."

Elaine turned away and paced. Bull remained, facing Jenkins. Jenkins backed away and leaned against the office wall.

"Stand down, Bull," Hughes ordered. When Bull relaxed and returned to his chair, he continued. "Jenkins acted under orders. And he did damn well, right up until he was faced with a Hobson's choice. Fortunately for you, Elaine, he made the right choice."

Elaine spun on her heel. "Fortunately for me?" She looked at Jenkins. "What does he mean?"

Hughes answered. "Who do you think coshed and tied up that Goran bloke? Who left the footprints in the blood?"

No wonder Cranwell had closed the investigation so quickly. He'd told her about the anomalies as if they were true mysteries. Goran, the huge hit man, trussed-up like a pig, lying unconscious on the pavement in front of the brothel. A smeared puddle of her blood and broken teeth on the table, as if someone had inserted their fingers in her mouth and cleaned out her airway. Footprints in the blood, leading through the kitchen and out the back door. She remembered almost nothing of the assault—or the events immediately before it. Cranwell had said they thought perhaps there was someone else in the house, some unknown, decent person who had witnessed the assault and tried to help as best they could.

She studied Jenkins. She remembered him with a shaved head, which accentuated his large ears. Since then he'd let his hair grow out and was now clean-shaven instead of sporting a three-day stubble.

But the biggest change was his demeanour. She saw no sneer,

no aggression in his eyes. "You scuttled your mission to save my life?" He met her gaze, then looked to the side.

"I'm not that noble," Jenkins said. "There was no choice to make. But what he said is true."

Could she reconcile the insolent, slovenly Jenkins she had known with this quiet, confident man leaning against Hughes's office wall? Perhaps, but it would take time. He'd have to prove himself. Elaine turned back to Hughes. "I'll need another outside set of eyes. I want Liz Barker. I suppose I'll be working with Jenkins too."

"Is Barker ready?"

"I want someone I know."

"Right then, you have her. Call them in, Bull." At Bull's astonished look, Hughes tilted his head at Jenkins. "He watched all of you arrive. You're wearing an earpiece so you expected to communicate with someone. Costello and Barker are probably freezing unless they found a friendly way to keep warm. I'll send out for coffee. It's going to take awhile."

Elaine wanted more specifics. "Where will we begin, sir?"

"You need to ask?" He arched an eyebrow in the direction of Jenkins, who still leaned against the wall, with his arms folded. "Jenkins tells me you've shown an interest in one of our targets. And we think Bull and Costello have been talking to you about another."

Elaine considered. Had she been that close to the truth? And what about the argument she'd witnessed only the night before? Hughes was waiting for her answer. "Jack O'Rourke. Novak."

THIRTY-THREE

Thursday morning, Kensington

"You say you represent a relative?" Blonde Helmet asked. Elaine figured the estate agent's layered and lacquered coiffure would hold its own in a North Sea gale, competently deflecting any blown debris that threatened to crack her skull. The woman was dressed in sleek black, accentuated by the red soles of her Christian Louboutin pumps and her forest green and royal blue Hermes scarf. A gold bangle bracelet jingled on her left wrist. It was all part of the costume rich buyers expected.

Blonde Helmet checked her diary. "Who is it you said, Ms. Speranza?"

Elaine ignored her and inspected the glaring white walls of the murder house's entry hall. Early in the week, the crime scene teams had finished their work, and the property had been released to the estate company. Elaine wanted to see the location but didn't want word to get back to Novak that other cops had been interested in his investigation.

Before they'd arrived, she'd instructed Liz to act as if the estate agent existed only on the fringe of their perception. Rather than try to dress up, she'd decided they would wear pressed jeans with jackets. As she had told Liz, "We'll dress down as if we don't care what people think." She only owned one good suit, and it wouldn't pass muster in the role she was playing.

Elaine held the estate agent's business card in the light from a window. "Boxe-Berkshire. Rings a bell. I believe my grandfather knew the owners at one time. Decades past, of course. I wonder if it's the same family." She looked a question at the blonde, who shrugged.

"Wouldn't know. Reg, the bloke who runs our office might. I can ask, if you like."

"That's all right. Don't bother him. Probably some Saudi prince or Russian oligarch by now. She slid the business card into her jacket pocket, and lied. "Ah, to answer your question. My cousin, Lady Fiona Paternoster. Viscountess Waleham. She feels isolated in Hampshire and wants central digs." Fiona was the only woman she knew whose family even approached the wealth required to purchase a property like this. It was touchy going, but she wouldn't have to keep up the deception long. Elaine decided to intercept any deeper enquiries. "She's in the Turks and Caicos and asked me to run up a short list of properties to visit when she returns in a month."

Blonde Helmet peered at Elaine. "She'll need to move quicker than that. This won't be on the market long. It's a bargain at three and a half million pounds." She looked Elaine and Liz from top to toe.

Liz had been busy scrolling through her smartphone. "Three point five's a steal in this area." She showed Elaine a screen. "I think this is the house where that chap was murdered." At Elaine's surprised expression, Liz continued. "All over the news last week, ma'am. The price was, umm . . ." She swiped her finger a few times. "Three point eight until then. Not been a lot of recent interest, I suppose."

Blonde Helmet's squint tightened. "We're still refinishing the walls and floors in the back room, but I assure you—"

"Why don't you wait here? We'll walk this floor ourselves,"

Elaine suggested. "Then you can show us the upstairs." She and Liz turned and walked down the wide central hallway, leaving the estate agent standing speechless.

They entered the room Bull had told them was the murder scene. Canvas tarpaulins hung from scaffolding along two walls and spread across the floor, covering any remaining blood-stains. Tile-cutting equipment and paint paraphernalia sat against another wall.

The agent had followed them. She sounded anxious, "We need to leave. The property isn't ready to be seen. I normally wouldn't have opened it for you, but you said on the phone you were in a hurry. I'll ring you once we've completed the repainting."

Elaine smiled at Liz. "I'm sure it will all be put right before too many days go by. Back garden? Through here?" She unlocked the kitchen door and stepped outside. It was as she had imagined from Bull's description. The herbaceous border along the house wall, the landing spot of Fiona's vomit, the garden shed, the paving blocks. She re-entered the house.

Liz checked the screen of her mobile and touched Elaine's arm. "Eleven thirty, Ms. Speranza."

Elaine breezed past Blonde Helmet on her way to the front door. "I think I've seen enough. It's too large. Fiona almost never entertains. Thanks so much. We need to have some lunch before we go to another appointment."

The agent's face reddened. "There's no Lady Fiona Patter . . . pitter, is there? What are you, reporters?"

Elaine managed to look taken aback and smile at the same time. "Reporters? Oh, heavens no. Wouldn't be caught dead in a newsroom. And the name's Paternoster. From Anglo-Saxon days. Means "our father" in Latin." Blonde Helmet glared. Elaine continued. "Don't be embarrassed, it's a common mistake. I assure you my cousin exists. Check DeBrett's. We have your card, in case."

Once they were on the pavement, Elaine said, "The back garden was as Bull and Costello described it. Not hard at all to get in and out. Paved, so there would be few tracks, especially after a rain. Shame about the interior, though."

"Yeah. Already being plastered and painted." Liz made a wry face. "Although I'm not sure I wanted to see the stains. I wish we could meet La Veuve and Lydia Anstey."

"Me too. The Anstey woman is interesting, but it would be too risky. We'll rely on Costello's description for now."

They paused just across the street from the Onslow Arms. "Tell me about Kerry," Elaine asked. "Mild Down's syndrome?"

"Right. Bull said not to underestimate her. Apparently the two of them hit it off well. He and Costello have met in the back room of the pub a couple of times. She's always very attentive."

Kerry was behind the bar when they arrived at the Onslow Arms two minutes later. Elaine extended her hand. "DCI Hope. You must be Kerry. DC Bull speaks highly of you. This is DC Barker. Did a messenger leave a parcel for me earlier?"

Kerry smiled and produced a zippered bag from under the bar and handed it to Elaine. "By motorbike. He was all in black. Asked my name, gave me the bag, then left. Bull said you were tall. You certainly are." She studied Liz. "He didn't say nothing about her, though."

"Thank you, Kerry. He didn't know she would be with me. Is there someplace DC Barker and I can talk privately?"

Kerry showed them to the small room at the back and asked if she could get them something. Elaine ordered an orange juice.

Liz pondered before deciding. "A bottle of your best Vesuvius water," she said, smiling broadly. "Bull laid some in at the flat. Said it did wonders for his digestion."

It took Kerry a moment to respond. "Yes, alright. Chips? Crisps?"

Elaine lifted an eyebrow at Liz. "An order of chips between us. I'm a bit peckish. Thanks, Kerry."

When Kerry had gone, Elaine leaned across the table. "Now, let's get clear; then next steps."

"Okay, I'm your liaison with Bull and Costello. You're to stay away from them."

"No contact unless absolutely necessary. I've emphasized to them their first job is to find the killer. Second, they report on progress and Novak's behaviour." She unzipped the bag and extracted four mobile phones, each wrapped with a slip of paper. "We each get a burner. The numbers are programmed. I'll keep this one, you take one, and give those to Bull and Costello."

Liz inspected the three phones, pocketed one, and left the other two in the bag. "Right, Chief. Last night you told Hughes I'd be on Novak."

Elaine motioned at Liz's flame-red hair. "Get a dye job. Brown. Wear a hat until then."

Liz stared, her mouth open. Kerry entered, carrying a tray.

"An orange juice, a fizzy water, one chips." Kerry set the items on the table and pointed. "Pepper, ketchup, and vinegar."

"Thanks, Kerry." Elaine sipped her ale and continued. "I mean it. I'll approve the expense. With that hair you might as well shoot off fireworks. I'll wager every copper on the force knows about your hair. So it's brown hair, jeans, loose, dark clothes."

Liz still looked dubious. "But I'm not entirely clear, guv. Why were we at the house? What were we looking for?"

"I wanted to get a feel for the crime scene without tipping off Novak. I don't know what we're up against. Hughes thinks this murder could be connected to money laundering in the real estate industry. He thinks Novak could be involved—disrupting the investigation, obstructing, enabling a cover-up. I think the murder was a message that someone isn't afraid to kill. So if Novak's bent, I'll not have your life or this operation jeopardized due to vanity. Clear?"

Liz didn't look pleased, but nodded. "Clear, boss. I'll get it done this afternoon. What about the Anstey woman and the French widow?"

"All we have that links Novak to Lydia Anstey is Costello's nose. You'll be the one to verify they're an item."

"Are you going to tell Novak that Bull and Costello came to you? When you meet him tomorrow?"

Elaine had expected Liz to ask her this. "I want him to think my reason for the meeting is to tie the murder victim to the Sreckos. He's bound to know I want to take them down."

"So nothing about talking to Bull?"

"You do realize he probably already knows. He likely warned them off me just to put the idea in their heads. Nothing I can do about that. I'll tell him the pathologist, Kumar, told me. I've worked with him for years."

"Sorry, boss. I'm just worried about Bull." Liz studied the bubbles in her fizzy water, turning the glass with her fingers. Elaine waited. Liz poured more fizzy water into her glass. Bubbles crackled, droplets arced above the rim. "What will you do about Fiona?"

"The murder's not my investigation, Liz. It's Novak's." Elaine sipped her ale, and shifted her gaze past Liz to a Hogarth engraving on the wall. A bear and a bulldog. Some kind of bull-baiting allegory? "I called her this morning. Told her about Hughes's operation, said I wouldn't grass on her. Not yet anyway. That it's still up to her to decide. I think she'll come clean."

"And Jacko?"

"It's up to Novak to haul that toerag in."

"Jacko'll give her up in an instant. Then what? It's bound to come out that you knew."

"So what? I'm pretty much beyond help. Don't worry about me."

Liz reached out and touched Elaine's arm. "Don't say that, Chief. Can't be true if Hughes wanted you to run this op."

"That's one way to look at it. Or he needed a scapegoat."

Liz slid her glass to the side and leaned forward. "If he did, then it's all of us for the chop, isn't it? But he organized it, so when it goes pear-shaped, he'll go too. If, I mean. Think about that."

Elaine looked more closely at the Hogarth print. It was titled *The Bruiser*. The bulldog in the print looked angry. The bear held a tankard of ale and looked at the bulldog affably. She sighed and turned her attention back to Liz. "I haven't figured out who's baiting whom yet."

"Not sure what you mean, guv."

"Just a nagging thought. Things are rarely what they seem. You go get your hair done."

"I'll do my hair myself. But, guv, what was so important about seeing the house?"

Elaine shook her head. "Less you know, the better."

Liz bristled. "Don't pat me on the head and call me a good girl! Why?"

Elaine considered. Loyalty. She hadn't done such a good job of protecting Liz on their last case. And Liz had a point—they were a team.

"Sorry. I had to ask," Liz said. "Why not top the poor sod on a derelict industrial site where the body could lie for days before anyone noticed? Why ruin the drawing room of a four-million-pound flat? Who decided that?"

THIRTY-FOUR

Thursday night, Brentford

Elaine curled up on her sofa with the remainder of the Malbec that Bull and Costello had brought on their previous visit. She stretched her legs and noticed Scratch looking at her from where he lay on the armchair across the room. He was twisted in a way only cats can achieve, belly up, his back legs splayed, his spine twisted so his front legs hung over the cushion's edge. Relaxed. She'd fed him.

She felt relaxed too, but her lack of tension seemed out of place. Since she'd agreed to work with Hughes, she was in a higher-stress situation, with more at stake than she'd had at the College of Policing. She realized it was because she was back at work, in her element. Her life was changing. Or rather, she had a chance to change it if she got a good result with this mission.

Had Peter felt this way when he went back to work after he recovered from his burns? Even now, years later, Peter hadn't fully recovered from the damage to his muscles and skin. He'd probably never fully recover from losing his wife and daughter. Yet he'd made decisions that moved him along the path he wanted to travel.

He was a good man, a man who was determined to move away from the abyss. Productive, caring, seeking to give love.

He'd delivered an angry sermon to her that rang with purpose. About how learning to give and receive love was the way back from grief and pain. Recognize that what you think you need may not be what you truly need. Make the decision to move forward. Do it. It sounded trite, but it was so hard to do.

And late tomorrow afternoon she'd meet with Novak, who was angry she'd talked with Bull and Costello. She'd never met him in person before, but on the phone he sounded like an officious little git. She knew how to play that type. She'd told him she suspected the Sreckos had been involved in the murder, and she had approached the detectives as part of her rogue investigation. He'd laughed and said he'd be happy to meet face-to-face.

So tomorrow would be interesting. For most of the day, she'd be meeting with Liz, going over logistics and procedures for the obs on Novak. She'd insisted Novak meet her at Nelson's Glory, a pub only a mile up the road from Liz's flat.

It also happened to be her favourite pub, the one where she and Peter had frequently met. Was that also a reason she'd insisted on meeting there?

She looked at Scratch. "Much to think about, laddie. Time to get ready for bed." Elaine rose, took her wine glass to the sink, and dropped the empty bottle in the bin. Scratch followed her and watched from the bed as the steam rose from her shower.

Friday morning, Brentford

Elaine sat at her kitchen table and poured herself another cup of coffee. Scratch lay on the floor, stretched in a sunbeam that streamed in through the French doors. She'd received a report early in the morning from Jenkins, who'd been watching Jacko the previous night. She read it through twice while munching buttered toast. What he described couldn't have happened to a more deserving person. Perhaps that's why she'd read it twice. She chided herself for the wicked thought, but only gently. The idea of Jacko being on the receiving end of a bit of rough held a certain attraction. The karmic wheel did come around, eventually. She brushed crumbs from her fingers, picked up her burner, and dialled.

Jenkins answered, "Yep."

"Interesting about Jacko. Your report from last night says two blokes assaulted him outside an illegal casino. Tell me what you left out."

"Not much," Jenkins replied. "Casino's in Fitzrovia, north end. We've known for some time he frequents it. Owes thousands. I've heard the place hasn't been shut down because a lot of high-stakes international wanking goes on there. So to speak. Not much for gambling, myself. Don't see the point."

"Me neither. So, two thugs beat him up, then took him inside. You left before he came out."

"You don't have any right to get on me about that. I don't report to you. I told Hughes I had to get home. I hadn't made arrangements."

His emotional flare puzzled Elaine, but she didn't pursue it. Instead, she said, "Sorry if I touched a nerve. I didn't mean anything by it, just a statement of fact. I wonder if he made it home."

"Hold on a mo'. Let me check." She heard Jenkins tapping a keyboard. A final heavy clack told her Jenkins was one of those persons who loved the committed finality of the "Enter" key. He was back a second later. "The CCTV tap shows his Jag's not at his house. Maybe he had an early court appearance." Elaine heard more clicking before Jenkins continued. "Wait for it . . . no, his schedule's clear for today. Interesting."

"Right. I'll have Bull or Liz take a run by the casino to see if his Jag's there."

"Any other questions?"

"I'm meeting with Novak this afternoon. I'll keep you posted."

"Listen. Novak's a shite with one agenda. Himself. Don't give him anything he doesn't earn." He rang off.

Elaine glanced at the time on her phone. She was meeting with Liz in an hour. As she brushed her teeth, she reflected that the Jenkins of today was diametrically different from the Jenkins she'd known months ago. Respectful. Professional. Perhaps it was time to show him more respect in return.

THIRTY-FIVE

Friday afternoon, Southwark

Elaine inhaled the familiar yeasty fug of the pub and stared into the dark pint in front of her on the table. Nelson's Glory was a traditional hand-pulled, oak-panelled, dart-boarded bit of England that her father had frequented during the family's early years in London, before he'd inherited the shoe business and moved them to Glasgow. She took a sip of the stout, its sweet, earthy tones flowing over her tongue, the bready aroma creeping up the back of her throat. Her tongue licked the froth from her upper lip.

She'd revisited the pub in the days after she'd joined the Met, as a nod to her deceased father and an attempt to establish a pied-a-terre in her new city. Fred, the now aging barman, had remembered her dad and welcomed her. Although she'd moved from the neighbourhood a few years later, she returned often to recharge, to watch the people of Southwark pass through. These days it was very often half full of tourists seeking a quiet pint or pub meal after the clangour and bustle of nearby Borough Market.

Most recently, it had been a meaningful place to meet Peter. They'd met here on their first date, if that's what it was. She'd been engaged in a murder investigation and hesitant to see him, wanting to put this persistent American behind her, expecting to have a polite pint and end the evening with a rushed goodbye-see-you-around. She lifted her gaze to the empty seat across the table. They had sat in this same nook. He'd been lighthearted and undemanding. A gentleman who instinctively understood the boundaries of a woman he respected. Inquisitive about her past and her future, interested but not prying. He'd stayed away from her present, knowing her devotion to the job and that she couldn't discuss the case—especially not with him.

Her eyes returned, downcast, to the pint. The memory of their first date cascaded into later, richer images. With him at the piano, playing Cole Porter tunes, improvising lyrics, laughing when they ran out of rude rhymes. Sitting at the kitchen table, listening to him philosophise about the horrors of mushy peas. In his bed, locking eyes and then mouths as their passion grew. Curled nude together in his big chair, silent, the scent of their lovemaking gathering warm under a duvet, the lights of Canary Wharf in the distance. She knew he was the kind of man who, once committed, would care for her until death. She had never told him she loved him. She didn't know if the reason was that she was honest—or afraid.

Why had she chosen this place to meet Novak? She needed her wits about her, and all the sentiment had become distracting. Hadn't she known the effect being here might have on her? A movement at the edge of her vision brought her back to the moment. Novak must have arrived.

"Hello, Elaine. I've been watching you stare at your pint for five minutes." Peter slid into the nook across from her. "I didn't expect to see you here." His blue eyes scanned her startled, open-mouthed face. He sipped his half-full pint of red Irish ale.

She struggled to find her voice. Finally, she took a deep breath. "I didn't expect to see you." She glanced at her mobile, lying on the table. Seven fifteen PM.

Peter sat back against the red leather and crossed his arms. "You're waiting for someone."

"Why are you here?" The question spilled out before she could stop it.

"I'm not stalking you. I stopped for a quick pint after work."

After work? She searched her memory. He'd taken a new job at Guy's Hospital three months ago. "Ah. You're not at Saint Stephen's anymore. Guy's is only a few blocks away."

"I come here a couple of times a week, but I never sit in this nook. I told myself I wouldn't unless you were here too."

"Yet you come anyway." She took a sip. "They have good beer."

"Yeah. We had good times here." He unfolded his arms. "For years I let fate, or whatever you call it, control me. Whatever happened wasn't my call. Iraq, the burns, losing Diana and Liza. I hadn't gambled, but I'd lost. I told myself my life was in someone else's hands. It was easier to accept that way. It kept my needs in check. The work was enough for a while. I met you, took a risk, and thought I'd won you. Then I lost both my job and the woman I loved. Again."

"I'm not completely gone."

"Aren't you? I wonder." His eyes gauged her face, the corners of his mouth turned up in a slight smile. "Perhaps not completely."

"I told you months ago that I had things to do before I could come back to you."

"Things to do. I know you needed time to recover, and maybe you felt like you couldn't trust a man to help you. I get that, but I admit it hurts that you couldn't trust me. You know what I think? I think those things you have to do involve pacing around in your own little prison cell."

"Really! And you know so much about it!" No sooner had she spoken than she realized what she'd done.

"What do you think I did for years? I paced. I didn't go anywhere, I stayed pissed off and measured walls and paced."

"Peter, I'm—" she began, but he ignored her and ploughed ahead.

"Life fucked me over!" He waved his hands in the air. "I thought to hell with everything! And after a couple of years, when raging hadn't helped, I made up something else. I told myself I was damaged. That I'd be alone forever. I kept trapping myself."

"You said there'd been a few other women before we met."

"There were a few. I told you they'd pitied me, but maybe it wasn't that. Maybe I wouldn't let them in."

Months ago, when she had offered passion, he had accepted it and returned it. She looked out the window. A fine drizzle floated down, shining the pavement. Overcoated pedestrians opened umbrellas or held their briefcases over their heads. Some ignored the misty drops and walked on.

When Peter spoke again, his voice had calmed. He reached out and placed his hand over hers. "Each of us builds our own cell, and we each hold the key. We let ourselves out when we're ready."

Am I ready? Have I lost the key? Here he is. She felt desirous but hesitant, like she'd felt the day she'd started university at Durham or the first time she'd walked into an incident room as a fresh young detective. She'd built a life and career facing challenges, but those challenges had been external. Now, her own heart and mind challenged her.

A cough caused both of them to look up. Novak stood at the end of the table, shaking his head, his black coat folded over his arm. "Such touching sentiment, both of you. Perhaps you should take selfies. If you're finished with the pop psychology lesson, Dr. Willend, I had an appointment with DCI Hope."

Peter didn't move. "I'm not done. You can wait over there somewhere. At the bar. Until we're finished."

Novak's voice edged into a police command tone. "This is official police business."

Peter didn't look up. "And this is official people business. Just guessing, but you're late, aren't you? What, twenty, thirty minutes?" He sipped his ale and made eye contact with Novak. "I don't know who you are, but you gave up your spot in line, so you'll be polite and wait your turn."

Elaine spoke, "DI Novak, give us a few minutes."

Novak scoffed and held his warrant card in front of Peter's face. "DI John Novak."

Peter laughed. His usually soft Texas accent hardened into a drawl, loud enough to carry across the room. "Well, my goodness. Look what we have here. A real live detective inspector. I don't know how, but you know my name already. Must be a real good detective. And you don't seem to care that DCI Hope here, your superior officer, is watching you make an ass out of yourself."

Peter slid from his seat and rose to his more than six-foot height. He looked down at Novak, who was a full six inches shorter. Conversations in the pub went quiet as the patrons became aware of the confrontation. Fred, the barman, stepped from behind the bar. Elaine motioned to him to stay back and slid to the edge of the nook, ready to intervene if it was called for.

Peter looked over Novak's head and scanned the attentive faces of the pub's few patrons. "In fact, everybody's watching you. Wondering what you'll do next. Will you be cool? Will you panic? But you know what, Mr. DI Novak? Whatever you do, you need to realize that warrant card doesn't give you the right to act like a fuck-witted douchebag."

Elaine stood and took gentle hold of Peter's hand. "It's alright," she said. In the same low voice, she told Novak, "It's best that you wait outside. I believe Fred, the barman, can find you a table under the awning." Novak sneered, so she continued. "Dr. Willend's right. I'm your superior officer, and I have some business to finish. Do as I ask until I'm ready for you, or I'll write you up for insubordination."

"You wouldn't—" he began, then looked up at her.

The barman had moved behind Novak. Elaine nodded at him. "Thanks, Fred."

"No worries, Ms. Hope." Fred motioned Novak to follow.

They sat as the barman escorted Novak out. Peter's solid presence across the table brought back the images she had visualized only a few minutes earlier, and triggered the sense of rightness she had felt. "I'm so sorry. You caught me by surprise, being here. I shouldn't have chosen this place to meet him. It was convenient, is all." She took his hand and twined her fingers in his. "But I'm not sorry I'm here. It's helped me find some perspective. I was thinking about us earlier, when you sat down. I've treated you badly. I . . ." Emotion closed her throat. She sniffed and blinked.

Peter squeezed her hand and spoke just above a whisper. "After what happened, you don't need to apologize. I know you need your space. I just want you to know what I've discovered. I held the keys to the cell I'd built. You hold yours too."

"Is moving to Texas part of your escape?"

He placed his other hand over hers. "Part of it. It's a fresh start for my career. I have to get it back on track. London's not the place."

"I'm a British cop, darling."

"And I love you for it." He lifted her hand to his lips and held it there. She felt the softness of his skin, the warmth of his breath. His closed eyes expressed a contentment she longed for herself. He finally opened them and laughed. "A cop, of all people, ought to know where the keys to our cells are."

She squeezed his hand. "I have a job to do, my first mission in months. It's an important one."

"I'm sure it is, for the Met and for you." He pointed at Nelson's exhortation before the fleet went into battle at Trafalgar, carved in the oak beam above the bar. "England expects . . ." He tipped his head to the door. "Fuckwit's part of it."

"Meeting with Novak is no replacement for being with you, but I need to see him now."

"Right. We'll talk soon."

She nodded. "Of course." He kissed her forehead, caressed her neck with his hand. She took it and held it to her lips. Her eyes followed him to the door, and she allowed that, right now, he looked as good as he had that first time they had met, nine months ago. As he passed under the awning, Novak stood and spoke. Peter ignored him and walked past, into the rain. She was still watching when Novak sat down across from her.

"Wasn't that touching."

Elaine watched Peter board a bus that would take him west on Southwark Street. She knew that in a little while he would take another bus that would cross Blackfriars Bridge, north towards his home. She didn't understand why he insisted on taking buses and not the tube. Perhaps she would ask him some day. She turned to face Novak but didn't reply.

He tsked. "You were reckless, you know. Getting romantically involved with a witness. Rutting like a ferret with a former suspect. All your years in the service, never set a foot wrong, but you go and boink the guy you released not a week after you make DCI. Definitely a yellow card, lady. Maybe red."

It wasn't that particular recklessness she regretted. "Grass me up, then."

"No use. Everyone knows, all the way to the Commissioner. I figure they're saving the lash for when you really cock it all up."

She'd had enough of his crap. "You didn't ask to meet so you could piss on me."

"Maybe a bit. You're either admired or despised. Not much in between. I admire you. You don't take shit from anyone; you're a mix of—"

"Why, DI Novak? One more chance or I bolt." She moved to get up.

Novak gestured appeasement. "I know you've talked the case over with Bull and Costello. I want to talk it over with you. There's more to it than you might think."

"And you're afraid I'll really cock it all up for you and send you to the sausage factory. Help me think right and maybe I won't."

"What have those two told you?"

Elaine gave a sardonic laugh and looked around. The pub was empty except for two customers seated at the other end of the long room, engaged in their own conversation. She drained her half-pint and signalled the barman. "Another half of the same, please, Fred." She looked at Novak, who nodded. "Two, then. We might be here awhile."

After Fred had set the beers on the table, she said, "I'll start. You were in the NCA and got reassigned to a murder investigation. Your team was cobbled on the fly, including Bull and Costello. Costello's a brand-new sergeant, but he's running the incident room. I can see doing that if Murder Investigation is a bit short-handed, but we're no more short-handed now than we ever are. When things get tight, we bring in some likely candidates from other parts of CID, ship in some uniforms, and keep going. But we don't bring in a new senior investigating officer from another organization. So I'm interested. I asked myself why this murder is different."

He smirked. "Because it touched on an operation we're running."

She sipped her ale and placed the glass carefully on the table. "Come on. We who? I don't want to have to pull teeth. Metaphorically speaking, of course."

Novak leaned back and looked at her with hooded eyes. "Don't get melodramatic with me, Hope."

Insubordinate ass. "I'm DCI Hope or ma'am to you, Novak.

NCA or not. And melodramatic means something different to a crazy woman on a mission than it does to you." She leaned across the table. "You'd do well to remember that."

She continued in a quieter voice. "You asked for this meeting, so you're buying. Talk."

"Financial Crimes, NCA. Money laundering. National, not just London. The Home Office gives national oversight. The mayor's office is concerned about Lights Out London."

"And the poor headless sod lying in the mortuary triggered your Operation Whatsit?"

"Operation Wedge, as in thin end of. We think they fucked up by killing him." He took a sip of his ale. "Quite good. You know your beer."

"They?"

Novak shook his head and smiled. "The dirty money flows into tax havens in the Channel Islands, or the Caribbean, somewhere offshore."

"But they aren't satisfied with just stashing it. They want to grow it."

"True. But remember, these people do it so they can live the high life. Fancy cars, big cigars, and beautiful women they need to find nests for. World-class shopping and clubs to entertain them. So they scrub-scrub-scrub."

She sipped her beer. "And come to London. You must have heard the same presentation I did last week. All interesting. But it doesn't answer my question. Why a special team?"

"Why does the Met ever form a special team?"

"Don't be coy, Novak. I'll make it easy. Complete this sentence with a sensible answer: The Met formed a special team because . . ."

"There are those in law enforcement who profit from the money laundering. We needed a team outside of any particular chain of command."

"So, police corruption. Any chance of a result?"

"These things are sensitive. We have to tread lightly."

"You've had a good team for over a week, and that's all you can say?"

"Let's cut the crap. My case has nothing to do with your Srecko obsession, so stay away. Period. I don't want to hear of you snooping around, meeting with your two puppies. You're on the sick. Act like it. If you freelance this one, you'll be out on your sweet arse."

A corruption investigation masked as a murder enquiry made no sense. Who was Novak investigating? From what Bull and Costello had told her, she couldn't tell where he was pointing the investigation. Was he trying to expose a murderous cop?

Elaine drained her glass and stood. "Is that why you called this meeting? To threaten me?" As she walked towards the door, she waved to Fred and jerked her head towards Novak. "Later, mate. It's his shout."

THIRTY-SIX

Friday evening, Mortlake

Fiona checked her mirror and changed lanes. The traffic on the M3 was moving north towards London at a steady pace. She would be at the Mortlake house soon.

She'd called Jonny before she'd left and told his voicemail she would be home by seven PM and needed to talk about something important. He hadn't replied, so she rang him again. Jonny's voice message sounded over the radio speakers, "This is Commander—"

She ended the call just as the Range Rover's tires thumped on the expansion joints of the Winchfield railroad bridge. Two miles later her phone chirped, and Jonny's name displayed on the screen. She pressed the button on her steering wheel.

"Hello, Fee. Can't be home by seven. I'm in Oxford. Conference with the Thames Valley Police. What do you need?"

"I need to talk. In person, conference or no. Something's happened and I—we—need to take care of it. I'll meet you at home. When can you be there?"

"Where are you? It sounds like you're driving."

"On the M3, back from Waleham. I'll be there in about an hour."

"Can't you tell me over the phone? We're on a short break."

The man was truly self-centred. "Jonny, I already said. It's . . . it's something that can—what am I saying?—that *will* affect both our lives. Probably your career. We need to talk."

"Jacko?"

"Something to do with him. I need your help, and you need to listen."

She heard voices in the background, then Jonny, muffled. Maybe she should just blurt it out. Maybe telling him wasn't as complex as she thought. "Jonny—"

He was back. "Alright. I can leave in an hour. I'll call you when I get to the M4."

"Jonny!" He'd rung off.

She jabbed at the red icon on the display. He'd leave in an hour and a half, more like, if then. A glance at the dashboard clock told her it was just past six PM. She'd be lucky if he got home by nine thirty. She shifted in the seat and focused on the road ahead.

The dashboard clock said 6:47 PM when she turned the engine off. The house was dark. It wouldn't be the first time Jonny had forgotten to leave the upstairs landing light on. She retrieved her large damask travel bag from the boot. Halfway up the garden walk to her front door, she stopped.

The motion detector, which normally flooded the front garden with light when someone entered the gate, hadn't triggered. She waved her arms, but no light. She retrieved her mobile from her pocket, swiped its flashlight app and held it high in front of her.

The front door was ajar.

Fiona fled back to the Range Rover, scrambled inside, and slammed the door shut. She started the engine, breathing deeply to control her panic. Where to go? The Ship pub was only two blocks away. There would be bright lights and people. Neighbours, maybe.

She parked at the pub less than a minute later, backing into a space in the row of cars that lined the street. Still behind the wheel, she dialled Jonny. Voicemail, damn the man. She ended the call without leaving a message. Her breathing was almost back to normal, and her thinking was clearing. The situation would be difficult to explain to the 999 operator. She'd keep it simple and to the point. They'd probably think she was daft if she mentioned murderous gangsters.

She identified herself as the wife of Met Commander Jonathan Hughes and gave her personal code word, *Trooper.* After determining she wasn't in immediate danger, the operator said they would queue the call to the next available officers. It would probably be a half hour. They would notify Jonny.

But what if someone was lying in wait inside the house? She may have just placed officers at risk. Elaine would know what to do and say. She pressed the speed dial.

"Fiona, are you back in London yet?" Elaine's voice was guarded.

"Thank God you answered. I need your help. I'm back, but the house has been burgled. What should I do?"

"Are you in danger? Where are you?"

"I didn't see anyone, and I didn't go in. I'm in the car park outside The Ship pub. It's just down the road from our gate."

"Okay. Stay where you are, and I'll request an armed response team. How do you know the house was burgled?"

"The front door was open, and the lights on the security system didn't come on. They should come on automatically."

"Right. I'll warn the officers." Silence for a few seconds, then Elaine asked, "Have you called Jonny?"

Fiona sighed. "Yes, but he didn't answer. He's supposed to be on his way back from Oxford. If he left when he said he would, he'll be here around nine thirty or so. The 999 operator said they would call him. Can you meet me here?"

"You'd be safer with an armed officer."

"What would I say to an officer I don't know? I can talk to you, Elaine!"

"I won't abandon you. You don't have to say anything more to the officers than you told the emergency operator. I'll explain the danger to the gold commander and ask for an Armed Response Vehicle, but they may want someone besides me to be with you. Remember, I'm officially on leave. I'll do my best to get assigned. Just trust me. I'll call you back once it's all in place." Elaine rang off.

Trust me. In Fiona's experience, honouring that phrase hadn't paid off. Elaine seemed afraid to commit. What wasn't she saying? *Trust, my arse. It's time to hide and watch out for myself.*

Fiona looked up and down the road. The moon was almost full. To her left, Chiswick Bridge glowed above the Thames, crowned by the twinkling headlights of passing cars and buses. Tall, slender cypress swayed along the opposite bank of the river. Just across the road to her right, the abandoned Stag Brewery loomed dark, casting a deep shadow on a brick ramp at the foot of the street. Rowers and scullers used the ramp to carry their boats to and from the water. Perfect. She idled the Range Rover to just past the ramp, then backed slowly down. Straining her neck to see out her lowered window, she manoeuvred as close to the water line as she dared. From the driver's seat she could watch the street in both directions, including the pub and its parking area. She raised the window, turned on the seat heater and watched.

THIRTY-SEVEN

Friday evening, Brentford

"Who's the gold commander tonight?" Elaine needed to engage a higher authority as quickly as possible.

"Assistant Commissioner Collins is nominal gold," the 999 operator replied.

Elaine gritted her teeth. "You said 'nominal.' Who's his deputy?"

"Commander Kenwood, ma'am."

"Please put me through."

A few seconds later, Kenwood was on the line. She gave a quick recap of the night's events and requested an ARV.

"An ARV for a burglary? Why?" Kenwood needed convincing before he sent armed officers to a scene.

"Because Commander Hughes's wife may be in mortal danger, sir. If you can trust me, I'll explain later. But we need action now."

Kenwood didn't reply immediately; she could hear his breath in her earpiece. Finally, he spoke. "Why did she call you and not Hughes? Aren't you on compassionate leave?"

Was she on compassionate leave if she was working with Hughes? How much should she reveal? "I'm not yet back on the sick. She called Hughes, but got his voicemail. She called me next because . . . because I was involved in something that happened last week, sir. She trusts me."

"Seems like an awful lot of trust flowing in your direction, Hope." Kenwood was probably asking himself why he should believe her. It's what she'd do. He needed more than just her word.

"Yes, sir. If you can contact Commander Hughes, tell him it's about Operation Spectra. He can explain—"

"I have no idea what Spectra is." Kenwood hesitated again. "Right. I'll issue the orders. Hold the line while I conference emergency services."

A few seconds later he was back on, talking with the 999 operator. "Send the closest ARV, with one on standby. All available officers in Barnes Common and East Sheen to converge as backup and traffic control. DCI Hope is silver commander. Put it in action."

"Executing now, sir," the operator replied. "Sergeant J. Holloway is listed to be bronze commander, sir."

Elaine took a deep breath and exhaled. She'd worked with Jamie Holloway and thought him to be among the best. "Thank you, sir."

She dumped her half-eaten salad in the bin. On her way down the stairs, she pulled on her donkey jacket and clipped her radio to the collar. A couple of pats on the coat pockets made sure everything was in place—her asp snuggled in the right pocket next to her wallet and warrant card. She dialled Fiona as she walked to her car in the parking garage under her building.

"An ARV and several officers are en route to your house. They'll seal it off. They've named me silver commander, so I'll be there in twelve, maybe fifteen minutes. Stay put and watch for a police car. Where are you exactly?"

A pause before Fiona answered, "No, I'll flash my lights when I see your BMW. No one else."

So trust wasn't flowing from Fiona. "Okay. Fair enough. Just sit tight. I'll be blues and twos. Hang on a minute while I switch to hands-free."

"I'm okay for now," Fiona replied. "I'll call if something happens." She rang off.

Elaine turned on her blues as soon as she exited the parking garage gate. She turned left onto Brentford High Street, hit the siren button, and upshifted to second gear, holding the engine RPM high. Already, radio chatter was beginning as officers were advised of the situation and rerouted.

Elaine turned her attention to her driving. A clear space ahead, a parade of shops on the right. Up to third gear now. Carry-outs, a bookmaker's, and a food store reeled past. Over the radio an ARV gave an estimated time on scene of four minutes. A bus clogged her lane a hundred yards ahead. She eased to the right for a better view, saw an oncoming car, and pulled back behind the huge vehicle. When the bus moved left at a stop, she was clear.

Once past the McDonald's, Brentford High Street opened ahead of her, wide and fairly straight as far as the Kew Bridge. To her right, the dark open space of Waterman's Park, which ran along the Thames, meant no worries about vehicles from that direction. Elaine kept her speed steady at about fifty miles per hour, relying on her lights and siren to clear her path. Her mind reverted to Hughes and Novak.

Fiona's doubt had stung, but in her defence, recent loyalties had betrayed her. Fiona was in trouble because her own weakness and a series of bad decisions had turned a dilemma into an existential threat. True, the woman was working her way out of it and deserved help. Elaine had helped her, but none of Fiona's troubles were Elaine's fault.

After hearing Novak's claim of an NCA corruption investigation, she'd re-evaluated the story Hughes had told her. Which one of them was lying? Both? Neither? She was sure she wasn't getting the whole truth from either of them.

Novak had the power and hierarchy of the NCA behind him. How else could he have pulled the team together? From what she'd learned from Bull and Costello, he might be bent. Bent or straight, he struck her as the kind of cop who marched to his personal agenda.

Hughes could be doing the same. Despite his betrayal of Fiona, to Elaine he felt straighter than Novak. He'd manoeuvred her extended leave and given her control of an undercover operation. Somehow, he'd managed to enlist Jenkins, whose exact status she didn't yet understand. Was he MI5 or an operator from some other shadowy group? Either way, Hughes must have had budgetary approval to hire him from somewhere high up in the Met, or maybe even the Home Office. Was she now in the middle of a power struggle between the NCA and the Met?

Hughes, Novak, Fiona. Did any loyalty she owed to those three override her personal goals? If so, who to trust?

She slowed at the intersection before Kew Bridge. Cars and buses moved aside as she veered right, blue lights flashing and siren blaring, past the old hotel and across towards Kew Green. She needed to report. "This is DCI Hope, silver. Southbound A205, ETA seven minutes. Firearms officers and responders, seal off the house front and rear, and wait. Electricity may be tampered with."

"Received, silver. This is bronze. Where is the victim?"

The voice on the radio belonged to Sergeant Holloway. As bronze commander, he was responsible for direct supervision of the officers on the scene. "Hi, Jamie. Good to hear your voice. Victim left the scene. I'm on my way to collect her."

"Received, ma'am. Hughes checked in with gold command. His wife's not answering her mobile."

"Received." Elaine set a steady, safe speed and resumed her thoughts. Picking the wrong side would be death to her career. It would end any chance of finding out who had betrayed her and of bringing Anton Srecko to justice. Even if she picked the right side, there were no guarantees. And frankly, neither Hughes nor Novak rang completely true in her mind. In spite of Fiona's weakness and her degrading affair with Jacko, she seemed to Elaine to be no worse than a good woman gone astray, a decent person committed to changing her life. She deserved help.

Only one path felt right. Who would she be, if she wasn't there for Fiona?

She steered the BMW around the hard right turn at the bottom of the North Sheen Cemetery. Two minutes more. Her communicator clicked.

"Bronze. Lane and house are secure front and rear. Instructions, Silver?"

"Do not enter until I'm there with Mrs. Hughes."

"Received."

Blues flashed through the intersection with Clifford Road, a few hundred yards ahead, moving north towards Fiona's house. Instead of turning to follow them, she continued straight through the intersection. Past the new brewery, she slowed and turned left down a narrow, walled lane overhung by plane trees. At the end of the lane, the Thames glimmered in the moonlight. She turned off the siren and parked crosswise, blocking the road. As soon as she got out of her car, headlights flashed by the river. A dark Range Rover crept out of the shadows and stopped next to Elaine.

Fiona emerged. "Nine minutes. What do I do now?"

"Leave your motor here and ride with me. Hughes has been trying to call you."

"I left him a message after I spoke with you. Told him what a shite he was and that he and I are done. I'm not interested in what he has to say."

"Did you tell him about the murder?"

"No. Too complicated for the phone."

"Right then, park your beast, and get in."

Once inside the police cordon, Elaine sought out Sergeant Holloway and introduced Fiona. Holloway took Fiona aside to ask her questions about the layout of the house, then gathered his officers for a briefing. Within minutes, torches flared around the back corner of the house, and a few seconds later a light shone from the window above the front entrance.

Holloway spoke softly to Elaine and Fiona, who stood near him. "The electricity main was off, but the intruders put an axe through the security system conduit. My advice, Commander Hughes needs to invest in an upgraded system with battery backup. We're going in now."

Using a bullhorn, Holloway shouted, "Armed police. Put your weapons down and come out." After ten seconds, he shouted again. When he still got no response, he motioned to his officers, who advanced to the front door, pushed it open, and entered the house. Voices from the house began shouting, "Clear! Clear!" A few seconds later, lights appeared through windows on the ground and upper floors.

Holloway led Elaine and Fiona into the house. The air had a sickly sweet scent, like spilled perfume. Despite that, whoever had broken in appeared to have left the home's contents intact. Elaine had expected to see wanton destruction, but in the front reception room the furniture and bookcases appeared undisturbed. Ceramics and small bronze sculptures were intact, apparently in their places.

"Do you see anything missing?" Elaine asked.

Fiona shook her head. "Nothing apparent. Everything looks in order. Don't burglars usually turn out drawers and cabinets?"

"What's the smell? It's too thick for air freshener."

"It's my perfume."

An officer motioned to Elaine from the foot of the stairs. "Ma'am, I think you need to see this." He pointed up.

Elaine and Fiona followed him to a bedroom door, which he opened. The perfume stench increased noticeably. Fiona took hold of Elaine's arm. "It's my room." When they entered, the shock affected them far beyond the odour.

The intruders had rampaged through her room. Chairs had been smashed, curtains pulled from the windows. Make-up and perfume jars had been opened and emptied. All the drawers from her dresser had been turned out and lay splintered on the floor. Their contents, mostly lingerie and knit items, had been ripped apart and scattered throughout the room, along with all the bed linens.

It was the bed, though, that chilled Elaine. The mattress had been ripped open, probably with the large kitchen knife that protruded from it near the head of the bed. The slash had been stained a deep, rust-red colour.

"Ma'am?" The officer who had opened the room pointed behind them. "On the wall."

Elaine and Fiona turned. Elaine's knees went weak. Her right leg nearly collapsed as Fiona leaned into her. Together they swayed, off balance. The officer reached out and took Elaine's arm to help steady them.

"Are you all right, ma'am? Do you need a chair?"

"No, thanks. I'll be fine." She put her arm around Fiona, who stood with her mouth wide open, staring at the rust-red letters scrawled across the wall's cream-yellow surface.

KILL U BITCH!! Slashes of crimson pigment had run down the wall in rivulets that puddled on the floor.

THIRTY-EIGHT

Friday night, Brentford

Hughes ran his fingers through his dark hair. "Fee, someone has threatened your life. How can I help you if you won't let me?"

"I'm not going to talk to you, and I'm not going anywhere with you, Jonny. I told you, we're done."

Fiona and Hughes stood in the sitting room of Elaine's flat. The Mortlake house had been sealed as a crime scene, and the forensics technicians wouldn't be finished for several hours. When Jonny had suggested they go to a hotel, with a police guard, Fiona had flatly refused. She instead said she needed to think, and asked if they could go to Elaine's flat. Elaine agreed, as long as officers were stationed at the entrances. Yet even there, Fiona had refused to answer Hughes's questions, despite his exasperated attempts at persuasion. She stared out the French doors into the night while her husband stood a few feet behind her.

The new threat made quick action imperative. Elaine saw no choice but for Fiona to give her testimony and move into witness protection. She sat silent, watching Hughes grow frustrated and Fiona become more intractable. She weighed how to end the stalemate without violating Fiona's trust.

"If I may suggest . . ." Elaine sat forward and cleared her throat. "Emotions are running high. With all due respect, sir, perhaps Fiona will speak with me. I'll record what she says and send it to you. If she's agreeable, that is." Fiona's quick glance told Elaine she agreed.

Hughes didn't notice. "I have to ask, Hope, why are you involved? Why did my wife call you?"

"We met outside Gionfriddo's the other night. I suppose I should have told you, sir. Someone accosted her on the pavement, and I happened to be there."

"Gionfriddo's?" A look of fear crossed Hughes's face. "You didn't bother to tell me this? Either of you? Elaine, I'm giving you a chance to recover your career, and this is how you show your grat—"

Fiona spun away from the door. "It's always about you, isn't it, Jonny? You don't do anything out of concern for anyone else. You lied your way into our marriage. You make me sick with your posing and your deceit. Just shut the fuck up. I'll talk to Elaine. She'll do the right thing, and it won't be based on her ego. Now I want you to go away. I won't say a word until you do."

Elaine needed keep things moving forward. "Sir, I need time to brief Fiona, and we need to keep her safe. Perhaps you might discuss what to do with AC Collins?"

Hughes resisted the idea but mumbled agreement when Fiona refused to budge yet again. After he'd gone, Elaine motioned Fiona to sit at the kitchen table, and began. "Consider this a rehearsal. I'm going to ask you a few questions, and I expect answers. When you answer, don't volunteer any information I don't specifically ask for. Understood?"

She turned on the record app of her mobile phone and began asking questions about what Fiona had done and seen on the night of the murder—short, simple, step-by-step questions, carefully leading her through the evening's pertinent events. She stayed well clear of questions about Fiona's sexual relationship with Jacko.

After Fiona related her stealthy walk home from the station,

Elaine asked, "Why did you think we'd arrest you for not report-ing the murder?"

Fiona cleared her throat. "Jacko. He said it was perverting the course of justice to run like we did and not report it imme-diately, and we could get prison." Her face was slack, tired. "He's a Crownie. I didn't know any better. I never talked about legal-ities with David or Jonny."

"What else did Jacko say?"

"He said he didn't tell them who I am because he was trying to protect me, but I know him. I'm his bargaining piece."

"Do you know who 'them' is?"

Fiona shook her head. "No. All I saw was the one guy, and he was in a balaclava, dressed in black, head to foot. With the shotgun."

Fiona wrapped her arms around herself, gripping her body. Her voice rasped, "He asked if Jacko was trying to bribe him with me! Not for the first time! Displaying the goods!"

Nothing Elaine could ask would extract more truth. She stayed silent.

"And he said you weren't part of the debt."

"That's right. He was clear on that."

It made sense based on what they knew about Jacko's gam-bling debts. The murder was an execution, staged to intimi-date him.

"Okay, then. Right now we just wait until Hughes calls back. You'll get protection, and Collins should allow a neutral safe house given our suspicions about Novak."

"I want to get this over with and move on." Fiona stood and paced the length of the kitchen. "I got fucked over because I was too bloody weak to stand up for myself and make my own deci-sions. Now I've got two shites to deal with, and I've had enough. It's ended and it bloody well won't happen again."

Fiona stopped pacing and sat at the table across from Elaine.

"I gave up control when I agreed to this sex farce." She

leaned over the table. "I've been fucked by that bastard at least once a month for almost two years now. Forced to do disgusting things. Two years of anger and shame and guilt, consuming me. I strayed from who I am."

Elaine sat silent. Most would judge Fiona and not even consider what she'd endured. Abused by that pig because she felt helpless to demand otherwise.

"Last year you were raped and disfigured by that criminal, and that's horrible, something no woman should ever have to endure. Now you're hard. Angry. You said you've got this justice mission. Vengeance, more like it. I saw that board in your bedroom. I think this mission, your hate, is eating you alive."

"Right. What's your point?"

"If I can change, you can too. You said Peter's a good man. Maybe he can help you."

Elaine's burner buzzed. It was Hughes. "I talked to Collins, and he won't budge. You're to deliver Fiona to Kensington nick as soon as possible. Novak's waiting."

Elaine couldn't believe it. Hughes had failed. "That's outrageous, sir. Her life's been threatened. Why wouldn't he agree?"

"We don't have anything solid against Novak, and the Met can't show favouritism just because she's my wife. So it falls back on police protocol. Novak's the SIO—he'll interview her and decide what to do."

Elaine thought it was a load of bollocks. Something else was going on. Had Hughes even tried to talk to Collins? Was Hughes running Spectra as a rogue operation?

It was time to leave. She had no choice but to play it out.

Forty-five minutes later, Elaine stopped her BMW a block short of the entrance to Kensington nick and turned to Fiona. "Right, then. You understand? Once more, quick. Novak's an abrasive git, and he'll try to get under your skin from the start, so what do you do?"

Fiona stared straight ahead through the windscreen. "Don't

get emotional. Never answer quickly. Think and breathe before speaking. Stick to the facts. No more, no less."

"And?"

"Answer questions directly with short sentences. Stick to what I saw and heard. Don't expand on anything, don't volunteer anything, don't apologize for anything."

"Good. What else?"

"Don't speak unless spoken to. Don't speak for Jacko or anyone else. Don't give opinions, even when asked." Fiona sighed. "He'll press me about the affair, won't he?"

"Definitely. Novak and whoever's with him will switch between empathetic and bullying. Don't let them pry lurid details from you. Just don't answer. If he asks about Hughes, say he needs to talk to your husband."

"What if he says he won't protect me if I don't talk?"

"He'll say that, but when he does, laugh at him and tell him you know he's bluffing. You're the wife of a Met police officer, and you've been threatened. If he abandoned you, he'd never set foot in an English nick again. The Met will protect you, no matter what he says. He'll say he's with the NCA and has special powers. Doesn't matter. Everyone will back you, all the way up to the Commissioner herself. You're scared for your life, and you haven't broken any laws. Got it?"

Fiona nodded. Elaine studied her face. At first, Fiona had been emotional, nervous, sighing, her voice shaking at times. But in the last fifteen minutes, she'd calmed. She appeared to be as ready as could be expected for having so little real prep time.

Elaine continued. "Whatever happens, don't lie. If they catch you lying, it throws everything you've said into doubt, and they'll spend hours picking it apart. You can be charged, and you might do time at Her Majesty's pleasure. If you're being pressed and you think you're losing control, focus on something important to you."

"Right. Andy, Stella, Peg, and Fritz." Fiona looked straight ahead and smiled. "I'm ready. Let's go."

"After you identify yourself, before you answer any questions, what do you ask?"

"I ask if I'm being charged with an offense, and if they say yes, I ask for my solicitor and clam up."

"And?"

"Don't ask for a lawyer if I'm not being charged."

"Right." Elaine rang the desk sergeant and identified herself. "We'll be there in two minutes."

Novak and several uniforms attended the car when Elaine pulled up to the entrance. She got out and started up the steps to the nick, but Novak blocked her way. "You can go in, Hope, but you can't watch or listen. I won't allow it."

"What? Are you daft? I brought her in. I've got a—"

"A right to be there? You bloody well don't. I decide. You're not on this case, nowhere near, even. Which makes me wonder why you're bringing in the poor little wretch. Why did she call you? Why not Hughes?"

Elaine stared down at him but didn't answer.

"No beefy barman to back you up here? You're supposed to be on the sick, so at least fake it. Go home and drink some cocoa. Shag your American doctor. I don't give a bloody toss what you do as long as you're not anywhere near my witness."

THIRTY-NINE

Friday night, New Scotland Yard

"Novak's being a shite, as expected. He won't allow any of us to observe." Hughes sat at his desk, twisting a paper clip, staring at the photos on his office wall. "It's his prerogative. He said we'll get a transcript."

"What about the safe house?" Elaine glanced at Jenkins, who stared at Hughes.

"I told him he had to put Bull on one shift, Costello on the other. Otherwise, I call in Security and Protection. How long has it been?"

"Fifteen minutes since the last time you asked, sir. They've had her just over two hours." Elaine watched as Hughes's paper clip broke. He flicked it in the direction of the waste bin, picked up another, and began worrying at it.

"You rehearsed her, right?" Hughes asked. "On the way here?"

Elaine only narrowly avoided rolling her eyes. "As much as I could. She knows to clam up if they start to stray away from the immediate investigation." It was as polite a way as she could think of to say, "I told her to keep you out of it." She looked at Jenkins, who did roll his eyes.

Hughes was too busy staring at the wall to notice either of

them. He harrumphed and continued to fidget. Finally, he threw the paper clip on his desk and began to pace.

Jenkins stood. "I don't see any reason for me to be here. It's after midnight, and if I don't get some sleep, I won't be worth a bloody thing tomorrow."

Elaine took the cue. "Same here, sir. We all need some sleep. Tomorrow could be a busy day." They both started for the door.

"You're leaving?" Hughes looked surprised. "What about Fiona?"

"Nothing much we can do," Elaine replied. His wife was safe, so why all the worry? "We'll follow up in the morning."

"What if he won't tell us where she is?"

"That's why we have Bull and Costello," Jenkins said. He made eye contact with Elaine before speaking to Hughes. "It might be best if you don't know, sir. The fewer who know, the better."

"What are you implying? Do I need to remind you both that we're investigating Novak for corruption?"

Jenkins shook his head and left the room without responding.

"It's standard procedure, sir," Elaine said. "Usually need-to-know. If there's nothing else, I'm for home too. I've gotten precious little sleep these last few days."

As she left, she heard Hughes muttering under his breath. She caught up with Jenkins at the lift down to the parking garage. "God, I couldn't take his fretting much longer. Something's odd about it. Over the top."

Jenkins pressed the button for the lowest level, which was reserved for those without offices in the building. "From the recording you made, it's not like she's going to jail. You don't think she lied? Left anything out? Something he knows about?"

"No. She's determined to put it all behind her. Hughes, Jacko. The last thing she wants is to cock it up by lying."

"It's not like he's a devoted husband. Him and Cranwell, all these years."

Elaine heard the words, but it took her brain a few seconds to react. "You're saying Hughes and Cranwell are a couple. I hadn't put it together, but it makes sense. Something Fiona said. How long have you known?"

"A couple of days. A retired detective I know told me it's not widely known."

The lift opened, and they emerged into the gray concrete of the visitor car park, empty now except for their cars. Elaine walked with Jenkins towards his black Saab.

"I feel powerless working outside normal procedures. I thought Spectra was a real operation. Doesn't look like it now that we've crossed into the murder investigation. I don't think Hughes talked to Collins at all."

Jenkins scoffed. "I agree. I think Hughes is running some kind of cover-up. I'm just glad he got Bull and Costello on the protection team."

"Fiona told me Jacko's been blackmailing him for years." She felt an obligation to share what she knew with Jenkins. "I think he's afraid she'll let slip the reason. Jacko told her that years ago Hughes covered up an evidence cock-up to protect Cranwell. She said a murderer got off because of it. If she lets that out, this whole operation is buggered."

Jenkins stared into space, clearly taken aback. After a few moments he shook his head. "Well, I guess we'll find out when we get the transcript. Or when Professional Standards pays a visit to Hughes. Nothing to be done right now."

Saturday morning, Brentford

Elaine woke and looked at her phone. Five hours sleep. A luxury. Scratch lay heavy across her ankles, so she decided to let him sleep. It wouldn't be long before his insistent mews would signal he was ready for breakfast.

Lately she'd felt bad about Scratch's breakfast. Sometimes, in the last two weeks, she was out the door so quickly in the morning, poor Scratch missed breakfast entirely. Fortunately, she kept a small bowl of kibbles on the floor next to his water. Judging from the numbness in her feet, her neglect hadn't affected his weight. Maybe she wasn't such a sluggard at keeping him happy.

Could she keep Peter happy? Maybe, if they lived in London. Her flat would be too small for Peter's Bösendorfer piano, though. Could they share Kate's house? That wouldn't be too bad for a while. Kate was solid, brilliant, and worldly. The woman had some depth. They'd connected during their talks last summer at the cottage in Devon.

But Peter would be in Texas.

Her burner pinged. "Good morning, Liz. Tell me good news."

"Morning, guv. Bull's confirmed the address where they're keeping Fiona. I'll text it to you. Costello's on until seven tonight; Bull takes over until seven in the morning. He said Novak was outraged the witness protection team specified them. Said it was because of you. Called you names I won't repeat. Very personal."

"It's mutual. You have obs on Novak today, right?"

"Yep. I'll pick him up at the nick."

"Okay. I'll be at Hughes's office, reviewing Fiona's statement. Transcripts ought to be ready. I seriously don't look forward to that. Hughes was an emotional wreck last night. I think he was more worried about himself than he was about Fiona. She told him she's going to leave him when this is over."

"I don't know if that's a shame or not," Liz said. "Sometimes I wonder if love and marriage is worth it. Just leads to misery much of the time."

"Hmm." Elaine didn't know what to say to that. "I need to put some clothes in the wash before I leave. Anything else?"

"Out of jeans and jumpers, eh? I'm off, boss." She ended the call with a giggle.

"Jeans and jumpers, my arse," Elaine said to a silent phone. "I wear the best clothes Marks and Spencer offers."

Moments later the text message with an address in Hanwell appeared, an area only a few miles from her flat. Elaine forwarded it to Jenkins.

FORTY

"Looks like she did a great job. Told Novak what she saw and heard, and clammed up when she needed to." Elaine set the transcript of Fiona's interview on the desk, and swivelled her chair to look at Hughes. He stood with his hands clasped behind his back, gazing out the window at The London Eye across the Thames. "Sir?"

"What? Oh. Yes, she did herself proud. Didn't know she had it in her."

Elaine figured that was why he'd married Fiona in the first place—he thought she was weak. Malleable. Maybe she had been, then. Hughes seemed calmer this morning than last night. Perhaps he'd gotten enough sleep or, more likely, had medicated.

"Who's watching this morning?" he asked.

"Costello until evening. Then Bull overnight."

"Liz?"

"On Novak. She should be checking in shortly." They had covered this ground a half hour ago. Was Hughes stressed or over-medicated?

"Do you suppose they gave us the entire transcript?"

"I have no way of knowing for sure, but it didn't appear

edited to me. Sir, I'm going out for a walk and some fresh air. I'll check in with Liz and Jenkins."

"Ah. Any word on Jacko?"

Not since yesterday morning, sir. I'll call Jenkins about it and let you know if there's any news." She left the office as quickly as she dared.

Elaine turned up her collar at the chilly wind and walked north on the Victoria Embankment. As usual, she stopped and stood silent for a few moments in front of the Battle of Britain Monument, then walked on.

Hughes was probably afraid that Fiona had spilled about the blackmail. She couldn't blame him. It didn't matter that his and Cranwell's transgression had happened decades in the past; once it was known he had perverted the course of justice, it would be the end of his career and very likely Cranwell's too. Policing was an unforgiving profession.

She dialled Jenkins. "News of Jacko?"

"His car wasn't at the casino. He didn't turn up for court today, and he's not home. We're checking ANPR records, but nothing yet. They could have masked the number plate or replaced it."

Elaine thought for a moment. "Doesn't make sense to kill him. The usual method is to make him pay off some of it, but let him keep enough debt to maintain their hold. I'll have Hughes ask for his bank records. Where are you?"

"Hanwell Cemetery, about two hundred yards from the safe house. I can see it, just. Can't get much closer without attracting attention. What about Novak?"

"Calling Liz next. I'll let you know if she has anything."

Liz had nothing to report. Novak had been at the nick all day long. Perhaps Bull and Costello would have something to report tonight. Elaine turned back towards New Scotland Yard. She'd take Jacko's bank records home and spend the afternoon going over them. She couldn't stand another minute with Hughes. The man was 'round the bend.

Saturday afternoon, Kensington

Where the hell's Novak? Liz checked the rear-view mirror and frowned. She was wearing a dark blue knit cap, and the strands of mousy brown hair protruding from under it triggered memories of her Aunt Mae, who had given Liz bloody hell the only other time she'd dyed her flame-red curls.

When Liz was thirteen, she'd wanted to go Goth with some friends. The resulting raven black curls had looked so alien to her, she'd cried for hours, like she'd lost herself. Her Aunt Mae had grabbed a handful of her own unremarkable locks, and waved them in front of Liz's eyes. "Look at this! Every time you go out, there are people who covet your hair! Women who would pay thousands for a wig made from it. What were you thinking, child?" She had gone on about it for ten minutes, until Liz had fled upstairs, wailing.

She should have bought a wig. Liz tucked the boring strays under the cap and resumed watching the mirror. A knock on the passenger window startled her. A young uniform cop motioned her to lower it.

"Hello, ma'am. I notice you've been stopped here awhile. May I ask your business?"

He was about the same age as her. "One moment." She retrieved her warrant card, opened it for him, and smiled.

He smiled back. "Excellent likeness, DC Barker. Do you need any help?"

"Obs," Liz whispered. She continued smiling but shook her head, then jerked it to the right a couple of times. Maybe he'd get the idea and move on.

His smile grew to a grin. "I see. I'm PC Stafford. Derek. Don't hesitate to call me if you need anything." He continued up the pavement.

Ten minutes later, Novak's gray Volvo exited the parking area behind the Kensington nick. She started her car as he passed her, waited a few seconds, then began the tail.

Dusk was gathering by the time Novak turned into the forecourt of a house in Saint John's Wood. She texted the address to the group's burners, then grabbed her notebook, got out of the car, and walked up the pavement. With her phone, she casually took a photo of a small block of flats across the street, made a note, then moved along to another house, again making a note.

She crossed the street and walked past the house Novak had entered. Three cars were parked in the forecourt. She photographed the house, being sure to get the cars in the photo, and continued walking. It was dark by the time she returned to the warmth of her car.

A few minutes later, Novak emerged from the house with a short, muscular woman Liz took to be Lydia Anstey. She clicked a couple of photos as the two walked to Novak's car. They were immediately followed by two men in dark business suits. From across the street, Liz took a couple of photos of the men, then walked quickly to her car. By the time she got there, Novak's car had left the forecourt and accelerated away, followed closely by a blue Peugeot.

"Shit. Get moving, Barker." Liz started her wheezy Astra and began her pursuit. She kept the two cars in sight fifty yards ahead and speed-dialled Elaine.

FORTY-ONE

Saturday evening, Brentford

Elaine put down the papers she'd been studying and answered the burner. Liz was calling.

"Guv, Novak picked up a woman at a house in Saint John's Wood. I think it's Lydia Anstey. Two men in a blue Peugeot left the house with them. I've got obs on them now. Hold on."

"Are you sure about all of that?"

"I'm sure it's a blue Peugeot. The woman looks like Anstey. Short, husky. Fits Costello's description. I didn't ask for her ID, but I'm damn sure I'm right."

Elaine chuckled. "Calm down, Liz. I wasn't doubting you. I'm as excited as you sound."

"Sorry, guv. Looks like they're stopping. Pulling into a car park. Hold on—let me check the address. It's Novak's flat."

"Drive on by. Don't stop."

"I've done this before, guv."

"Relax, Liz."

"All due respect, boss, but you're the one who needs to relax. I've turned around and have eyes on the car park. Instructions?"

"Wait and watch."

"They're standing around the Peugeot talking. I'll take some snaps for posterity. Now they're going inside. Any other news?"

"Jenkins has eyes on the safe house. Jacko and his car are missing. I've been trolling through his bank records. They make interesting reading." Elaine stopped as a thought struck her. "Anstey. I need to look something up. Don't end the call."

Elaine shuffled through the papers on her kitchen table until she found the list of companies and people she'd made for Joanna. She traced her finger down the columns, checking each tick mark. There it was. Why the hell hadn't she noticed it before? "Baker Anstey."

"What, guv? Anstey?"

"Mm-hmm. Baker Anstey." She opened the spreadsheet on her laptop. "He's one of the directors of Boxe-Berkshire. And he's also known to IRG. The Sreckos."

"Jesus, guv. Do you think—hold on. The two men are leaving. Don't see Novak and the Anstey woman." She started her car. "I'm after them. They've turned westbound on Marylebone Road."

"Westbound, you say. Whereabouts?"

"Just coming to the Marylebone flyover at the A40," Liz replied. "They're moving fast, guv."

"Right. I'll call Bull and Jenkins." Elaine imagined a map in her mind. The A40 would carry them west with pretty good speed. Were the men going to the safe house? It was too much to be a coincidence. Better to be safe. "Stick with them and give me a bell if they turn off. I'm going to ring Bull."

Bull called before she could dial. "Strange things, guv. Jones, the DC on duty with me, got a phone call and went in the other room. When he came back, he said it was the desk sergeant at the Ealing nick. Said Novak was there and wanted him to pop over to pick something up. I argued with him, but he left anyway. I'm not feeling good about this. I've only got an asp."

"Jenkins is armed and he's got eyes on the house. I'll tell him to join you, so watch for him." She repeated what Liz had told her about the two men in the Peugeot. "I'll call Hughes for backup, then I'm on my way."

Jenkins answered on the first ring. "Just about to ring you. Something odd. Bull and the other relief officer showed up at seven. But just now the other officer left. It's only Bull and Hughes's wife in the house. Not standard procedure. I want to move closer."

"Right. I want you in the house. Bull's expecting you." Elaine relayed the information about the two men Liz was following. "I've got bad feelings right now. I'm going to arrange backup."

"Doesn't feel right to me either," Jenkins said. "I'll move in. Wish we had radios."

"True, but then someone could eavesdrop. I'm calling Hughes for backup."

Hughes didn't answer. Elaine left an angry voice message, then rushed to pull on her donkey jacket. She patted the pockets for her wallet, warrant card, notebook, and asp. She'd left her mobile on the table. She stopped, remembering the number Cranwell had given her the previous week. It was worth a try. She dialled.

"Hello, Elaine." Cranwell's voice was even. "How can I help you?"

She took a deep breath. "We have a serious situation sir. I need someone to authorize armed backup. DI Novak has Commander Hughes's wife in protective—"

"Whoa, Elaine. Slow down. I'm aware of Novak's investigation and that you and your team are working with Hughes on his Operation Spectra. Why do you need armed backup?"

How did he know they were working with Hughes? It didn't matter—there was no time to ponder. As she walked to her car, Elaine explained what Liz had witnessed and the situation at the safe house. When she was done, he repeated what she'd told him.

"Yes, sir. You've got it. I think all that's too much for coincidence, sir. Bull and Jenkins are there with Mrs. Hughes. Jenkins is armed. It could get violent."

"I agree. I'll set armed backup and medical in motion. You'll be on scene, so do what you need to do. And Elaine, I'm taking over from Hughes. You'll report to me now. Keep me posted, especially with anything regarding Novak or Hughes. Understood?"

What the hell? What next? She had no time for questions. "Yes, sir."

Seconds later, Elaine turned north on Boston Road and switched on her blues. Cranwell had said to do what she needed to do, but what was going on? Hughes had been acting strangely since the burglary. Had he stepped 'round the bend? Been relieved of command?

No way to know. No point dithering. Actions alone count. If her bad feeling was wrong, she'd never get another chance to salvage her career. If the feeling was right, she might be saving lives.

Her mobile warbled, and she pressed the button on her hands-free. "I'm on my way, Liz. The other copper deserted Bull. He's alone. Jenkins is armed and will be in the house in minutes.

"Okay, guv. Still on the A40. Maybe fifteen minutes away. Should I call for backup?"

"It's done. I couldn't get hold of Hughes, so Cranwell's ordering it."

Ten minutes later, she switched off her blues and turned into a narrow close that contained the safe house. Cars parked on both sides left only a single lane open. She backed into a spot at the end. A siren wailed in the distance. Cranwell's backup would likely come from the Ealing nick, two miles east on Uxbridge Road. She waited, listening, but the sound slowly receded to the west, away from her.

Inside the house, she gathered Bull, Jenkins, and Fiona together. "We have two objectives," Elaine said. "Protect Fiona, and arrest anyone who tries to harm her. Backup's coming, but it's best to get her away from the house. We have maybe four minutes."

Jenkins asked, "Hughes ordered backup?"

"Couldn't reach him. Cranwell."

Jenkins laughed. Before Elaine could ask him what was funny, Bull's mobile chattered.

"It's Jones." Bull held up a finger. "What? Are you coming back? When? Who?" He pocketed his phone. "He says he's delayed. Two other officers are on their way. Be here in a few minutes." He shook his head. "He's not a copper. Should have asked to see his warrant card when we first got here."

Jenkins spoke. "Elaine, get Fiona to your car, and get away. We'll be just behind the hedges on the side of the house. I'll cover the front, Bull can take the back."

Elaine and Fiona ran to the BMW. When they got to the car, Elaine turned in time to see Bull and Jenkins slither through a gap in the hedge. The house was dark except for a light in an upstairs bedroom and one at the front door.

Elaine had just sat behind the wheel when headlights appeared at the end of the street. "Damn. Get down." Both women slid down. Elaine fished in her pocket for her asp, finally freeing it. The approaching headlights glared in the windscreen. The sound of an engine grew closer, until it was no more than a few feet away. Car doors shut, male voices murmured. The front garden gate squeaked.

Elaine lifted her head just high enough to peer out. The Peugeot, its headlights now off, sat half on the pavement, driver's door open, engine idling, blocking the narrow street. Two dark figures approached the house. One stood to the side of the front door, his hands down in the low ready position, holding a handgun. The other man slipped into the shadows, moving towards the back of the house. In a few seconds, the first figure tried the front door and slipped inside.

"Psst. Boss." A whisper, then Liz's face at the car window. Elaine opened the window.

Liz pointed at the Peugeot. "You're blocked in, guv. What do you want me to do?"

"You and Fiona hide in the cemetery and stay there. Back-up's on the way. I'll deal with the car."

Elaine slipped out of the BMW, crept to the Peugeot, and switched it off. After pocketing the key, she flicked open her asp and moved into the shadow of the garden wall, crouching on the pavement next to the front gate. A glance over the wall revealed the intruders had turned on more lights. By now, they must know the house was empty.

Elaine took a deep breath and focused on the weapon in her hand. Its black metal rods were telescoped out to the full two-foot length, ending in a steel button about the size of a pound coin. She wiped her palms on her jeans and tightened both hands on the knurled grip. The shaft weighed heavy, solid in her hands. Used to its limits, an asp could crack bone. Used without restraint, it could kill.

The front door opened, and yellow light streamed through the slats in the gate, splaying bars of light and shadow over the pavement just in front of her. A male voice spoke, low, excited. Foot-steps clicked on the garden walk, moving in her direction. Elaine took another breath and adjusted the position of her feet, twisting her body, extending her arms. She would have one chance with her asp, and then she had to hope that Jenkins and Bull were quick. She would not hold back.

"Armed police!" Jenkins shouted. "Put down your weapons and lie on the ground! Now!"

An exclamation, then three gunshots. Another yell. The gate flew open, dark trousers moved across Elaine's vision. She swung the asp as hard as she could against the man's kneecap, untwist-ing her body with the effort. A crunch as bone splintered, a scream as the man toppled, face down.

Elaine leapt on his back, yelling at him to stay down. He still held the gun and twisted, raised his arm towards her. She swung again, and he grunted and went limp. The gun skittered into the shadow under the Peugeot. Sirens wailed in the distance.

Grunts and yells behind her. Elaine turned to see Bull and a large man grappling by the door of the house. She ran towards them, asp high. Bull lost his footing and slipped to his knees. The man raised his pistol. Elaine swung with all her might, striking the man's wrist, knocking the gun from his grip. She recovered and struck again, this time catching him in the face. Blood erupted from his mouth. He collapsed, moaning, as Bull scrambled to his feet. The sirens were closer now.

"Thanks, guv." Bull pulled out his handcuffs and snapped them around the second man's wrists. "You'd best cuff the one over there. He might get up." They walked to the garden gate and looked down. The man lay moaning, his leg twisted under him at an unnatural angle. Bull shook his head. "And then again, he might not. Give me your cuffs—I'll do it."

Blue lights flashed in the street. Sirens stopped. Elaine looked around. "Where's Jenkins? Jenkins!"

FORTY-TWO

Saturday night, Hanwell

She ran to the hedge and slipped through the gap. Jenkins lay against the grassy bank, holding his thigh. "I think it clipped an artery." His voice sounded soft, tired.

Elaine shouted, "Code Zero! Officer down. Over here!" She laid her hands over his leg and pressed. Blood seeped between her fingers. "Hurry!" Rustling sounds in the hedge behind her. A calm voice at her side. Hands on hers.

"We'll take it now, ma'am. We've got him."

She rose slowly to her feet. Fiona. Liz. She turned back through the hedge, towards the blue lights. The two women stood near an ambulance with Bull.

"Elaine, Are you all right?" Fiona looked horrified. "The blood . . ."

Elaine nodded. "It looks like Jenkins took a bullet. Bleeding pretty bad. Medics are with him. Who's in charge here?"

A short, swarthy officer in uniform walked up to them. "Inspector Bell, Ealing tactical response. You must be DCI Hope. Are you hurt?"

Someone handed Elaine a towel to wipe her hands. "I'm fine. Not my blood. There's a gun by the door and another under the Peugeot. And one with the wounded officer behind the hedge. He's not police. I think he's MI5, or something like that. Please see to him. If you have any questions, DC Bull and DC Barker can fill you in."

Elaine took a deep breath and pointed to Fiona. "This woman is in witness protection, and I need to get her to safety. The two men in handcuffs came here to kill her. If a DI named Novak contacts you or shows up and tries to take over, don't listen to him, don't let him. It's your crime scene, Bell. Tell him to ring DCS Cranwell. I'll brief Cranwell on what's happened. Got that?"

"Yes, ma'am. DI Novak to ring DCS Cranwell."

She fished in her pocket for a business card and the Peugeot key. "My number's on there. Can you please ask one of your officers to move that car out of the way? I need to get her out of sight."

Elaine kept her blues on until they were out of the neighbourhood. A half mile away she pulled into a dark parking lot next to a derelict store. "Are you okay?" she asked Fiona.

"Yeah." Fiona took a deep breath and exhaled. "Do you think Jenkins will make it?"

Elaine shook her head. "Dunno. The medics got there quickly. I think so."

"Good. I think so too. What do we do now? Are you going to call Jonny? I don't trust him, Elaine."

"Alec Cranwell told me Jonny was just relieved of command. Cranwell's in charge now. He told me not to call Jonny. And if he calls me, I don't have to tell him everything. Or anything."

"Alec's taken over from Jonny? Is it always this crazy? Who to trust?" Fiona stared out the windscreen.

"Right." Elaine faced Fiona. "Something's bothering me, and I need an answer. You gave your testimony. I read it and thought 'Flying colours. Well done, that woman.' So that's over, but why do they still fear you so much they would do this?"

"I saw the killer's face."

"I thought you said he had on a balaclava. You couldn't recognize him."

"Not then, later. When they tried to kidnap me. His voice. The French accent. He's the guy who jumped out of the van."

Of course. "You haven't seen him since."

Fiona shook her head. "Those two men tonight are too big. Where are we going?"

Elaine looked at her burner. "We'll talk about that in a minute." She pressed the number for Cranwell. "Sir, It's Hope. The situation is under control at the safe house. Fiona's safe, with me."

"I spoke with Inspector Bell. We need to talk, Elaine. I can't arrest anyone yet. I need more rope to tie it together. So continue to protect Mrs. Hughes. Do you know where you're taking her?"

Careful, Lainie. "Not yet, sir. Have you heard how Jenkins is?"

"He's on the way to hospital. Lost a lot of blood. Haven't heard beyond that. We've called his wife."

Called his wife. "Sir, you knew about Jenkins, what he was doing, didn't you?"

"I can't comment, Elaine."

"Operation Spectra. It's rogue, isn't it?" she asked. Cranwell didn't answer, so she continued. "I know about you and Commander Hughes, sir. Knowing that makes our conversation difficult. Do you understand?"

"I do. Two things and I have to go. Call Hughes and tell him about his wife. Summarize the situation, answer his questions. Don't mention me. As far as he knows, he's still in charge. And find a place to hide from Novak. The two of you aren't out of danger yet. I need some time. Don't tell anyone where you're going—just call me when you're safe. Like I said, we need to talk." The line went dead.

"What? What's wrong?" Fiona's voice sounded anxious.

"Nothing wrong, just odd. He wants me to ring Jonny to tell him you're safe."

"Whatever. I don't mind if Jonny knows I'm safe. But I won't talk to him, and I don't want him to know where I am."

Hughes picked up immediately. "I just heard. Is my wife all right? Can I speak with her?"

Who told him? Damn. "She's safe, not injured. She doesn't want to talk to you right now, sir."

"Let me speak with her, Hope."

"Sir, I can't force her to talk to you. She's safe."

"For the last time, DCI Hope, I want to speak with my wife."

Fuck you, Jonny one-note. What about Novak? "And for the last time, sir, she said no and I can't force her. Novak sent the hit men to the safe house. Barker followed them to Hanwell. You need to arrest him, sir."

"Don't lecture me." Hughes was silent for several seconds. "Keep this to yourself. We don't need it bandied about until we have him in custody. Do you think that means Novak's behind the Kensington murder?"

"Dunno if he's behind it, but he may be involved. I might suggest an all-ports, circulate his photo."

"For the last time, don't tell me what to do, Hope. I know what I need to do. Right now, Novak's on his way to Kensington nick. Where are you taking my wife?"

Always "my wife," never "Fiona." "She and I are going to discuss it. Somewhere safe."

"Waleham House would be good."

"Might be too obvious. We'll think of something. Good night, sir. We'll call once we're settled in."

She rang off, and snicked the car into gear. The car. "Christ! We need to ditch this car. He'll run the number plate on ANPR."

"There's my Range Rover, if it's not clamped."

"Excellent. To the pub, then. Didn't you leave it there?"

FORTY-THREE

Saturday night, Mortlake

Elaine drove the big Rover in silence for fifteen minutes, twisting through Richmond, always trending south. Elaine's personal mobile warbled. It was Peter. She asked Fiona to put it on the speaker.

"Hi, Peter. I'm busy right now. Can we talk maybe tomorrow?"

"Fuckwit called. He asked if I knew where you were. Anything you need help with?"

"No! He called you?"

"Yeah. Said you were in danger and he needed to warn you."

"What did you tell him?"

"What could I tell him? I said I had no clue. He didn't believe me."

"If I'm in danger, it's from him. Shit! I'll text you from another phone. Hang up, now!" She ended the call.

"What was that about?" Fiona asked. "So that was Peter. Who's Fuckwit?"

"Yep, Peter. Fuckwit's Novak. Good story how he got the moniker. I need to text Peter from the burner. But first, take the battery out of my phone." She handed the phones to Fiona. "Ready? I'll dictate. Text, 'He knew you would call me.'"

Seconds later the burner pinged. It was Peter.

<Trace location?>

Elaine chuckled. "Yep, the boy's sharp. Send, 'Yes, need place to hide.'"

Ping.

<My house>

Elaine laughed. "Really sharp. Why didn't I think of that? The place is a fucking fortress." At Fiona's puzzled look, she added, "His sister's a diplomat. A spy. Really."

"Wow. And I thought being married to a cop was cool." She paused. "David, I mean."

Elaine wondered how cool it could really be. "Text him, 'Tell Fuckwit I won't tell you where we're going.' Then text, 'We'll be at your place in an hour.'"

Ping.

<Will do. Go get em>

Ping.

<Love u>

"What did I tell you? That guy has your back," Fiona said. "What makes the house a fortress?"

"We had to search it last year during a case. That's how we met. I don't know all of it, but it's got really heavy doors and multiple layers of security systems. If someone tries to breach the doors, a Special Air Service squad shows up. Or someone like that. It's what he told me."

"No!" Fiona began giggling. "That would be a hell of a surprise!"

"If Novak finds out we're there, he'll probably just station a car on the street. Even if he wants inside, Peter will make him get a warrant first. If his sister Kate's involved, they'll never get the warrant. But we've bought some time. I need to think."

Why had Novak chosen to brazen it out instead of running? He surely knew the assault at the safe house would point suspicion at him. But if he'd been careful with the planning, and the two thugs weren't caught, nothing would be traceable back to him.

Would anyone believe Liz's story? Elaine couldn't remember if Liz had taken pictures.

Traffic had gotten thicker, so Elaine slowed. "Okay. Can you call the contact marked 'RH' on the burner phone? That's Liz."

When Elaine asked after Jenkins, Liz sounded fraught. "He's still in surgery. The doctor in A&E said the bullet ripped his femoral artery. The medics at the scene got it clamped, but another few minutes and he wouldn't have made it. We sent a car for his wife. And, guv, two large, quiet men have settled in the waiting room. They're wearing earpieces."

"Doesn't surprise me. Just steer clear of them. If you see Jenkins, tell him we're behind him. What else?"

"Costello's at the incident room, but Novak isn't there."

"One more thing, did you get pictures of Novak and the two goons who attacked us?"

"Several."

"Right. Send them to me first chance you get. Call me when you have news of Jenkins."

The burner pinged. It was Peter.

<Done. Kate knows ur coming>

It pinged again.

<Fuckwit asked if Fiona ok>

Elaine thought for a moment, then said, "Text, 'Tell him she needs medical attention.'"

Ping.

<Really?>

Elaine laughed and said to Fiona, "If Novak thinks you need a doctor, he might waste time looking for us in hospitals. Text him, 'No, its a delaying tactic.'"
Seconds later, the mobile pinged again.

<See u soon>

FORTY-FOUR

Saturday night, Highgate

"You're safe here. Nobody's getting in this house unless Corporal Redmond there lets them in." Kate indicated the beefy, black-clad soldier standing against the wall in the sitting room. His sub-machine gun hung loosely from a shoulder strap. "I requested protection."

"I'll make another round of the property, ma'am," Redmond said to Kate, "before DCS Cranwell arrives." He moved through the kitchen and disappeared down the steps to the basement.

Fiona shivered. "It's like a thriller movie."

"We only do it to impress," Peter said. "Would you two like to clean up before Cranwell gets here?"

Fiona nodded, but Elaine shook her head. "This is Jenkins's blood. I won't wash it off just yet."

After Kate showed Fiona to the lavatory, Peter asked, "Can we talk?"

At her nod, he took her hand and led her up the stairs. Peter's second-floor bedroom was as Elaine remembered it. They stood before the panoramic floor-to-ceiling window overlooking London. The distant lights of Canary Wharf twinkled through the clear night outside. His huge channel-back chair, the duvet folded over its arm, invited her to surrender to the passion she had felt growing in the last two days.

She didn't resist when he took her hand. "I want you to join me in Texas for however long you can. I've arranged a house on Lake Austin. Quiet, herons, water lilies. There's a separate cottage on the shore. You can dive in from your bedroom veranda if you want. You'll have privacy, space. You can even bring Scratch. I've checked."

"He's an urban cat. But he does like looking over the water." She took his other hand. "It's just . . . it's like I said. I'm a British cop. I believe I was born to be one. I don't know how the arrangement would work or how long I would last in Texas."

"I'm not asking for a commitment. I'm the one who changed direction. I know you have to decide what's best for you. This is an open invitation, whatever you feel like you can give. Look at it as an interlude before you go back to work. I just ask you to please give me this time with you."

He wants me. On my terms. No man has ever loved me like he does. Touch him, Lainie. Show him you're willing to give.

The intercom on the wall beeped. Corporal Redmond's voice said, "DCS Cranwell has arrived."

Elaine pulled Peter close, laid her forehead on his shoulder. "I have a case to wrap up. We'll make some plans then, darling." She kissed him on the cheek. "I can't wait to see your home town."

Saturday night, Kensington

Novak's high-pitched yelling grated on Costello's nerves. He held his mobile away from his ear as Novak raged. "First that fucking American ass says he hasn't heard from Hope, then he says Hughes's wife needs medical attention. Have you found Hope and the other bitch yet?"

Costello rolled his eyes and yelled back. "No!" He gathered himself. "Sir. No location on Hope's phone. She must have removed the battery."

"There has to be something that shows where she went. I'm on my way in. Check ANPR for Hope's number plate. Then get the CCTV from the cameras in the area around Hope's flat. And Hughes's house. Before I get there."

"Right, sir."

Novak breezed into the incident room thirty minutes later. "CCTV?"

Costello pointed to a young, uniformed woman seated in front of a large video monitor. "PC Nelson, sir. IT boffin. We've been having trouble with the network connections. Just bringing it up now." He and Nelson had spoken with Elaine and Cranwell before Novak arrived.

Nelson grimaced. "Hold on. It was here. Lost connection again."

Novak fumed as Nelson's fingers tapped away at the keyboard. "Hurry up, woman. Time's critical. Can't you do it any faster?"

Costello made eye contact with her and smiled.

"The IT folks must have been reconfiguring the routers today, sir," she said. "Network's always a bit twitchy after they do that. Lots of times the IPv4 to IPv6 address conversions aren't fully repopulated, and I have to re-initialize the routing tables, and—"

"Would you just shut the hell up!" Novak shouted. "Get it working, PC whatever-your-name-is!" He paced back and forth behind her.

"Nelson, sir. PC Olivia Nelson." She had a soft, deep voice that Costello found attractive. "And if you curse at me, or call me 'woman' in that tone of voice one more time, or yell at me again, sir, I'll file on you. It's not the way you should treat a fellow professional." She folded her arms and looked at Costello. "I don't have to put up with it."

Costello took a deep breath and nodded. "Just bring it back up as soon as you can, Nelson. I'm sure you're working as fast as possible. One can only repopulate as quickly as the bits and bytes allow."

Novak's face was the colour of a deep sunburn. "What are you saying, Costello? You don't know shite about what she's doing, so quit babbling."

Nelson said, "Here it is, sir. Four of them. This one shows the entrance to DCI Hope's flat. This one's the intersection leading to Commander Hughes's residence, this one's on Mortlake High Street, and this one's—"

"Move." He motioned to Nelson to vacate her chair. "I'll take it from here. Just leave me with it." He glared at Costello, who smiled back.

"Let us know if you need something, sir. Or if it breaks again. PC Nelson and I will be in the canteen."

They stood close to each other at a vending machine. Nelson leaned against Costello, her hip brushing his. She asked, "Was that performance worth a bottle of wine?"

Costello put his arm around her shoulder. "Indeed. Plus a standing ovation and a bouquet."

She closely inspected the choices in the machine. "Oh, wouldn't you know? No wine. Pity." Her deep blue eyes met his. "I expect some later. But don't throw bouquets at me, Sergeant. People might talk."

"Costello. Simon?" Bull's voice came from the direction of the canteen door. "I hate to interrupt, but we're to meet the guv and Cranwell in the incident room." He acknowledged Nelson with a nod. "Philip Bull. Most just call me Bull. Better hurry if you want to be in on the fun." At Nelson's quizzical look, he continued. "We've seen the guv like this before. No better show than when she's got her suspect cornered."

Cranwell and Elaine waited in the corridor outside the incident room with two uniformed officers. Elaine spoke. "Before we go in, Jenkins just got out of surgery. He'll have a long recovery, but it looks good." She nodded at Nelson. "I'm DCI Hope."

Nelson held out her hand. "PC Nelson, ma'am. Simon, Sergeant Costello, speaks of you often." She glanced at Costello before she continued. "Um, ma'am, did you know you have a blood smear on your cheek?"

Elaine's eyes narrowed. "And on my jacket and trousers, and under my fingernails. I want the bastard to see what he caused. And good work with the CCTV."

Elaine's burner phone pinged once, then again and again. She swiped the screen a few times and grinned as she held it up for Cranwell and the others to see. "Liz's photos of Novak with the goons. We've nailed him."

The few detectives in the incident room watched and murmured to each other as the procession of officers, led by Elaine, marched through to where Novak sat in his glass-walled office, studying his computer screen. Elaine and Cranwell stood in front of his desk. Bull blocked the doorway. Costello and Nelson watched through the office window.

Novak spun his chair to face them, and leaned back. "So, whose party is this? I'm sure I didn't issue any invitations."

"DI Novak, can you tell us where you were between seven and eight o'clock this evening?" Elaine asked.

"Seems these days you've always got backup, Hope. Not like before, eh, Bull?"

Bull bristled. "Just answer the guv."

"And here I sit, thinking I'm your guv, Bull." Novak tutted. "What's become of loyalty these days?"

Elaine placed both hands on Novak's desk and leaned across. "Where were you?"

"At my flat. I have a witness who can place me there."

"Lydia Anstey, I suppose. Were any others there at that time?"

Novak's eyes narrowed. "It's possible. I wasn't watching the clock."

"Perhaps we could ask one of these blokes." Elaine placed

her mobile on the desk, with the photo of Novak and the two hit men displayed. She swiped the screen. "In fact, we have pictures of them following you from Baker Anstey's house. Do you recognize the car in the photo?"

Novak looked away, his eyes scanning Costello, Nelson and the two uniformed officers.

"I don't need your answer. There's only one way this ends, Novak. Stand up."

Novak didn't move.

Elaine took a step to the end of the desk. "I'd love to grab you by the scruff and pull your crooked arse out of that chair. One more time. Get up."

Novak stood. "Get it over with."

"Pathetic." Elaine moved behind him and clicked the handcuffs closed. "DI John Novak, I'm arresting you on suspicion of conspiracy to commit murder. You do not have to say anything, but it may harm your defence if you do not mention, when questioned, something which you later rely on in court. Anything you do say may be given in evidence."

She said nothing more as the uniforms led him away.

EPILOGUE

A week later

When Elaine arrived at the address on the slip of paper, she was sure there had been a mistake. The concrete-walled building looked nothing like a hospital. The heavy steel door only opened after she'd been grilled by a faceless voice. Once inside, she signed an acknowledgement under the Official Secrets Act, pressed her thumb to a biometrics pad, and got scanned for metal and God knew what else several times.

The nurse escorting Elaine through the featureless corridors was professionally pleasant, offering only innocuous replies to questions. Elaine had known some physically fit nurses in her day, but "Nurse Smith" went a bit beyond fit. Her biceps and flat abs indicated she followed a strenuous workout routine. Perhaps she was more than a nurse, like Jenkins was more than a cop.

Nurse Smith finally indicated a half-closed door and stepped back. The room was larger than Elaine expected, twice as large as a regular National Health Service hospital room. Jenkins lay in a hospital bed. A frame suspended his heavily bandaged left leg.

"Wrong leg," Elaine said. "I could have given you advice if you'd been shot in the other one." She smiled and extended her hand to the small, birdlike woman who sat in a wheelchair next to Jenkin's bed. "I'm Elaine Hope."

The woman held out her hand, which was soft and had a slight tremor. "Roxy. Arvel speaks highly of you, DCI Hope."

"Completely unwarranted."

Roxy spun her chair away from the bed. "I think not. I don't want to appear rude. I would love to stay and jabber, but I have a treatment scheduled in ten minutes. I'll be back in about a half hour. I know the two of you have a lot to talk about." She wheeled her chair out the door and pulled it closed behind her.

When Elaine turned back to Jenkins, he was still looking at the door. After a few seconds, he said, "Multiple sclerosis. Started about six years ago. It comes and goes. This week, it came. He picked up a small container of orange juice from his bedside tray. "So, I thought this case was very strange."

"And that's all you want to say about your wife?"

"For now. You may have another chance to get to know her. Roxy and I have something to talk to you about when she gets back. Fill me in on what's happened in the last week. What about Cranwell and Hughes? My contacts told me they were an item, but Cranwell didn't say a thing when he brought me on board. Then he went and undermined Hughes."

Cranwell brought Jenkins on board? "Yeah, but according to Cranwell, they haven't been an item for over two years. Jonny Hughes traded him in for a model with fewer miles on the clock. He had to keep that a secret for a very good reason. So, how's the food here?"

"Come on, Hope. I don't want to have to twist your arm."

"I owe you lots of aggravation, Jenkins. If that's your real name. His new amour was AC Collins's son. And AC Collins didn't know."

"Jeez-us! There's a career-limiting move. The kid's less than half his age."

"Mm-hmm. Jonny never told Fiona. And our money-grubbing Crownie Jacko found out."

"Tangled webs, Elaine. Where's Jacko? Alive or dead?"

"Alive. Beaten unconscious. Fingers and ribs broken, the works. Same goons who came after Fiona at the safe house. Jacko spilled Fiona's name right away, but they kept beating him. Finally dumped him outside an A&E in Essex. No ID, unconscious. Took two days to find him. He'll confess to blackmail and tax evasion."

"Hughes?"

"No prosecution. Too much bad publicity. Forced early retirement."

"What about the murder?"

"Looks like we were right. The hit men had the impression Dragan Bosko wanted revenge against Anton Srecko for killing his son. He made threats, demanded compensation. They tapped Duclerq as the killer. The poor sod was killed in that house because Jacko said meeting in East London wasn't convenient."

Jenkins shook the container of orange juice. "You were after Anton Srecko, then you crossed over to the murder investigation. Decided to leverage the team. What was the connection?"

Elaine considered whether she should disclose Joanna's role. She said, "I'm not big on motive, but Bosko gave us a reasonable one. We knew the method, so my next question was opportunity. Why that house? Then I got information that Srecko and Anstey were connected through real estate holdings."

"You have a snout." He smiled and took some sips of orange juice before continuing. "Could have been coincidence."

"Thou shalt not believe in coincidence. One of my commandments."

"I tagged Anstey but didn't have time to follow up. Tell me about him."

"Baker Anstey. Rich, connected, very powerful. He owns the gambling syndicate Jacko owed money to, along with money laundering services, probably smuggling, and who knows what all. His legit real estate business makes piles of cash, and the Sreckos help him launder it. We have nothing to stick on Baker Anstey. Not yet anyway."

Jenkins said, "Novak was head over heels for Lydia. He had to play her daddy's game to keep her. Duclerq?"

"Mid-level muscle. We caught him yesterday, trying to get on a fishing boat in Ramsgate. No confession yet. Between Fiona and Jacko and forensics, we'll have enough to convict."

Elaine could tell Jenkins was tiring. "It was Hughes who brought Novak on board, right?" At his nod, she leaned close. "You were working for Cranwell, but he doesn't have the rank to pull many strings. He was your handler. Who do you really work for? I doubt it's MI-5 or -6. But this hospital you're in makes me think it's something like that. MI-8.3?"

Jenkins pulled on the small trapeze dangling over his shoulders, lifting his body slightly higher in the bed. "Have you thought about what you'll do when you return from the sick?"

"I want to know. What's all this about?"

"In good time. Answer the question. What will you do?"

Elaine laughed. "Short term, I'm going down to Hampshire to visit Fiona for a few days. Then I have a date with a tall Texan. Long term, Cranwell has some ideas, but I'm probably more non grata than ever in the Met, so I don't know."

"Have you considered janitorial work?"

"Can't say I have."

Roxy's voice came from behind her. "Then let us try to educate you about it, Ms. Hope." She wheeled her chair next to Elaine. "Some find it fascinating."

The next day, Hampshire

Elaine walked the heath over grass still brown with winter, between patches of heather. Deer, grazing at the edge of a copse, lifted their heads at her steps. Rabbits wound quick, erratic trails through the undergrowth. Grouse leapt into sudden, startling flight from hides not two yards in front of her. A hawk wheeled in the clear, cold sky.

Life here at Waleham House was so different from London. She'd balked at first, when Fiona asked her to visit. But in afterthought, she'd enlisted Liz to feed Scratch and accepted.

Thumping hooves told her Fee had joined her. They sat in the grass and talked while Trooper munched, his teeth crunching and grinding local botanicals.

"Jonny won't contest the divorce, so I'll get the decree nisi in a month and should be completely free in less than a year."

"You're going to New Zealand?"

"For a while. The kids and Peg talked me into contacting my brother. Turns out he's wanted to meet but felt guilty about the years of neglect. We're going see if we can work out a different deal with the estate, because I don't plan to marry again. Peg and Fritz won't budge, and I can't leave them alone here. I've got money put away, maybe still get the inheritance, and the gallery will bring a decent price. We're thinking about turning Waleham House into a retreat. Renovate, put in a pool. Golf nearby. Host conferences. Do horsey events. Plenty of space, a big house, close to London and Devon. It has lots going for it."

The two women sat silent until Fee continued. "What about you? Peter loves you."

Elaine lay back and stretched her arms over her head. "I'm going to Austin. He knows I have some recovering to do. He's got a house on a lake. I'll stay there, swim, rest. He knows I'll come back here after my leave's up. Then we'll see how it works out. It's open-ended."

"You'll be a British cop."

"It's what I am, Fee. I'd go nuts doing anything else. I have a couple of offers here. I've been asked to do some janitorial work."

Fee looked puzzled. "Janitorial work? Like cleaning buildings?"

Elaine laughed. "I can bloody well clean up without pushing a broom."

Acknowledgments

I would like to thank my critique partners—K. P. Gresham, Gogi Hale, Bill Woodburn, Jan Rider Newman, Dan Roessler, Connie Newton, Nona Farris, Linda Ritzen, and Martin Barkley—for their comments and suggestions.

I extend heartfelt gratitude to my old friend Nigel Powell, not only for sharing his deep knowledge of British nuance and habit, but also for his unwavering support through difficult times. We'll soon share a pint or two of real ale in Seer Green or Padstow, or wherever we find ourselves. My shout.

Deb Rhodes of BetterBetaReads was indispensable for helping me untangle Elaine's relationships with Peter and Fiona. Thanks again for your help, Deb!

As always, my appreciation goes out to my agent, Elizabeth Trupin-Pulli; my editor, Anne Brewer; and her assistant, Jenny Chen, for their guidance and support.